KING OF THE DARK

PRINCE ASSASSIN #1

ARIANA NASH

King of the Dark, Prince's Assassin #1

Ariana Nash - *Dark Fantasy Author*

Subscribe to Ariana's mailing list & get the exclusive story 'Sealed with a Kiss' free.

Join the Ariana Nash Facebook group for all the news, as it happens.

www.ariananashbooks.com

PROLOGUE

And the three gods, Etara, Aura, and Walla
proclaimed a griffin must forever
hold the flame.

CHAPTER 1

he Stag and Horn pleasure house had once been a glittering jewel among the stores and inns lining Loreen's ancient, winding streets. When the city had been in its prime, Niko had been too young to venture inside. Back then, he'd asked his pah about the beautiful people coming and going from the house's fancy stained-glass doors. Pah had promptly smacked him across the head so hard his left ear had rung for days. Only when he was older, and had been drafted for war, had he crossed the Stag and Horn threshold for the first time, knowing one thing for certain: he could not die a virgin.

What happened after had left an impression, given him a new appreciation for the male form, and cost him his first month's military wages.

Niko considered his younger self to be a fucking idiot. He hadn't died on the front lines, but it wasn't for the vicious elven force's lack of trying. There had been plenty of opportunity for sex among the soldiers too. All of it free. Although, in the end, Niko had paid with his heart.

Eight years later, now with twenty-three years and a whole lot of war behind him, he was back at the pleasure house, his head full of shadows as dangerous as those cloaking the streets, and nothing about the once-grand city of Loreen was as he remembered, including the Stag and Horn. The jewel had decayed from a precious gem to costume jewelry.

Pretty people still worked the tables, but their ruffles had frayed, their hair had fallen loose from the multitude of sharp pins, and the paint on their lips had smeared across their cheeks. Patrons were passing spice from hand to hand, openly snorting the blue powder from tabletops, not caring that the drug had officially been outlawed years ago.

The house had become a parody of itself, and Niko wished he hadn't come at all. He shouldn't have been surprised. All of Loreen, the city and the land of the same name, was similarly neglected. The city had neglected its people, and it had good reason, the Royal family had neglected it too. Defeat was everywhere—in the peeling wallpaper, the spluttering streetlamps, the hungry beggars, and the sad-eyed orphans.

Most nights he woke drenched in sweat wishing he'd died alongside his brothers-in-arms so he didn't have to suffer the shame of returning home with the bitter taste of defeat forever on his tongue. Or maybe that was the mead. He picked up his tankard and frowned at its contents. The drink truly was vile.

"I hear they water it down with piss," a cool, civilized voice said beside him. A heavy-hooded riding cloak cast a thick shadow across the man's face, revealing only a smooth, sharp chin and the small uptick of thin, pale lips.

Niko hadn't seen him take the seat at the bar. Either he moved with the grace of a snake, or the mead was more potent than he'd realized. Perhaps both. Whatever the case, having seen how far the Stag and Horn had fallen, he didn't plan on purchasing any company tonight, fearing he'd catch crotch-lice and lose the contents of his pockets in return.

"I'm not interested," he grunted, sparing the man a glance. Criminals hid their faces. Niko had no time for wretched thieves.

The stranger placed a plump red velvet money pouch on the bar. Its contents clinked, fat with coin.

Niko wet his teeth with his tongue, preparing to tell the prick that if he couldn't see how Niko wasn't a whore, then he was either blind, or stupid, or both, when the flash of the man's ruby signet ring caught his eye. A gold stylized griffin set into obsidian. The royal emblem. The sight of it should have inspired pride and loyalty. He should have dropped to his knee and kissed that ring. But he'd charged into battle with that damned griffin on his breastplate, like a fucking target for every elven blade and arrow. He'd witnessed friends die for that griffin. And it had all been for nothing.

Niko tightened his fingers around the tankard, wishing it were the handle of his sword. Good thing he hadn't brought his blade or else the royal bastard might find himself missing that finger and its ring. Of course, such thoughts were fantasy. Whoever this royal was, he wouldn't be walking Loreen's streets alone at night.

A quick scan of the crowd revealed two potential palace guards, similarly cloaked, making fine wall ornaments while watching Niko's back. One had pale blue eyes and a sandy blond mop of hair that had likely grown out since his soldiering service, and the other had red hair cut close to his skull. With faces like theirs, they'd make good money in the Stag and Horn.

"For this coin, you will kill a man," the smooth royal voice said, reminding Niko he wasn't alone.

Niko lifted the tankard to his lips, smiled, and took a sip. "I'm not an assassin."

The royal leaned in so close Niko could smell the sweetness of rosewater. "You are whatever I order you to be, or nothing at all," the man said with the confidence born of having never been denied.

How lovely it must have been to bathe in rosewater. The closest Niko had gotten to such a thing was washing elf blood off himself in a stream.

The royal still had his hand on the money pouch. His fingers were smooth, lean, nails precisely rounded, more accustomed to delicate maneuvers like playing the harp or signing royal decrees of surrender. They'd snap like twigs under Niko's rough grip. Despite this man's physical weakness, he had all the power in the building, perhaps in the city, depending on which royal he was. There were several possibilities. Not the king. He never left the palace and his health had been deteriorating for years. That left one of three princes.

Niko hadn't seen them in years, and then only once during a parade. He had climbed onto the rooftop of his father's forge and watched the shining procession pass beneath. The young princes had passed by too, all three atop huge white stallions. Chins up, backs straight, resplendent in royal colors. They'd all been boys back then. A few months after, the eldest prince was shipped off

6

to some retreat, keeping him safely hidden as war descended on the land. He'd returned only a few months ago, according to local gossip. By-the-Three-Gods, Niko couldn't recall their faces, but it was unlikely a prince would visit the Stag and Horn to buy the services of ex-soldiers. It had to be some low-level royal, then. One of those leeches who clung to their name because it had more power than they'd ever earn through blood and sweat.

"Have one of your guards kill your unfortunate victim." Niko dismissed him, finishing his sour drink. He moved to leave when light fingers clasped his wrist, pulling him back with surprising strength. Niko grabbed the bar, regaining his balance, only to freeze when the man's next words brushed his cheek.

"Refuse me and I will have you flogged." The venom with which he spoke was genuine. This royal was not bluffing.

Rage shattered Niko's already cracked restraint. He didn't have much patience left, and this prick was already on Niko's last nerve. He twisted his grip, capturing the man's wrist. The royal gasped. Niko caught a glimpse of pale blond before the royal turned his head away, hiding beneath the hood.

His anger was a curse, and lately he'd been losing control of it. It unraveled, Niko's control slipping. "I obeyed for years," he hissed at the royal. "I lost everything for the Caville name!"

The royal's thin wrist creaked inside his grip, the bones about to break. He'd done enough for the griffin. He'd lost everything. And this gilded fool thought he could wave a bag of coin around and buy Niko's loyalty? So typical of the royals. What they could not buy, they destroyed.

Niko shoved the man off his stool and trapped his body against the bar, pinning him rigid. Long, lean legs and hard muscle didn't yield. He felt like a drawn bow, but he had enough strength to capably resist. Niko leaned hard into him, ramming a knee between his thighs. The royal's chest heaved, breaths ragged.

The commotion had roused a few shouts from the crowd. Niko didn't care. The royals still lived their luxurious lifestyles while their people succumbed to the elves. They were cowards, all of them. "I am not for sale."

A bone in the man's wrist shattered. He cried out and a gleeful surge of pleasure brought a smile to Niko's lips. The royals needed to suffer for betraying their own people. A broken wrist wasn't enough.

Hands clamped around Niko's upper arms and yanked, wrenching him off the vulnerable royal.

"Arrest him!" The royal's words lashed like a whip. He clutched his wrist to his chest, but he'd managed to keep his hood in place and his face hidden. Only his straight white teeth, bared in a snarl, were visible.

It didn't matter who he was, just that he was hurting. Niko lifted his chin, wishing he'd thrown a punch into that jaw as well. For the soldiers that had lain dying in their own steaming entrails. For the screams he heard at night. For the flutter of that gods-awful blood-soaked griffin banner staked into the ground amidst mounds of cold, stiff bodies. He'd have killed this royal for free, he realized, and laughed at the insane thought. Perhaps it was the mead, or perhaps it was everything else, because nothing had made any sense since returning to this damned city.

"Where shall we take him, Your Highness?" one of the guards asked.

"The dungeons. And throw away the gods-damned key!"

"Yes, my prince."

Niko laughed harder. One of the three princes, then. Perhaps it would also be his last night alive. If death had finally caught him, he welcomed it. He just hoped it would be the prince with the broken wrist who gave the order to take his head, so he could look him in the eyes and drag his soul to the depths of the infernal underworld with him.

CHAPTER 2

*T*he palace cells were rammed wall-to-wall with thieves and whores and the mad who prattled to themselves, earning the restless ire of the bigger prisoners.

Numerous fights broke out. Niko had already broken up a scuffle between one of the men and a young fool, but gained no thanks from the lad he'd saved. The brute delivering the punches had likely served at the front line. Niko knew the sort. He'd commanded many of them. They dealt with fear differently, turning it inward into anger. As soon as Niko had ordered the man to stand down, he'd backed off. No others had bullied the lad since, but they would, eventually—when Niko was removed from the cell for sentencing.

Although it seemed the prince had forgotten him.

His stomach gnawed on itself, indicating several days had passed, but with no windows in the cell there was no way of knowing how many. Water pouches were thrown between the bars every morning and food was slopped from buckets into a trough by snickering guards, like the prisoners were no better than pigs.

Pigs would have been better treated.

The contents of the troughs looked a great deal like contents removed from their shit-bucket each morning.

"You," a guard grunted. "Hey!" He slammed a hand against the bars, making Niko look up. "Yeah, you. Over here. Stand at the gate, face away. Try anything and I'll break your knees. Got it?"

Niko crossed the cell, then turned his back on the guard. He let himself get dragged from the cell, his eyes briefly falling to the lad chittering to himself in the corner. The brute might kill him while Niko was gone.

He caught the brute's eye, and the man leered, confirming Niko's fears. All Niko had done was mark the poor boy as prey.

Manacles locked around his wrists, linking him to the guard by a length of rattling chain. The elves had broken similar chains, ripping them apart like each link was made of paper. They'd massacred his regiment right after, leaving him alive to pass on news of their victory. The tricks had been the worst part of battling elves. They did not fight like soldiers. They fought like shadows, like nightmares. But they could be beaten. They had been gaining ground until—

"Get moving!"

He was marched up spiraling stairs and down a cold, dark corridor into an antechamber filled with bustling palace staff. The rich smell of cooked meats and vegetables had his mouth watering. His stomach knotted. Gods, he was starving.

A set of tall, narrow doors opened ahead and the guard

shoved Niko through into a rich, overly decorated columned hall. Silk draped from the ceiling. Candles flickered in their branch-like candelabra. The table—longer than the height of most houses—sat mounds of food, more food than Niko saw in a year. A veritable feast for the lords and ladies present.

He bared his teeth to see such bounty, ignoring his grumbling belly.

"Is this the one?" a booming voice asked. The man to whom that voice belonged had been leaning over the end of the table, basking in the guests' attention. He straightened to his impressive height and sauntered toward Niko. White-blond hair was cropped to his jaw in the typical short Loreen fashion. Half the gazes in the room followed. "From your description, brother dear, I was expecting a giant!"

The crowd tittered.

Niko couldn't see who this man's brother might be, but given his swagger, the fine, gold-embroidered clothes, and the griffin ring he wore, he was clearly a royal. Likely one of the princes, though not the same prince whose wrist Niko had broken.

"Hm." The prince stopped a few feet in front of Niko. He had a narrow face, thin lips, and was quick to sneer. "A soldier. We owe you a debt. It's a shame you didn't beat them."

If he expected Niko to acknowledge him or his words, he'd be waiting a long while.

The prince sipped his wine, eyeing Niko over the rim of the goblet. It was said the royal brothers were a trio of vipers even before the war. Now they'd matured, their venom had become more potent.

"Why am I here?" Niko asked, tired of standing on display.

"You're here..." a voice said, the same smooth voice Niko recalled from the Stag and Horn. He came into view from behind his brother. "... to serve."

Niko was reminded of the three princely boys he'd seen so long ago and recognized this one's sharp face: Prince Vasili, the eldest of the three. Dressed in an ocean-blue silk jacket and trousers embroidered with gold, he'd had his servants pin his long, silver-blond hair back at the sides, leaving a lock free to rest over his right eye. When he leaned over a chair—and its occupant—to retrieve a bowl of grapes, the length of his hair trailed down his back to his waist. The current fashion was short hair. Elves wore their hair long, and few wanted to emulate elves. Vasili clearly didn't care what others thought of him.

Niko recalled exactly how the man's figure had felt when he pressed onto it. He got a better look at Prince Vasili's design now that he was adorned in a slim-fitting suit, and he'd been right: The prince was lean, his strength not in muscle, but in movement. He'd be lethal with a blade. Quick and light. Niko now wondered if he ever learned to wield a sword or if he had always relied on the palace guards to protect him.

This prince was no longer a boy atop a white steed. He'd changed a great deal since Niko had seen him, not least because of the scar slicing through his right eye, rendering it blind. He'd hidden it with the hood when they'd met in the pleasure house, and he styled his hair to cover it now, but there was no way to completely hide such an injury.

He approached, carrying the bowl of grapes in his left hand. His broken right wrist he held behind his back.

With a nod from the prince, the guard unlocked Niko's manacles. Niko rubbed at his wrists. He hadn't been in the restraints long, but it was long enough to chafe.

Vasili lifted the bowl. "Now serve Amir and I."

Was this a joke? Niko glanced at the crowd. They watched on, curious. Lords and ladies and dukes and viscounts—some intrigued, some already bored of Niko's arrival, turning away to continue their conversations. Was Niko expected to perform in some way?

"Don't you have servants for that?"

Vasili's thin mouth twitched. "You are my servant now. So, serve."

Prince Amir, who had approached first, snorted and moved on, more interested in the guests than his brother's game. But Vasili's attention wasn't waning. He stared at Niko, his one eye a frosty blue. He looked like a shard of glass, all angles and fine lines that would cut anyone who dared get close. "Well?" he snapped.

These people, this feast—did they even know how many lives had been sacrificed to keep the elves from their doors? Did they even care? Families had lost generations. Fathers and mothers gone, orphanages overflowing. And the royals feasted and laughed, growing fat in their glistening palace.

"Serve yourself."

Several guests gasped. Some murmured excitedly. Vasili huffed a soft laugh and gently set the bowl back down on the table. When he straightened, his eye shone with cold, hungry menace. What had this prince seen to make him so callous?

A sudden blow poured pain across Niko's cheekbone, whipping his head to the side. He staggered, startled by the prince's backhand. The aftermath throbbed through his face.

Vasili turned away. "Return him to the dungeon."

He dabbed at a tickle on his chin moments before the guards caught his arms again and yanked them behind his back, hastily reapplying the manacles.

Blood dripped onto the polished marble floor. The prince's rings had sliced open his cheek.

Rage boiled in his veins. He considered unleashing all his disgust at these people, but a loose tongue would likely see itself cut off. The princes were cruel. He'd heard it, but hadn't believed the extent of their brutality until now. All the Cavilles were cruel. All but the queen, who'd died, leaving behind an ailing king and three vipers in his nest. They were supposed to be guardians of this land and its people, but these royals were parasites, feeding off it instead.

The guard dragged Niko back through the bowels of the palace, unlatched the manacles, tossed him into the cell, then heaved the body of the lad out. Niko had known it would happen, but it all seemed such a waste. A familiar and potent fury silenced all the reasonable voices in his head. He lunged for the brute and slammed his head against the stone wall until bone shattered and he stopped moving.

The next morning the guards dragged that body out too.

16

CHAPTER 3

*I*t had been a week. He'd begun eating the foul slop dumped into the trough yesterday, mindless with hunger. Others came and went from the cell, but Niko was ignored. He whittled away the hours fantasizing of all the ways to kill a prince. Given the brothers' reputation, they probably had wine tasters, so poison was out of the question. He had no weapons either. His sword likely still rested in the closet of the room he'd rented for a month. Getting close to the prince would be easy enough. Both times they'd met, he seemed to recklessly put himself within striking distance, but his guards would be a problem.

If Vasili had his manacles removed again, it wouldn't take much effort for Niko to wrap his fingers around the man's thin neck and choke the life out of him.

He growled at his own thoughts, despising himself.

He'd once loved his city and its royals. Fought for them, believing it was right. His soldiers had fought too. They'd all worn the griffin on their chests with pride.

Where had it all gone wrong?

When the guards came for him next, only he and two others remained in the cell. His wrists were manacled behind his back again and like before, he was marched through the servants' areas—but this time, they all wore black and spoke in hushed voices.

Had the king finally succumbed to his ailments? Did that make Vasili, the eldest, the king now?

That was usually the natural order of these things. But Vasili had been absent for almost as long as the war, safely hidden away. His path to the crown could be contested.

"Who died?" he asked.

"Keep moving," replied the sandy-haired guard with the kind blue eyes from the pleasure house.

He'd find out soon enough. It wouldn't be Vasili; Niko had never been that lucky.

The guard escorted Niko up many staircases into the lighter, cooler parts of the palace where huge windows overlooked the glistening city, then stopped in a chamber adorned with gold-threaded furniture most people never got to see. It was an entirely different world from the blacksmith's cottage where Niko had been raised.

The doors opposite them rattled open, and a plainly dressed man carrying a messenger bag walked out, scowling at Niko before moving past him.

"Send in the mercenary," Vasili's melodic voice chimed.

A shove, and Niko entered another chamber, this one decorated with the same elegance, but larger in every way. The prince leaned against the wall beside a sunlit window, his mourning clothes dark as a thundercloud. He held a glass of wine in his left hand, while his right rested on his thigh. The sight of the bandage around the prince's right wrist summoned a smile to Niko's cracked lips.

Vasili glanced over, as though he'd forgotten he wasn't alone, and sneered. It seemed to be his preferred expression. "He reeks."

"You said to bring him right to you," the guard said flatly.

Vasili waved him off, but did it with his left hand, sloshing some of the wine from the glass. He didn't seem to notice or care how the wine dribbled over his fingers. He walked up to Niko, his keen eye riding over Niko's filthy clothes, making some kind of assessment. "What is your name?"

"Nikolas," Niko croaked. If he was going to die, then at least the prince would know the name of the man he'd sentenced.

"Family name?"

"Yazdan."

"Trade?" His gaze dropped again, scrutinizing, roaming, reading, assessing. *Dissecting.* "Before you were a soldier."

"Smith."

He sipped his wine and took a step back. "What kind?"

"Blacksmith."

The prince nodded to himself. "Do you still forge?"

"No." Niko was not about to reveal how he'd been too young to properly learn the trade before the war broke out, and when he'd returned, there had been nothing left of Pah's forge, just rubble around a chimney stack.

Vasili's smile was shallow, cutting a slash across his face. He took a second step back, appraising his catch. "Uncuff him."

The guard fiddled with the manacles until, with a

freeing click, their weight was gone. Niko rubbed his sore wrists, working feeling back into them.

"Shall I leave?" the guard asked.

"No." Vasili's smile grew sinister. "This one will try and kill me given a chance. Won't you, Nik?" He downed his wine without waiting for a reply and sauntered across the room. His sloppy stride suggested he'd consumed more than one glass that morning. "I offered you coin before; now you don't get a choice." He reached for the bottle with his left hand and refilled his glass, spilling the last few drops. "My brother is dead. You will kill the man who killed him."

Niko continued rubbing his wrists, giving his hands something to do while his thoughts turned over.

"Why?" he asked.

"Why what? Kill a man?"

"Why ask me?"

"You don't know?" Vasili snorted. "I heard all about your altercation in the cell. You protected a lunatic. Did it make you feel better, throttling the man who killed your charity case, or did you murder him because you were angry and he was convenient?" The prince grinned again. "Truly, I'd like to know."

Niko gritted his teeth and turned his face away. He should not have laid a hand on anyone in the cell. He wouldn't have, but lately his nerves and fury ignited like a spark. It had been harder and harder to keep himself controlled. Like with the prince in the pleasure house. He'd lashed out and his mistake had brought him here among these royals—people he despised in a world that wasn't his.

Vasili strode closer, his long legs quickly eating up the

distance between them. "I asked you... Nikolas." He peered into Nikolas's eyes and blinked. "Because I recognize a killer when I see one. And if you speak of this task outside of this room, nobody will believe you."

He could lunge now, wrap his fingers around Vasili's neck and maybe end it, but what good would that do anyone? The elder prince would be dead, but one prince would remain. The king still lived, and there were probably half a dozen other Cavilles lined up, eager to wear the crown, and all were a curse upon this land.

Vasili wet his lips. Niko watched the viper's mouth part, watched the tip of his tongue stroke over his bottom lip. "You've thought about killing me," the prince said. "Many have. Many more dangerous than you. Yet here I stand, very much alive." He seemed to gain a twisted sense of glee from that statement, then threw back his second glass of wine in several gulps. His throat undulated, so delicate for someone full of poison.

Suddenly the prince whirled and launched the glass at the wall. It shattered spectacularly, raining jagged fragments across the floor. Vasili laughed, but there was no humor in the sound. Just madness.

Niko glanced at the guard. The man hadn't flinched, staring across the room completely unfazed. It seemed this was normal behavior for the prince.

Vasili flopped into a chair, elegant limbs sprawling. He rested his right wrist gingerly over his waist. "Toss him back in the cell until he agrees."

Niko swallowed, dread filling his empty gut.

The guard grabbed his wrists. He couldn't go back there. If he went back, he'd get weaker, and then he'd have no choice at all. He yanked an arm free of the guard's fingers.

"Come on, now," the guard grumbled, reaching again. "Back we go."

Niko ducked the guard's arm, plucked the shortsword from the guard's sheath, hearing him shout, and bolted for Vasili.

The prince didn't move from the chair, barely even twitched, so when Niko fell over him—the guard's blade drawn back to plunge into the prince's heart—he did not expect to feel the bite of steel at his throat. But there it was, freezing Niko rigid.

"Hm." The prince licked his lips and tilted his head. His eye widened, drinking in Niko's murderous glare. "A free lesson, from me to you. Call it a gift. I'm always one step ahead, Nik." He flicked his wrist and the blade nicked Niko's skin, drawing his blood for a second time.

The guard barked something. A dull thump stole Niko's vision, filling it in with throbbing blackness, and the last thing he saw as he plunged into unconsciousness was Vasili's cruel smile.

HE AGREED to the prince's order two days later, delirious from hunger. The same sandy-haired guard who had escorted him everywhere led Niko through more palace corridors, all of them blurring into one long stream of opulence. It was dreamlike. If Niko could pretend this was all a nightmare, then whatever happened here didn't matter.

Hot, damp air brought him back into the moment.

Niko blinked at the sunken baths behind the guard. Steam rolled off surfaces scattered with rose petals, and clung to tiled walls. Water streamed into pools and ran into drains recessed into the stone floor. They were alone, which seemed unusual for the size of the bathing house.

The guard reached up to unbutton Niko's rancid shirt.

Niko grabbed the guard's gloved hand, holding him back, and met his gaze.

He was out of his heavy armor and instead in a simple tunic and trousers. Had this moment arrived two weeks ago, Niko would have tackled him. He'd be a match physically, but he didn't have the look of a man accustomed to violence, despite his profession. But two weeks into his prison sentence and Niko could barely stand without swaying on his feet. He was in no condition to fight. Not without food and water and rest.

"The prince wants you clean," the guard said.

"I can bathe myself."

The guard lowered his hand. "I'm sure you can. But if you slip and injure yourself, it'll be my head the prince takes."

They both knew which prince he was referring to, and it irked Niko to know Vasili was able to issue commands without being present.

His shirt buttons vexed him. His fingers didn't seem to want to obey, his body slow to respond. If he'd been fed, he'd be more able, but cleanliness was apparently more important than starvation. Even so, Niko wasn't about to allow a stranger to disrobe him. He had some pride left.

The guard stepped back and folded his arms, clinically observing while Niko stripped naked and descended the steps into steaming water. His entrance sloshed water over the sides. He sank his shoulders beneath the surface. The heat was unexpected and welcome, kneading into sore muscles like warm hands.

A room full of hot baths seemed surreal. He couldn't imagine how they were heated. A natural spring, perhaps. He couldn't remember the last time he'd indulged in a hot bath. Before the war, surely. Sighing, he leaned back against the pool's edge. Flushed and light-headed, his body was warning him to wash quickly before he passed out—but by the three, it felt divine.

A sponge hit the water, splashing his face. He grabbed at it and wrung water through it a few times. "Thanks."

"Don't thank me," Vasili said.

Niko whipped his head around to see the prince making his way around the bath. Most lords had boots with metal heels to announce their presence wherever they went, but Vasili's boots barely made a noise on the stone. Vasili didn't announce. He lurked like the snake he was.

"Clean the filth off yourself," the prince said with a flick of his pale hand.

He'd been about to, but having Vasili command him made him hesitate. He'd been a good soldier, able to follow orders and issue them, but hearing this prince's dismissive tone summoned a petulance Niko hadn't known he'd possessed.

"Your betrayal cost me a brother." Vasili stopped at the foot of the bath and tilted his head. His hair fell over his damaged eye, almost hiding it completely. Tilting his head must have been a habit formed either to hide his eye or to help himself focus better. It suggested the wound was old enough for him to have adapted. "You owe me your service, mercenary. That is what you are now? A blade for hire?"

"Mercenaries are paid, not beaten." Niko dragged the sponge across his face, scraping the natural fibers across his beard. It did feel good to rid himself of the grit and stench that clung to him from the cells. He let his eyelids droop.

"You'll pay with your life if you betray me again."

"I can't betray those who haven't earned my loyalty."

Vasili's laugh was hollow, like the man it belonged to. He knelt at the foot of the bath and dangled the fingers of his left hand into the warm water, circling a rose petal, making it spin. "Honest words such as yours will cost you your tongue. I advise you keep them to yourself from now on."

Niko bit his tongue to keep from telling the prince to go fuck himself and focused instead on washing across his chest. "May I speak freely?"

Vasili lifted his chin, brow raised in surprise. "I assumed you already were. Go ahead. Julian is my... personal protection. Whatever you say will never go beyond the three of us. Unless I wish it, of course."

The guard, Julian, was standing near the wall, away from the bath. He raised an eyebrow at Niko's over-the-shoulder glance, but said nothing. "You have access to assassins," Niko said, facing Vasili again. He didn't like having the prince leave his line of sight. The guard was unlikely to stab him in the back, but the prince might. "Why not ask one of them to kill your target?"

"Because it's exactly what they'd expect of me."

"They?"

He removed his fingers from the water, flicked them

dry, and straightened, tugging his finely tailored shirt into alignment. His single-eyed gaze roamed Niko's face again, then briefly dropped below the waterline to where Niko pulled the sponge over his navel.

The water rippled, obscuring Niko's nakedness, but even so, Niko still felt the crawl of the prince's eye. His skin crackled with discomfort. The gaze wasn't clinical, like Julian's. Vasili looked at Niko like a butcher deciding which prime cut to carve off next. There didn't seem to be any weapons about his person, but Niko hadn't seen the dagger the prince had pressed against his throat until it was already kissing his skin.

He touched his neck, brushing the scab hidden inside unruly stubble. The mark was small, but deep enough it might scar.

"If anyone asks you who you are, you say you are Prince Vasili's *doulos*."

"I'm what?" He couldn't have heard correctly.

"Simply that. You are mine. You have no name and no purpose beyond serving me."

"I don't understand. A doulos? I thought I was hired to kill someone?"

"All in good time, Nik."

Niko's brows pinched. Of course the viper would go back on his word. "I see the Cavilles are the same liars now as they've always been."

Vasili smiled. "You have no idea."

Niko stared ahead as the prince strode from the bathhouse.

His fingers gripped the sponge so tightly they ached. Doulos was a derogatory term reserved for criminal slaves —thieves that had been pressed into service instead of having their fingers severed as punishment for their crimes. He'd seen some of the worst offenders whipped in public and ordered to perform debased acts while a jeering crowd watched. He'd rather die than be so disgraced.

But it didn't matter what Vasili called him.

Once clean and fed, his strength restored, he'd flee the palace and the city. There was nothing left for him here, anyway. The lawless, gang-ridden coastal southern lands with its sunbaked city of Seran—named after the gods dumping ground for wrong-doers—were the perfect place to hide. He'd adapt, find a place among those people. Ships needed metalwork. He could turn his hand to black-smithing. It was less conspicuous than mercenary.

"Finish cleaning and get dressed," Julian ordered.

Niko measured his breathing and focused his mind, ignoring the way Vasili's presence alone had boiled his blood. He'd only have to endure him for a few more days; then he'd be gone and the Cavilles could bicker among themselves for all he cared. Perhaps the Cavilles' reign would soon be ended, because the elves would finally reach the city gates and paint the palace red with royal blood. Whatever happened, Niko would not be here to see it.

CHAPTER 4

*J*ulian showed Niko to the cramped doulos chambers and his cot set against the far wall, a long way from the door. It was an improvement from sleeping on the cell floor, but it was still a prison. Bars for windows made that clear.

The clothes waiting for him were scant at best, and clearly designed to make a man feel vulnerable. A tunic, belt, undergarments, and sandals. No pants, Niko's assets would be swinging in the breeze beneath the tunic. He usually slept in more. "This is ridiculous. I'm not..." he trailed off as the heads of the others in the chamber turned his way. They were all similarly dressed. Two men, one woman. Doulos. Criminals-turned-slaves.

Julian sighed. "By all means, complain to the prince when you next see him. I'm sure you don't need all ten of your fingers." He left Niko's side, and as he passed by the beds of the others, he said, "He's Vasili's." Like those two words were enough to strike fear into their hearts. It might have worked for anyone who wasn't a doulos, but the three didn't look at Niko in fear. Distrust, curiosity, and hatred gleamed in their eyes. Julian had just painted a target on Niko's back.

The woman approached first. "Fresh blood," she said. "What did you do?"

They were all smaller than Niko and not a threat on their own. But the three of them could overpower him. He missed his sword. "Broke Vasili's wrist," he said. "Also mentioned a few truths he didn't want to hear."

She laughed. "Oh sweetie, you're so green we could plant seeds in you." It was probably the most genuine laugh he'd heard in weeks. "Josephine." She offered her hand. "I stole some fruit and was stupid enough to get caught."

Niko grasped her wrist and they shook. "Well met, Josephine." He nodded at the others, acknowledging them. "My name's Nikolas."

"A soldier?" she asked.

"Not officially trained. I was drafted to the front line."

She appraised him anew. "We've all been assuming Vasili would never keep a doulos. He executes anyone who displeases him. He must like you." She withdrew to her cot, her smile growing as her gaze wandered over Niko's attire. "You don't seem his type," Josephine said.

"He has a type?" Now that he'd asked, he wasn't sure he wanted to know the answer.

She shrugged. "I just figured he had a kink for the more submissive types. You don't look like you'd bend for anyone. No offense."

The two men eyed him warily, but not without their

own kind of interest, probably assessing where best to stick a dagger.

"I don't intend on staying."

She laughed again and turned to the two men. "He thinks this is an inn! He's so special, he can leave any time." Her good humor vanished and Josephine's hooded eyes spoke of more than her words ever could. "Try the door and you'll find it locked. The steel bars at the windows are fixed in place. The only way out of here is in a casket. The Cavilles own you now."

He slept restlessly that night with Josephine's words haunting his dreams—or were they memories? Around and around the images flew, a spinning vortex pulling him under. Cold, dead hands jutting from mounds of the dead. Rivers of blood. Silent killers moving through the dark. Curved blades glinting in the moonlight.

He snapped open his eyes. His heart pounded. Slick sweat soaked his skin, sticking the thin sheet to him. The killers in his dreams weren't here. They were far away, on the borders. The war was over. There was peace between the races. Because King Caville had surrendered too soon.

One lone candle illuminated the dark, and there, in the shadows, he saw them. Figures moved like smoke, silent as they leaned over each cot, smothering the mouths of their sleeping victims, and drawing their deadly curved blades across their throats. Elves. Here. Impossible.

Blood scented the air, made it wet and heavy. He couldn't move. His body refused to obey. Thoughts came fast, demanding he run. There was no escape. The windows were barred; the only door, behind them. Closer they crept, no more substantial than ghosts.

The single candle snuffed out.

Niko jolted awake a second time, this time for real, gasping back into cruel reality in time to see candlelight lick off a blade raised above his chest.

With the dream still fresh in his head, he grabbed the wrist and rolled, twisting his attacker on top of him. The man grunted. Niko locked a hand around his throat and squeezed. The knife clattered to the floor. Niko had him now, and he would not escape. Someone screamed. The elf could not be allowed free, because it would kill and kill and kill and never stop—that was what they were. Monsters in the night. Monsters the Cavilles had invited into their land.

A pair of new hands grabbed his arm. Someone else yelled at him. But he had the creature in his grasp, and he'd never stop. Damn the elves for taking everything, for ruining it all. Damn them for taking Marcus, leaving behind his hollow, heartless corpse. They always took the hearts. Every single fallen soldier had lost his heart. Niko hadn't died like the others, but after finding Marcus's body, he'd lost his own heart.

A blow to the side of his head almost tore the consciousness out of him. He still had hold of the attacker. He'd never let go, not until it was dead. He'd kill them all if he had to. For Marcus. For revenge. The man's mouth gaped, his lips blue, his fingers clawing at Niko's grip.

Screams and hollers, then someone rammed a cloth over Niko's nose and mouth, and the world came undone in front of his eyes, unspooling and falling free. He fell with it, lost to the ravages of his own mind.

～

He woke in chains.

The guard who came to collect him wasn't Julian, and they weren't taking him into the palace, but outside into its courtyard where a colorful crowd stood fanning themselves beneath unrelenting sunlight.

His mouth tasted bitter, his throat was thick, and his head throbbed. He recalled the dream and more, wincing at the feel of the man's neck in his grip. There hadn't been any elves in that room. Just criminals and one had tried to attack him. Fuck if he knew why. Maybe to get back at Vasili. Maybe they always attacked the new one. Was the man dead? Had Niko killed him? Another life slipped through his fingers?

And now he was on his knees on a wooden stage, chained to metal loops so he couldn't flee, squinting into the sun with sweat dripping down his back.

"Fifteen lashes," Vasili said. Niko searched for him among the people and saw only strangers' faces peering back at him. Was this some kind of nightmare, an extension of those haunting him through the night? The sun on his face, the boards beneath his knees, it didn't feel real.

The first lash struck before he'd had time to brace. He barked a cry, falling forward onto his hands. The second lash landed too fast after the first, ripping a second cry from him. He almost buckled completely—the shock was more vicious than the lashes.

"Slower," Vasili ordered. "We might as well enjoy it if we have to stand in this wretched heat."

Niko's thoughts spun. His back blazed, and the flogger came down again. This time he barred the cry behind gritted teeth. And when the fourth lash landed, he barred that one too, swallowing it as he willed his body to relax. Fighting the whip-blows was useless, but he could lessen them if his muscles relaxed. Retreating inside his head, he thought of the time he'd first met Marcus. Marcus had been the quiet sort, preferring to listen rather than talk. He'd listened to Niko, and then brushed his thigh in a way that suggested there was more between them than being brothers in blood. He'd been too kind for war; he would have made a good teacher.

Thoughts of Marcus lent Niko strength. Did these people think a whip could subdue him? They were all pretty, fragile fools. When the elves came—and they would—they'd tear through Loreen's bejeweled high classes. Whipping a doulos achieved nothing. They should turn their spite on the enemy.

Blood soaked through Niko's thin shirt and dripped on the timbers beneath him. He took another blow, quivering in the heat and sweat and blood. This time, when he looked up, he found the prince dressed in black among the colorful crowd. Vasili didn't smile, just stared back and watched unblinking as every blow landed.

There were others here. Other royals, gentlemen and ladies with titles to hide behind. Prince Amir smiled as though he were watching some humorous performance. He leaned across to speak with his brother, but Vasili didn't hear, or deliberately ignored him. All Vasili's attention was drilled into Niko. Niko twitched and breathed and thought of better people in better places than this, because these lashes would end. All pain ended, one way or another.

The lashings finally stopped. Niko's teeth chattered, his body a trembling wreck, but he was conscious. Vasili nodded and promptly left as the guards unchained Niko from the loops. As he was unceremoniously dragged from the square, Amir's sly gaze caught his eye. The prince licked his lips like he'd just tasted something delicious, something he desired, and wanted more.

CHAPTER 5

*H*e didn't see any royals for the ten days it took for his back to heal enough that moving didn't immediately make him want to drop to his knees and heave his guts up. He'd spent many of those days lost to fever, but the palace healers had brought him back quickly from the worst of it, and had done a grand job of covering the weeping wounds until they'd scabbed over.

He was almost relieved to see Julian when he finally arrived to escort him through the palace. It seemed likely he'd return Niko to the doulos chambers, and if Josephine and the others hadn't wanted to kill him before, they would now he'd tried to kill one of their own.

"One of the doulos attacked me," he explained as Julian guided him down a corridor. Julian didn't reply, just stared ahead with the stalwart look of a man who followed orders like they were ordained from Etara, the goddess of earth and war. "Put me back in with them and I cannot guarantee the same thing won't happen again."

"The prince is very much aware of what you'll do, Nikolas."

Had Vasili anticipated this? No, that was too much of a stretch. He could not know Niko would be attacked, or how he'd react. Although, was it really so unexpected given how Niko had already killed a man in the cells? This couldn't go on. These were games to see what triggered Niko. He'd hurt someone else, someone who didn't deserve it. "I need to speak with Vasili."

"You will."

"Julian..." It was the first time he'd said his name, and he brought the guard to a dead stop in the corridor. He had startling blue eyes, the kind made for laughing, although he wasn't smiling now. His broad-shouldered stance could easily make him intimidating, but he didn't radiate violence like some men in his position might.

What had he been about to say? Niko cleared his throat. Now he had the man's full attention, he wasn't sure of his words. "Did I kill the doulos?"

"You certainly did not make a friend of him." The guard's mouth hinted at a restrained grin, and warmth touched his eyes. "He survived."

Well, that was good, wasn't it? "If you put me back in with them—"

"You're not going back there. Come now." Julian took his arm and urged him along. They walked in silence a while, turning corridors and climbing steps. "Some advice, if you'll listen?" Julian voiced it as a question, implying he'd noticed Niko's stubborn streak. "The prince is..."

Indecision made his gaze flicker. His fingers tightened on Niko's bicep. "... Complicated. Work with him, and you might survive this."

Work with him? He wasn't sure such a thing was possible. Vasili seemed to summon in him the urge to kill the moment the prince stepped into the same room. "I agreed to kill a man for him. The rest of this was avoidable—putting me with doulos. I'm not a criminal. It's on him."

"You agreed, yes. But he doesn't believe your word. I wonder why that is," Julian mused in a singsong voice, keeping his eyes ahead.

Niko stared ahead too, wishing he could see through walls to a way out. "He doesn't trust anyone."

Julian glanced over, his smile gone. "Prince Amir wanted you dead for attempting to kill another slave. Vasili saved you from the noose."

Saved him? Niko barked an incredulous laugh. "It's Vasili's fucking noose to begin with!"

Julian grabbed Niko's jerkin in his fists and yanked him face-to-face with startling strength. "Mind your words, Nikolas."

"Unhand him, Julian." Vasili sighed, having emerged from a gilded door at the end of the hall. "Bring him inside."

The room was different from the first he'd been invited into. That one had been overflowing with opulence. This was softer, somehow. The furniture and wallpaper weren't fighting for attention. Instead, cool, clean lines and colors complemented each other. It was probably the first room in the palace that didn't instantly give Niko a headache. Then there was the huge bed. Blood red velvet curtains draped from each of the posts. Black quilts were laid over it, pooling around it.

By the gods, it was hideous.

"Leave us," Vasili said.

Julian frowned. "I don't think—"

"Good. Don't. Go."

Julian reluctantly let go of Niko's arm, lingering like he had more to say, and finally left. Niko couldn't decide if Julian took his work as the prince's guard seriously or if there was something more between them. He couldn't imagine Vasili's sharp exterior ever thawing enough to let *anyone* close. Niko had found rocks with more empathy.

Vasili gracefully reclined in a chair, placed an ankle on his knee, and stared. His white-blonde hair curtained half his face, hiding the scarring. When he gestured, he did so with his right hand, proving it had healed enough for him to freely move it. "You understand how we can meet like this?"

"I..." Niko wasn't entirely sure of his answer. He wasn't sure of anything since the guards had dragged him to the palace dungeons.

Vasili rolled his eye. "You are my doulos, to do with as I please. Thus, you and I can be alone. In fact, it's expected of us. Come closer. I do not bite."

Niko took a few obligatory steps forward and stopped. This felt like a trap. Julian hadn't bound him, and there were plenty of ornaments and pieces of furniture that would make brutal but efficient weapons. He'd already spotted a large, beautifully decorated vase that would make a brilliant projectile. The broken pieces would make excellent blades.

"Were you, say, a mercenary, we would not be here," Vasili said, his words and voice elegant and smooth. "Were you, say, an assassin? We would not be here. Were you a lord or indeed a lady, we would certainly not be here, in my personal chambers, alone. As a doulos we can be in the same room, without anyone caring. Our conversations are private. Now do you understand?"

"Then...I am not your slave?"

"For the benefit of others, yes. If I wanted a real doulos, I'd find one far more willing to fuck without arguing."

A relief, for the most part. Niko sighed. If he could ease the tension between them, perhaps he could convince the prince he didn't need a handler in Julian, and then he'd flee. "I apologize."

The prince raised his eyebrow.

"For the wrist. And the trouble."

Vasili tilted his head and smiled. "How kind of you to admit your wrongdoing, but also bullshit. Still, I'm impressed you were able to say the words without spitting in my face. Now, sit."

"I'd rather stand."

Vasili blinked. "I'd rather I did not have to speak with you at all." He leaned forward, making his long hair slip from his shoulder. "I'd rather you were not in my chamber and I'd rather I still had two eyes instead of just the one. We would all rather things be different, so take the fucking seat, Nikolas, and save your energy for arguments worth having."

Nikolas grabbed a nearby chair, spun it around to face the prince, and sat.

"Don't worry," Vasili purred. "There will be many more chances for you to defy me."

"Am I here just for you to torment?"

He chuckled and rested an elbow on the arm of his chair, propping his chin on his knuckles. "What a delight that would be. But no. Carlo, my younger brother, did

41

not die by accident, as the gossip would have you believe."

He hadn't heard. Being locked up on arrival at the palace and then convalescing for the past few weeks meant he hadn't heard much of anything, and certainly nothing of courtly politics.

"His saddle was loose. The horse spooked. His body was found a mile outside the city. His skull was caved in, apparently from a fall."

He delivered the facts calmly, coolly, and utterly detached in a way that made it seem as though a stranger had died, and not his own brother.

"That horse was mine," he added. "His death should have been mine too. While I was...away, something insidious manipulated its way into my home and my family. It undermines them—us," he hastily corrected. "Observed as I am, I cannot root out this force without them becoming aware of my interest. That is clearly where you come in."

"Julian seems proficient. You trust him. Why not ask him to investigate?"

"Julian is" —he glanced toward the closed doors— "helpful where he is." Vasili held Niko's gaze, making Niko's insides turn over, as though the man had an uncanny ability to rifle through his soul and reveal things best left hidden. "You have not been subtle in your hatred of me, but that I can trust. I prefer the enemy I can see to the one behind my back."

There was an elegance to it, Niko supposed. If Niko wanted the prince dead, it wouldn't be with a knife in the back. "You clearly have suspicions as to who wants you killed."

He chuckled dryly. "My return was unexpected. Many

in my family would prefer I did not return at all. The palace, its people, it's all changed. And I see from your eyes that we finally agree on something."

Niko straightened in the chair. He'd always thought himself careful with his expressions, but Vasili's gaze had the unnerving ability to strip Niko's guard. "What makes you think you can trust me for this task?"

"I don't trust you," the prince said, as though that answered the question. Perhaps it did, but only by opening up more questions.

This man was like none Niko had ever met before. He claimed to be hunted, and yet he didn't look like a man afraid. If anything, he was the only person Niko had met who wasn't afraid. He reminded him of a fox among chickens. The kind that didn't kill to eat. It killed because it could. Niko knew killers too. He'd commanded many of them. This Caville prince was the kind who enjoyed the killing a little too much.

Niko shifted in the seat, briefly averting his eyes. "And at the end of all this?"

"You may leave," Vasili said, tone flat. "Rebuild your blacksmith's shop, forge a new life."

And how did the prince know his family's blacksmith's shop needed rebuilding? Coincidence, as most trades from outlying villages had ceased during wartime, or something more?

"Pah's shop was at the heart of Trenlake." The village name had the desired effect of making the prince's brow tighten. "The elves burned it down in the massacre, got right up to Loreen's gates. Killed everyone, including my parents."

The prince winced again and turned his face away. "Julian," he called.

The door promptly flew open.

"I wasn't there to protect them." Niko stood. "The elves hung them from trees. They weren't dead when they were strung up. Death never comes easy for their victims." The prince still faced away. The thin skin over his pulse fluttered lightly in his neck, and Niko found he wanted to twist the blade some more, make the man hear the horrors of war, make him *see* them.

Julian reached for his arm and Niko snatched it away. "You'd know that if you'd been here instead of hiding wherever your father had you holed up for safekeeping."

Vasili tore from the chair and lunged for the window. He braced an arm against the frame and bowed his head. "Take him away." His shoulders heaved, breaths coming fast.

Was it shame that made him turn his face away? Shame that he'd run from the war like the coward he was, while his people had fought for the griffin and died by the thousands.

Satisfied he'd done enough, Niko relented and left with Julian.

They walked two doors down from the prince's chambers. Julian shoved him inside and slammed the door behind them. "You need to learn to hold your tongue." The man's cheek twitched. "This is where you will sleep from now on. By all means, admire the view from the window. We're in one of the highest towers. Don't jump. You'll sleep on the lounger. The bed is mine."

The room was similar to Vasili's, if smaller, with an interconnecting door that possibly led through a second chamber and eventually to the prince's room. "This is your room?"

"It is. Vasili wanted to keep you with the other doulos to see what shook free since your last encounter was so fruitful. I suggested that may not be the most efficient use of your skills and offered to accommodate you here. You're welcome."

"How was my last encounter fruitful when I almost killed a man?"

"Multiple witnesses stated the man, a new doulos, tried to kill you, unprovoked, in your sleep."

"He did...." Niko drifted about the room. There were no weapons, at least none of the obvious kind. Minimal, neat, impersonal. This room either hadn't been Julian's for long, or he preferred to keep all personal items hidden out of sight. Probably to stop Vasili using them as ammunition. "I hadn't been sure at first. The dreams make it—" He cut himself off and reached a dresser mirror, only to find Julian's reflection watching him closely.

"Someone took a dislike to Vasili having a personal slave and decided to remove you," Julian said. "It could be connected to Carlo's death. We don't know. Doulos, by their nature, are feisty with each other."

"If Vasili knew I was attacked, why did he have me publicly flogged?" His back itched and ached at the recent trauma.

"For appearances. Most doulas are broken in early on so they know their place. He was lenient."

Acrid hate burned on Niko's tongue. These people, they were a different breed. The killer, whoever they were, had the right idea in attacking the prince. Maybe Niko would find them and help them eliminate all the royals.

What a thought that was. From soldier to assassin. But the idea didn't sit well with him. He had more honor than that. The Cavilles weren't worth his loyalty, but the innocent people of Loreen were. "Did you fight in the war, Julian?"

"I did," the man said, surprising Niko. He didn't have the hard eyes of those who had survived.

"Where?"

"Carlion Gap."

Niko turned and reassessed the man standing before him. He was well-built with enough muscle to make him a proficient warrior, but something didn't feel right. The Carlion Gap was one of the first border locations to fall to the elves. Loreen's forces hadn't been prepared. *Nothing* could have prepared them for the elves. He studied Julian again, stepping closer, and noticed the gloves. He'd been wearing them from the moment they'd met in the pleasure house, and though Julian was in a more comfortable uniform, the gloves stayed.

Elves often took more trophies than hearts.

"You escaped them?" Niko asked.

Julian worked his jaw and sighed. "I try not to think about it."

"I'm grateful for your service, even if the Cavilles are not."

Julian nodded and half-gestured at the room. "Don't touch my shit."

"Fair enough." Niko smiled.

"And don't get any ideas about fleeing," Julian added, dropping into a chair to unlace his boots. He used a thumb and finger, but the remaining gloved fingers stayed rigid. "I'll have to chase you down, and neither of us wants that."

He pulled the boot free, then added the second and neatly set them aside.

"Do you care for the prince?" Niko asked.

The question interrupted Julian's smooth movements, making him stall and look up. "It is my duty to protect the royal name, as it is yours, although you seem to have forgotten."

"I did not forget. They stopped earning my loyalty when the king surrendered."

"The king negotiated peace, and he had his reasons."

Niko leaned back against the windowsill and folded his arms. "I don't blame you for wanting this peace. But we fought back, and we were winning. Eight years and we were beating them until King Talos pissed it all away because he's a coward, just like the rest of them. Just like Vasili."

Julian's smile was a sad, sympathetic turn of his lips. He stood and fumbled with the buttons of his shirt as he headed toward the four-poster bed. "Get some rest while you can. Vasili keeps unusual hours."

"I rarely sleep."

"Neither does he."

CHAPTER 6

$\mathcal{N}$iko woke to the sound of whispers. At first, he'd thought the gentle ebb and flow of hissing was the wind through the trees and his mind had propelled him back to the frontline camp where fires fought off the dark, but not the elves. But the blanket thrown over him was not his own, and the lounger he slept on was far more comfortable than straw over dirt. Groggy, he blinked, clearing his focus while checking for the shape of Julian sleeping on the bed.

The whispers continued, although he couldn't make out any words.

He carefully folded back the blanket and padded barefoot across the room, grateful he'd kept his shirt and undergarments on. The sound wasn't in the room, but seemed to be coming from behind the connecting door. He was sure of it. The whispers grew louder as he approached.

Niko glanced at Julian. He could wake him, but wasn't entirely sure if the whispers were real or his own dreams misleading him again. He closed his hand around the door handle and gently turned it. The door swung open with well-oiled ease to reveal a narrow, middle chamber with a sofa and a few chairs. No beds or wardrobes. Just a private antechamber leading to the prince's room. And it was empty.

He must have been dreaming after all.

A shadow moved under the prince's door.

Niko silently crossed the distance and pressed his ear to the door. Nothing.

Was the prince awake? Julian had said the man didn't sleep. What if the assassin were in the room right now? Maybe he should leave them be. *What a terrible shame the prince had died.* Although with Niko so close, he might get accused of being complicit in his death. If he were to die, it had better be for the truth and not wrongly accused.

The whispers started up again, louder this time. Niko grabbed the handle, twisted, and shoved the door open.

A shifting shadow with ruby-red eyes loomed over the prince's bed, clawed fingers poised to strike. Its head whipped around, glare fixing on Niko. The shadow rushed forward, slamming into Niko, sending him reeling. A breath-stealing sensation of crawling ice clutched at his throat and chest and froze his heart.

His legs hit something—a chair. It toppled, taking Niko with it, the shadow still riding his chest. The red-eyed glare burrowed into his own, screaming through his soul. By the gods, it was strong. Niko got hold of some solid part around its thin waist and pushed. His biceps burned, arms trembling, but inch by inch he heaved the shadow creature off his chest and gasped, finally able to breathe again.

"Back, fiend!"

Grit rained over Niko, some of it catching in his lips. Salt. It sizzled on the fiend's wispy skin, making the shadowy smoke bubble. The fiend screeched, darted free of Niko's grip, and shot like an arrow through the prince's chamber door. Niko launched himself off the floor in time to see it disappear out the window.

"You all right?" A hand landed firmly on Niko's back. Julian steered him toward the chair Vasili had been draped in earlier.

Niko grabbed the chair's arm. He concentrated on breathing through the remnants of that thing's death-grip on his lungs. He glanced at the bed. The sheets were unwrinkled. The prince wasn't here, and never had been.

Julian stood close to Niko's right, making him glance up. The guard's blue eyes were big in the dark room. "I'm fine," Niko grunted.

"Wait here."

Julian left and Niko stared at the window, its pane ajar. How had the creature climbed to the highest tower in the palace without being seen?

Julian returned later to find Niko slumped in Vasili's chair. "He's safe," he said.

"Good for him," Niko wheezed, still trying to make his lungs work. "What was that thing?"

"Our assassin."

Niko dragged a hand down his face and sighed hard. "He said nothing about *sorcery*."

"Did he not?" Julian mumbled, reaching for Niko with a gloved hand. His fingers landed gently against Niko's shirt, over his chest. The sudden touch stalled Niko's thoughts, emptying out everything that had happened. His head filled with notions that Julian's concern might be something more. Julian was shirtless, his chest smooth. A few soft golden hairs caught the ambient light from the connecting room. Niko's gaze fluttered downward to where his loose night trousers hung off his hips.

"Come on," Julian said, pulling his fingers back. "It won't try again tonight."

Niko almost groaned at the loss of the man's touch. Breathlessness and aches aside, he'd have welcomed more attention from Julian's steady hands. Niko might have taken them in his own hands and applied them to parts of him that so desperately missed the touch of another man.

Scanning the chamber a second time to distract himself, his eye caught the monstrous bed again. "He doesn't sleep in this room, does he?"

Julian slipped his fingers into Niko's hand and heaved him to his feet, then looped an arm around his waist. "Of course not."

The prince was far more sly than Niko had realized.

"I'm really all right," Niko protested, wishing he'd slept shirtless so he could feel the man's skin brush against his own.

Julian guided him to his own bed and urged him to lie back on the soft covers. The icy tightness in his chest sparked up again; probably bruised ribs. He wheezed his thanks and rested his head on the fine pillow. Would Julian climb on beside him? Wrecked as he was, the thought of Julian lying close, his firm body next to Niko's, had his cock taking an interest. He waited for Julian to speak, to say something about the attack or Vasili, but he only smiled and withdrew, readying the lounger where he clearly intended to sleep.

Candlelight stroked over the man's firm back and shoulders and down his waist. The rise of his ass looked firm too. Would he yield, or would he demand Niko yield for him? It was a good thing Julian had taken the lounger because there was no hiding exactly how much attention Niko's dick had taken in events.

Julian turned away and Niko drifted again, this time falling into a deep, dreamless sleep.

WHEN HE NEXT OPENED HIS eyes, sunlight poured into the room through the window.

The pressure on his chest was still there, and he winced as he gingerly climbed from the bed. His time in the cells had cost him physically, but his strength would return.

He was alone and checking his wrists for shackles, revealed he was still unrestrained. His gaze went to the door. Probably locked.

He spotted a washbasin and mirror and, after stretching his sore muscles, he made his way over. His grim reflection appeared as weary as he felt. He dragged his fingers through his short beard. A straight razor and soap lay on a towel beside the basin. He didn't recall seeing it there before, and he'd checked the room for weapons last night. Julian was the thoughtful type. But perhaps too trusting? A razor made a formidable weapon in capable hands.

He shaved, finding comfort in the familiar task, and ran wet fingers through his dark hair. The weight of his stare had been lost in his bearded appearance. Now smooth-shaven, his eyes regained the hardness that had helped him earn a reputation on the front—one he was not proud of.

He pulled his hair back into a short tail using the thin strip of leather left out for him. He'd always kept his hair short on the front. Elves would grab a soldier's loose locks and slice them from their scalps, more gruesome trophies for their collections.

"There is a face beneath all the fur."

Niko allowed himself a small smile at Julian's words as he came through the doorway, carrying a bundle of clothes.

"Your actions last night earned you a gift." Julian set the bundle on the dresser.

"Vasili suggested this?" Niko gestured at the clothes. He spotted a fine leather jerkin, the type squires often wore. It wasn't something he'd normally wear, but it was a huge improvement on what the prince currently provided. He couldn't spend another day in the doulos outfit.

"He didn't refuse."

Then Julian had suggested it and Vasili hadn't cared enough to comment either way.

Julian busied himself about the room while Niko stripped off the undergarments from last night and layered himself up in the fresh linen and leathers. With all the ties laced, he regarded himself in the mirror again and caught Julian's hungry gaze behind him. This time, he didn't look away. Was it hunger of a sexual kind, or just appreciation?

Niko began tidying the shaving implements, and rested his fingers on the razor.

"I wouldn't advise it, merc." He said 'merc' like he'd said 'doulos', the tone unfriendly.

Niko withdrew his fingers. As much as he didn't want to be here, he also didn't want to take a blade to Julian. As a fellow soldier, Julian was obliged to follow the prince's orders. Niko wasn't about to attack him for doing his job. There would be other opportunities to escape that didn't involve spilling Julian's blood.

"You don't like mercenaries?"

"No."

"Few soldiers have a prince to prop up their finances after the war."

"So frosty," Julian mumbled.

Niko observed Julian's reflection smile. "You serve Vasili and think I'm frosty?"

Julian conceded the point with a small laugh, the sound so very natural for him. After so much darkness, the easy laughter lifted Niko's mood.

"If you're well enough to argue," Julian said. "You're well enough to do some observing for the prince."

"What kind of observing?" He leaned back against the dresser, and this time Julian's attention was less clinical in its path roaming Niko's new attire. The warmth of that attention thawed the tension in Niko's veins. A beat passed, then another. Did Julian know he was staring? It had been a long time since anyone had paid any physical attention to Niko. After Marcus... Well, there hadn't been much desire after Marcus, just the need to spill elven blood.

"You'll see." Julian tore his gaze away and headed for the door. "Can I trust you won't try and flee the second we leave this room?" he said, holding the door open, his tone almost back to that of the palace guard. "You wouldn't get very far."

"For now." Niko brushed by him, needlessly touching to test a theory. He'd hoped to feel the man tense, or hear him react, but Julian merely smiled and walked on ahead, waiting for Niko to fall into step. Niko had imagined his heated interest, then. Likely the man just appreciated good clothes and a clean jaw.

"What was that creature last night?" he asked.

"A fiend." Julian kept his voice low. They passed by several servants bustling about the hallways, cleaning, tending fires, and doing the routine things the royals seemed incapable of doing for themselves. They acknowledged Julian with brief dips of their chins as he passed. He nodded back, noticing each and every one. Vasili probably ignored them all.

"And what is a fiend exactly?"

"Think of it like an arrow let loose from a bow. Only the bow is the sorcerer and the fiend is able to reach places arrows cannot. You know that child's song... How does it go?" He mumbled to himself in a vague tune Niko recognized.

"Something about the moving flame, or living dark. I can't remember."

He clicked his fingers. "It's old, from a different time when most everyone believed in the gods. The fiends were simple creatures, born of shadows. Myths say they are children of Aura, due to their shadowy nature, and they live for a single night and die at dawn. Others say they're elves corrupted by darkness."

"It didn't look much like an elf." Niko recalled talk of such phantoms on the front line, after several soldiers had died in their sleep. He'd disregarded it as superstition. "They kill their victims while they sleep?"

"Suffocate them," Julian's lips thinned as he pressed them together. "That one was meant for the prince."

Niko couldn't forget how the creature had tried to freeze his lungs. "Have they been sent for Vasili before?"

"Once. He moved from that room after the first attack."

"How did he survive?"

Julian's lips lifted, hinting at a smile. "He's difficult to catch unawares, as you've witnessed."

A knife plucked out of nowhere and pressed to Niko's throat was the perfect demonstration of how aware Vasili was. He likely slept on a bed of blades. Niko hoped never to see it.

"There's nobody you suspect?" Niko asked.

"Plenty we suspect, but none we can prove."

Considering how Vasili was the eldest prince and heir to the throne, the person most likely to benefit from his death was the remaining brother, Amir, the loud prince Niko had seen at the feast. Vasili's recent return would have ruined his plans for the throne. "Amir—"

"Careful," Julian muttered, nodding at another pair of servants. "Needless to say," he added once they were alone in the hallway, "Amir is of *interest*."

"If there's sorcery involved, that changes things."

"Whoever the sorcerer is, they don't have access to much power. Summoning a fiend is all we've seen from them."

Still, the practice of sorcery was unheard of now, only existing in ancient stories. But someone had discovered a way to harness enough unnatural power to summon a fiend and send it through Vasili's window.

"I need more to work with. If Vasili wants me to help him, he has to start helping me."

"He has been helping, in his own way."

"By having me publicly flogged?"

"A lenient punishment for almost killing a man."

"Who wants him dead, Julian?"

Julian shoved through a corridor doorway. "A better questions is who doesn't?"

More staff had filled the hallways, coming and going with trays of food and wine. The time for talk was over. Julian rested a solid hand on Niko's shoulder and leaned in. "Do as I say. You're here to observe. My job is to watch the prince. His is to be seen." He drew Niko toward a second, elaborately decorated door. "Can I rely on you to obey?"

He'd been willing until the word *obey*, and now he wondered what was expected of him. He nodded, and Julian opened the door.

CHAPTER 7

*S*unlight made all the colors in the room bloom like flowers in a meadow. Silk drapes fluttered in a breeze drifting through vast, open windows. Most of Loreen's elite sat around another huge table, this one cluttered with wineglasses and fruit.

Julian guided Niko down one wall toward a row of kneeling doulos. "Kneel," he said.

Niko's brief hesitation made Julian's eyebrows rise. He'd agreed to this, albeit under the threat of starvation. Ignoring the spike of pride trying to keep him from submitting, he dropped to his knees.

Had Vasili ordered him, his reaction might have been very different.

Julian left him at the end of the line and took his place near a column at the side of the room, seamlessly blending in with the other guards present.

People mingled. Laughter tinkled, some light and sharp, some deep and booming. At least Niko wasn't likely to be whipped. He just had to play along and *observe*.

Although what he was supposed to observe from his knees was questionable.

He stretched, trying to find the princes or anyone worth observing who wasn't full of air, but saw only a sea of backs.

"Did he fuck you yet?" the man beside him whispered.

Niko ignored the question.

"Dresses you like a doll, huh? You must be special."

Murmuring passed down the line of kneeling doulos.

"Does he order you to get yourself off while he watches?"

"Is it true he likes to watch?" another voice whispered. "Have you touched him? Is he scarred, like they say?"

Niko narrowed his eyes and fixed his glare on the grinning blond beside him. "Are you addressing me?"

"Who the fuck else would we be *addressing*, eh?" The young man wet his lips. "C'mon, what's he like? Does he even *have* a prick?"

Niko frowned harder and faced forward. The tittering continued, whispers and snickers over whether Vasili could get it up or if he liked to be tied, or if he just liked to take a whip to Niko and masturbate while doing so.

"Hush," a woman's voice piped up. Niko glanced over. Josephine's gaze met his. "Or we'll all suffer."

The man who had asked questions first rubbed his hands down his thighs as though he were wiping his sweaty palms dry. "Bet the elves cut his little prick off." He snickered. "And ate it, made the little bitch whine for his bitch mother—"

Niko's knuckles impacted the fool's nose, shattering bone. The doulos wailed and fell back into the others in a spectacular display of tangled limbs. A surprising amount of blood had spurted down the man's face and chest. Niko hit him in the throat this time to stop the screeching, and he wouldn't have stopped if viselike fingers hadn't pulled him off.

It was a relief. Now he didn't have to listen to the bastard's foul mouth. That *had* been satisfying. He smiled at his own thoughts and shook out his bruised knuckles as the guards manhandled him backward. Then he noticed the crowd and the look of horror on their faces.

He flicked his hand, making someone nearby squeak as blood splattered their fine clothing. They all stared at him like he was some wild animal. Maybe he was. He grinned, making a lord shudder and stumble back.

"You again." Amir stalked toward him, stopping an inch from Niko's face. The grip on Niko's arms tightened, holding him rigid.

"You just can't play nice with the others, can you? We have ways of dealing with doulos like you." He turned to the nearest guest. "Move!" As soon as they sprang from their chair, Amir swept the wine glasses to the floor, shattering most.

He plucked a serrated knife from the cutlery. "Hold him down."

Hands shoved Niko in the back, driving him forward.

The nearest guests scattered, but didn't go far, sensing a show.

Niko bared his teeth and dug his heels in.

"Spread his hand! Now!" Amir barked.

The guards pushed down. Thick fingers dug into his shoulders and pushed.

"*What is this?*" Vasili's voice cut through the ruckus like a blade. Everyone froze but Amir, who glared at

Niko, his blue eyes full of murderous intent and his cheek pulsing.

Julian stepped from the crowd, skimmed a glance over Amir, he faced Vasili. He didn't kneel, but a hesitation suggested he wanted to. Always the soldier. "It appears one of the doulos spoke ill of you, my prince."

Finally, Amir tore his glare from Niko, fixing it on his brother and Julian instead. "Your wretched pet broke mine's nose."

"It'll be your nose next, *prince*." The words were out of Niko before he had considered his precarious position.

Amir whirled. "How dare you insult me?! You are nothing! You piece of common filth—"

Vasili laid a hand on his brother's shoulder. Amir shrank under his touch, his bluster cooling, but rage still simmered in his eyes.

"Bring the doulos," Vasili said.

Some scuffling ensued. The man with the broken nose was brought to Vasili and pushed to his knees. He huffed clogged breaths through his mouth.

"What was said?" Vasili asked.

The man looked up and blinked. "Nudding."

"Nothing?" Vasili asked, his voice taking on a dangerous lightness. "I do not think my doulos caved your face in for nothing. He does have a tendency to have his fists win arguments for him, but not without reason."

Vasili crouched to the man's level and smiled like he'd just become the doulos's best friend. That look made the fine hairs rise on Niko's arms. "It's best to tell me now. Your punishment will be worse if I have to ask again."

Half the crowd was leaning in, feverishly whispering theories.

The man blinked, groaned, and finally sobbed. Niko almost felt sorry for him. The slurs hadn't been that bad. It was more mention of the elves that had snapped the frayed line of control in Niko's head, because he'd seen the doulos's words happen. Torture was never a joke.

Vasili straightened. "Is anyone going to tell me what was said?" His single-eyed gaze flicked over the crowd but avoided Niko.

"He said..." Josephine raised her voice and the crowd parted, letting her through. She instantly dropped to a knee. "He said the elves had cut off your...cut off your prick and eaten it." Her eyes flicked up. She blinked and looked down again.

The air chilled suddenly, or perhaps the ice was already in his veins and he'd just now noticed it. He turned his head and found Vasili staring at *him*. Gods knew why. Niko hadn't said the words. Then the prince lifted his chin and swallowed. "Is this true?" he asked the sobbing man at his feet.

The man's head jerked in erratic nods.

"I didn't know..." Amir trailed off. "I didn't hear—"

"Of course you didn't."

Vasili took the knife from his brother's hand, sank his grip into the sobbing man's hair, yanked his head back, and cut his throat in one clean slice. Blood dashed Niko's clothes and spattered those around them. Some gasped, but most stayed silent, frozen in place.

Vasili tossed the bloody knife onto the table, spattering more blood across the lily-white tablecloth, and strode from the room. It was minutes before the crowd carefully and quietly hurried away. It was longer when the body was collected, and longer still when the guards escorted Niko down familiar dungeon corridors.

This time, he was alone behind the bars.

He paced.

He should leave at the first opportunity. Just run. It was the sensible thing to do. Julian would come and unlock the cell. He'd let his guard down and Niko would fight him, if necessary. The Cavilles were insane. All of them. The city was rotten and cursed and he was done with them and it.

But then Julian was outside the bars, hesitating, his eyes haunted. "If you're concerned about the doulos, don't be. He was vile, said to touch children. Vasili has been looking for an excuse to kill him."

Niko frowned. Was that supposed to make him feel better? The entire gods-damned palace was inhabited by killers. If Niko spent any longer inside its walls, he'd lose himself to the same darkness. He wet his lips, seeking the right words to convey what he thought and wrapped his fingers around the bars.

Julian looked up. "Thank you."

"What for?"

"For standing up for Vasili."

"That's not why I hit him. I've seen elves cut fingers off men and worse. Such things are not for jest."

Julian pulled a key from his pocket, slipped it in the lock, flicked it over, and swung the door open. "Leave."

Niko hesitated, waiting for the trap to close.

"Just walk right out," Julian urged. "There's nobody else here. Nobody has to know I let you go. You slipped away and left the city."

It should have been that easy, but his thoughts kept

him rooted in place. He should leave, just walk right on out of this viper's nest and never look back, so why hadn't he left the cell?

"He'll punish you," Niko said. And knew it to be true.

Julian leaned against the open door, staring at the floor. "Probably."

Niko dragged a hand through his hair and tore out the leather tie. "Dammit!" He stepped across the cell's threshold, but he wouldn't be leaving, and by the gods, he hated how this damned place pulled him back in. Whatever fucked-up thing was happening inside this palace, he couldn't leave Julian. The prince could go fuck himself, but Julian didn't deserve to suffer because Niko had run away. He'd never turned from a fight, never backed down. He'd have never surrendered to the elves if it weren't for the king. And he wasn't about to surrender to this wretched place and its curse now.

"I'm not leaving until this is dealt with."

Julian lifted his head. Hope widened his eyes before the harder edge of scorn pushed that hope aside. "Why? Run, while you have the chance. There will not be another."

Niko sighed hard. What else did he have to live for anyway? His life was here, now, in this cell, in this moment, staring another soldier in the eyes so they both knew they didn't have to be alone. "I'm staying. On one condition."

Julian's frown made him look younger, he hadn't been prepared for Niko to stay... for him.

"What condition?" the ex-soldier asked, his voice so soft the vast, cold cells almost swallowed it.

"My sword."

"You want a sword? Vasili won't—"

"Vasili doesn't have to know, and not just *any* sword. My sword. It's in the room I rented. I'll give you the address." He offered his hand. "Are we agreed?"

"You're a fool," Julian clasped his hand around Niko's and smiled. "But I'll get your sword, Nikolas Yazdan."

CHAPTER 8

*N*iko woke early, alone in Julian's chamber. As far as he knew, Julian hadn't returned the night before. The bed lay undisturbed.

He dressed and shaved and decided to explore the palace before Julian could return and stop him. Corridors and staircases ran from one to another with no logical reasoning, likely due to the palace having been constructed around an ancient weather-beaten mountain. Its carved granite blocks followed rocky contours, making the palace appear to claw at the sky high above Loreen.

If this was to be the new battleground, he had to know its every inch. Servants regarded his passing warily. Some acknowledged him with a nod, but most ignored him completely. He assumed they knew he was Vasili's doulos.

Parts of the palace were guarded or sealed behind locked doors. He'd try again later with Julian.

By the time Julian found him, it was long past midday. Niko had rearranged the furniture in the connecting room between Julian's and the prince's room to create a work space. He'd borrowed pencils and paper from a helpful servant and used them to scribble notes about the palace floorplan and its inhabitants.

"Perhaps I wasn't clear enough, but you can't walk about the palace like you own it," Julian said by way of greeting, but the ire in his glare quickly turned to curiosity at the sight of Niko's notes. He drifted closer to the table and examined the papers and maps Niko had drawn. Exits and entryways. Servants' quarters, guest areas, entertaining areas, libraries, and private chambers. The more he'd scrawled, the more he'd come to understand how the Caville palace was a different place to the one that must have stood on the same foundations in ancient times. Generations of Cavilles had altered it over the years, sealing off redundant rooms, moving staircases to suit their whims, turning it into a maze for any visitor.

"There are gaps in my knowledge you'll have to fill," Niko explained, standing behind the table. "In fact, too much is unexplained. If the prince wishes me to help him find his assassin, I need answers beginning now."

Julian's pinched brow gave Niko pause. He'd forgotten he wasn't on the front line distributing orders. Here, Niko was nothing. Julian was his commanding officer and the prince was... Well, the prince was a sharp thorn in Niko's side.

"I can't help without intelligence on the enemy," Niko added, deliberately softening his tone.

Julian sighed and appraised the scattering of papers. "We'll need wine."

He left and returned a few minutes later with wine and

a tray of fruit. "We have a few hours until Vasili's council meeting adjourns. Time enough for you to explain all this to me." He drew up a chair alongside Niko and immediately began studying the maps and papers, asking questions whenever something didn't make sense.

"The sorcerer, whoever they are, clearly has knowledge of the palace to know where to send the fiend, correct?" Niko asked.

"Indeed."

"But they didn't know he no longer uses that room. So let's begin at the bottom—the staff who have access to Vasili's rooms. I want names of all those who personally serve the prince." He pressed his pencil to the paper and waited for Julian to reply.

"He doesn't have staff."

"What?" He looked up, catching Julian's shrug.

"He dismissed them as soon as he returned from his time away."

That seemed unusual. Why would a prince refuse to be served? Surely they all wanted to be pampered and have their needs met by others. Wasn't that one of the innate benefits of being the ruling class? "None? Nobody attends him?"

"Only you." Julian smirked.

Niko huffed a laugh. He'd serve the prince a punch to the face if it wouldn't result in him losing a hand. "What of the man I saw leaving his chambers?"

Julian's brow pinched again. He leaned back in his chair. "Man?"

"Yes. Dressed like a squire. Not dissimilar to how I'm dressed, so he's likely staff, but higher up? I'm not sure how the staff are managed, but I assume there are tiers of authority. The man was likely someone able to come and go as he pleases, but he still answers to the royals."

"I don't recall."

"You were there with me. You saw him leave the prince's chamber."

Julian blinked and looked at the ceiling. After a few moments, he shook his head. "No, I genuinely don't remember," he said, suddenly interested in the nearest note to him.

That was clearly a lie. "If you're going to lie to my face, at least make it convincing."

Julian laughed, leaned forward, and briefly touched Niko's hand where it rested over the palace maps. "I see he was astute in his choice to hire you."

"I wasn't hired. I was bound, brought into this vicious place against my will, and flogged for killing a reprobate who deserved to die." Niko considered pulling back, but Julian's gloved hand reminded him of how it had been months since he'd been touched in any meaningful way that didn't include beatings, floggings, or threats to his life. Just a hand on his, but it felt safe. He let Julian's hand rest where it was.

Julian shifted himself closer. His knee brushed Niko's as he leaned in to examine more notes. Only then, he lifted his hand to reach for the short list of names Niko had put together. "You write very well."

"Mah taught me. She was a seamstress to the Lady of Bucland Manor. Reading and writing were a prerequisite of working there." Why he'd said those things, he couldn't imagine. Julian hadn't ever asked him anything personal. Personal had no place at this table. Or in this palace.

"Ah, that answers how you gained your accent," Julian mused.

"I have an accent?"

"Sometimes you speak like the ruling classes. I assumed you were better bred than most soldiers." A small smile lifted the man's mouth, almost shyly, as though he were ashamed to have noticed such a thing. "I read, but my writing is... It leaves a lot to be desired."

Niko opened his mouth to offer to teach him and promptly closed it again. He had no intention of staying any longer than was necessary. Teaching the man wouldn't be fair when Niko was leaving this gods-awful place as soon as the assassin was found.

"Were you always a soldier?" Niko heard himself ask. Julian's knee brushed his again as he set the paper down. A sharp and unexpected desire coiled low in Niko's belly, awakening the same urge he'd wondered about as he'd lain in Julian's bed.

"No. I grew up on a farm." Julian shifted again and the contact was lost. He didn't offer any more information and reached for the palace map. "A good memory too, to note down all this from one walk."

Niko mourned the absence of his knee against his, as well as the brush of his hand. It was ridiculous. He was a grown man, not some starved adolescent seeking his first sexual encounter in the Stag and Horn. Yet a familiar, breathless thrill had taken hold of Niko's body, making a part of it rise in an inappropriate way. Desiring another man was common enough in Loreen, and what happened at the front wasn't so much a desire as a need, but desiring the prince's personal guard was something else entirely.

He grabbed for the wine and steered his thoughts back

to the task at hand. Julian had always been kind, albeit within the confines of his orders. Niko had no intention of returning that kindness with a foolish crush. He hadn't once shown an interest in Niko beyond professional courtesy. There was nothing between them, there simply couldn't be, and there were more important matters to consider.

"When did the attempts on the prince's life begin?" he asked.

"A few months ago."

"So, right after he returned from his *absence*."

Julian tensed. He stood and made his way around the table, deliberately facing away, reaching for a pitcher of water instead of the wine. Was it something Niko had said?

"Can you tell me where he has been for the last eight years?" Niko asked, observing the man's bicep flex as he poured himself a drink. Julian appeared to be trying to hold himself in check, guarding against slips in his mask, but his very act of shutting down revealed a great deal. The prince's absence was a taboo subject.

"No."

Niko waited a beat, hearing tension in everything unsaid. "Does the assassin have anything to do with the prince's absence?"

"I don't see how."

The secrets were frustrating, but Niko could no more force Julian to speak than he could get a straight answer out of Vasili. He had no choice but to work with the information they gave him. At least Julian did genuinely seem to care about stopping the assassin, unlike anyone else in the palace.

The topic of the prince's time away was clearly out of bounds. "Tell me about Amir," he said, hoping the different angle would open Julian up again.

Julian leaned back against the dresser and took a long drink of water before setting the glass beside him. Niko diverted his gaze from how the man's clothing pinched at his hips and hugged his thighs. He clearly trained, keeping himself physically healthy. Perhaps there might be a chance to join him during one of those training sessions. Gods, no, what a terrible idea. Niko could barely keep his thoughts from wandering now. He wouldn't be able to hide this startling attraction if he had to observe Julian flexing and panting.

"Amir is," Julian began. "He's direct, whereas Vasili misdirects."

Interesting description. "Did you deliberately put me beside his doulos yesterday?"

Julian's eyes widened. "Not I. That order came from Vasili."

"Why?"

"Amir's doulos is known to be vocal. Vasili wanted to know what the doulos would say about him, and likely what Amir was saying in their intimate times together. I don't think he expected the comments to be so frank."

Vasili had deliberately put Niko next to the loudmouth fool to shake something loose, like he had when insisting Niko sleep among the doulos. Niko may not have been Vasili's doulos in the normal way, but he was clearly being used. Unfortunately, he was no longer surprised by the levels Vasili would stoop to, in order get what he wanted.

"Who holds the power in the palace at the moment?"

"Prince Regent Vasili."

"Before he returned?"

"Prince Amir."

"Do the brothers get along?"

"To onlookers, yes, but to anyone who knows them both, not in the least. Carlo, the youngest of the three, was overtly vicious and didn't care who knew it. Amir has always been the louder, more flamboyant. He thrives when he knows he's the center of attention."

"And Vasili?" Niko already suspected he knew the answer, but he wanted to hear Julian's take. "You already told me he's complicated. But I need more."

Julian drew himself tighter together with an inward breath, carefully measuring his response in a few moments of quiet. "Vasili is difficult to define. Before he went away —it was before my time, but I've asked the staff—he was known to be the more stable of the brothers. He cared for his family, but like all Cavilles, he had a cruel streak. The older brothers once stripped Carlo naked and had him whipped in the private gardens. It went on for hours until the king put an end to it. The king dismissed it as boyish games, but the staff say Amir and Vasili almost killed Carlo."

Niko almost wished he were surprised. "Had Carlo done anything wrong?"

"If he had, nobody spoke of it. But even if he had, what kind of family does that to their own?" Julian appeared to want Niko's answer, but there was no answer to give. Only the one they both already knew. Cruelty was in the Caville blood.

"The king," Niko said, after their moment of shared understanding. "Tell me about him."

"Talos is of the old ways." Julian's tone lightened, the

subject more comfortable. "Talos Caville came into power at a young age, when his father was struck down by mental illness in his middle years. He took to it well, so I hear, but there are...rumors."

Niko raised his eyebrows.

Julian picked up his glass again and rested it in his hands. "It was said the boys had an elder sister. If it's true, all mention of her has been scrubbed from records and the older staff denies she existed. Even the pregnancy is said to be a rumor. If there was a girl, she clearly died. The queen withdrew into herself after that. The three boys came after, their births close together. The queen took her own life after Carlo was born. Carlo was raised by the staff. He was often considered the runt. I hear it haunted him some, made him strive to be crueler than the rest."

The picture Julian painted of Caville family life was not a pleasant one.

Niko studied his sketched maps and asked, "Where is the king now?" There were too many blank spaces to guess at the location of the king's chambers.

"I can't tell you that."

So, he knew? "Why not?"

"His location is a secret for obvious reasons." And Julian's tone was back to that of a neutral royal guard. The man clearly had two defined sides; personal and professional. His personal side liked to talk, until the professional in him shut himself down.

"For fear someone will end the king's life prematurely?"

"Indeed." He sipped his water.

"Has anyone attempted to kill the king?"

"There have been some instances of his staff

succumbing to sudden terminal health issues. Food-tasters, and the like."

Poison. "This place is rife with vipers," Niko mumbled, eyeing his lists, maps, and theories. He picked up a hastily drawn sketch of the Caville family dynasty. The royal line stretched back for centuries. Legends spoke of how the Caville blood was sacred, said to be blessed by Etara herself. Their history was full of heroes, warriors, honor, and pride. But then, most everyone's history glowed. Such was the privilege of the victor.

"When the king dies, Vasili inherits the crown, yes?" Niko asked distantly, his gaze still roaming the maps as though he could somehow join up all the lines and unlock all the palace's mysteries.

"He does," Julian confirmed.

"And until recently, in Vasili's absence," Niko looked over, finding Julian still relaxed against the dresser. The glass was empty and set aside. All of Julian's attention rested on Niko. "Amir had the king's ear?"

"The king's health has been sporadic for some time. Amir had begun to adopt the regent's duties, until Vasili returned."

"Does Vasili want the crown?"

Julian cocked his head. "He's Vasili. He's the heir. Choice doesn't come into it."

"Yes, but does he want to rule? There's a difference between wanting something and having it thrust upon you by birth."

"I don't know, honestly. I don't think anyone has ever asked him."

"I'm not surprised. He's not the most approachable person."

Julian smiled with a touch of irony, as he often did when referring to Vasili. "He is not."

Niko wanted to ask if there was something more between them. He could hide it in the line of questioning and Julian would probably answer, but their relationship had nothing to do with the assassin and everything to do with Niko wanting to know if Julian was available. And he'd already drawn a line through that.

"The preternatural element is one that doesn't fit. Lords killing lords, princes killing princes. These things are not unusual in history. But having sorcery in the middle of it..." He frowned and looked up as Julian approached the table. "It doesn't feel right. Which leads me to believe there's more you're not telling me." Like the identity of the mysterious man who had left Vasili's chambers.

"I agree, it's strange."

"Do you know of any sorcerers in the palace?"

"None. Sorcery is..." He chuckled, "It's normally a joke."

"In the city?"

Julian considered the question. "Some hedge witches, a man who claims to be able to commune with trees. I looked into them when the first fiend attacked. But they're nothing more than an herbalist and a madman. In fact, sorcery outside of the palace is virtually unheard of."

"What do you mean *outside* the palace? Is sorcery connected to the Cavilles in some way?"

"That depends if you believe the stories."

"Assume I do."

"The Caville bloodline is surrounded by myths. One such myth, according to the staff, is that the old kings somehow bestowed some individuals with powers and made them their personal protectors." He frowned at his own words. "I'm not sure how much of it is true." His expression indicated not much. "These old families... go back far enough and everyone has some kind of mystical ability."

"Well, someone clearly has access to preternatural forces, and they know how to hide. Which makes them dangerous." Would Amir hire an unknown sorcerer? Throwing a sorcerer into the mix would divert attention away from himself. The family liked to misdirect, although Julian had just told him Amir was more forthright. Unless, whatever or whoever was shouting the loudest was likely a distraction while the real culprit moved in the shadows.

Niko tossed his pencil down and rubbed at his forehead. Trying to unravel the Cavilles was like trying to second-guess the elves' next move. He'd spent nights and nights with his commanding officers, trying to understand the enemy, only for that enemy to attack where they least expected them.

"I'm..." Julian cleared his throat, drawing Niko's eye. "I'm glad he brought you here, although I regret his methods of doing so. This..." He gestured at the table. "I could not do this alone."

Julian's thanks was genuine and Niko smiled back at him. "There is a long way to go."

"I have a gift for you."

"Oh?"

Julian returned to his room and reappeared with the unmistakable package of a sword wrapped in a blanket. He set it on the table, on top of the notes. "I had your personal items brought to my chamber too. You're staying for a while so I thought you'd want to be comfortable."

Niko refrained from grabbing the sword and hid the relief from his face. He'd felt naked all this time without it. Although it had been part of the deal to work with Julian, he hadn't expected to see it again so soon.

"Thank you," he said, voice creaking. And now Julian was smiling, the expression lighting his face with genuine warmth. Would it be wrong if Niko stood, reached across the table, and kissed the man? There had been times under this roof that he feared he'd never have the sword in his hands again. The fact Julian had brought it to him, clearly against Vasili's wishes, meant a great deal.

"It's late. I must attend the prince," Julian said, glancing at the light outside the window behind Niko. "Tonight...we'll study your work some more? I'll help fill in some of those blank spaces."

"I look forward to it." The words were out before Niko considered how they might be taken. Fear kicked his heart over. But it wasn't too much to reveal he enjoyed Julian's company. They were working together and got along well. All purely professional.

Julian hesitated and Niko felt heat prickling beneath his skin. Thankfully Julian didn't question the familiar tone and left before he could notice the color rising on Niko's face.

Niko downed the wine and swore quietly into the empty room. He did not need to get distracted by Julian, not with Vasili breathing down their necks. If the prince so much as suspected Niko was warming to Julian, he'd use that affection against them both. Better to nip it in the bud now, and nobody would get hurt.

"Purely professional." Hearing it aloud made it real. Once this was all over, if he were still desperate for a fuck, he'd visit the Stag and Horn. Until then, and while he was under the prince's roof, anything personal was out of bounds.

CHAPTER 9

*N*iko spent the rest of the day adding to his notes, expecting Julian to return at any moment. The shadows grew long, so he lit the lamps, holding off the dark, but it was clear Julian wasn't returning to discuss Niko's work as he'd said. The prince had probably called him away. The questions would have to wait until the morning.

He'd fallen asleep in the chair at his worktable and woke with a start at the sound of Julian's chamber door closing. It was late, the night air chilly in the connecting room. He shut the window, latching it tight to keep any fiends out, and headed into Julian's chamber.

The single candle Niko had lit earlier struggled to illuminate the large room, leaving Julian in shadow by the bed. It wasn't until he got close that he saw how Julian's shoulders and back heaved.

"Are you hurt?" Instinct had him moving in to help, but he couldn't see any wounds or tears in his clothes, no evidence of an attack.

"It's fine," Julian grunted.

Niko grabbed a second candle and lit it, then set it on the bedside table. The new source of light revealed Julian was not fine. He breathed through gritted teeth, clearly in pain. His hair hung loose, sticking to his damp face.

"I'll be fine," he said again. "I just need some time."

"How can I help?"

"You can't." Julian finally straightened. He groped at his shirt buttons but failed to clasp them. Swearing, he slumped onto the edge of the bed and threw his gaze at the ceiling. "I just... just give me a second."

Niko wasn't going to watch a man suffer, no matter how stubborn he was. He moved to stand in front of him and began working to unlace the shirt's collar. They were loose, and a few gentle tugs pulled them apart. When Julian didn't protest, Niko began working the buttons free. If he wanted him to stop, he'd say it. Still, Niko glanced up to check.

Julian rested his head against the bedpost, his absorbing gaze reading Niko's face.

This was purely to help the man, and nothing more. It was certainly nothing intimate. Julian was in pain. The important thing was making him comfortable.

The shirt opened and Julian sat up, peeling the garment off his shoulders. He hissed as the fabric slipped down his back. But as Niko leaned in to help, Julian's eyes flashed a warning. Niko lifted his hands off, backing up a step to give him room.

He eventually worked himself out of the garment, swearing when the cuffs snagged his gloves. Julian bit the end of one gloved finger and pulled it off. "Please just leave me," he mumbled. "I'm all right."

Niko nodded and turned away, but the reflection in Julian's mirror revealed everything the man had tried to keep hidden. Soft candlelight flickered over angry welts marking his back. Lash marks. He'd been whipped, but whoever had performed the whipping hadn't broken the skin. The punishment was designed to be hidden.

Vasili. It had to be. No one else would dare touch the prince's favorite guard.

He turned back, facing Julian, tasting bitter anger on his tongue. "The prince did that to you." He failed to hide the growl from his voice. It wasn't a damn question either. He knew it with absolute certainty, especially when Julian flinched, his gaze downcast.

"Leave it, Niko." Julian's warning carried some conviction, but not enough.

Vasili had whipped him, probably naked or close to it, then sent him back here.

"What happened?" If he got close to Julian again, he wouldn't be able to stop himself from helping him, no matter Julian's protests. Niko hung back and watched him struggle with his trouser ties, fingers twitching at his sides to intervene.

"Nothing happened," Julian mumbled.

"Why did he whip you?"

"I said leave it." Julian finally tore the ties free and, with trembling hands, he shoved his pants down over his hips. The fabric pooled at his ankles.

His thighs were marked too, the skin angry and red.

Vasili was going to pay for this.

Niko swooped in, caught Julian's gloved hand and looped his arm around his waist. "Lean on me."

"You don't need to..." The moment he surrendered, all

tension fell from his body. He sighed and gave himself over to Niko's embrace. He shuddered from pain or maybe fear, possibly exhaustion. Niko held him like he'd held so many of the broken and weary who had sobbed in his arms.

Julian didn't resist when Niko readied the bed and laid him gently on his side on top of the cool sheets. Niko removed Julian's boots and set them aside, then maneuvered off his undergarments. He expected Julian to protest again, but he'd turned his face away to stare at the candle beside him, hardly acknowledging Niko's presence.

Niko gathered up the sheet, softly laid it over him, and retreated to the lounger at the far side of the room. Julian's eyes fluttered closed. His chest slowly rose and fell, and Niko fumed in silence, his thoughts full of pinning Vasili to a wall and taking a whip to the prince's porcelain skin, making him scream under every lash.

THE MORNING CAME and in the harsh light of day, Julian said nothing of the wounds on his back and thighs. He shaved and dressed in silence, ignoring Niko's lingering glances. Julian hid the pain well, well enough that Niko thought he often had to withstand such wounds.

"I need to see more of Amir," Niko said.

"Agreed. But first"—the man's easy smile lit up the room like sunshine, and after the horror of the previous night Niko's heart flip-flopped to see it—"breakfast."

Julian had a spring in his step that belied how he must have ached. They walked to a pleasant orangery in the eastern wing of the palace, where a breakfast had been set on a small table, apparently for Julian, as there were no others present.

"Sit." Julian urged, pulling out a seat for Niko before taking his own.

"This is nice."

Julian piled his plate high with pancakes and syrup and fruit. "Courtesy of Vasili. Enjoy it while it lasts." His pallor was a little milky, but otherwise, his eyes had brightened. In fact, he seemed more alert now than he did last night. Relief that he'd survived the whip and that it hadn't been worse? He almost behaved like a man set free of his bonds.

Niko loaded his plate and ate with gusto. The rations he'd been given as a doulos were meager and bland. The fruits here were juicy and plump and sweet, and so fucking delicious Niko returned for a second plate, asking, "Does he always feed you so well after whipping you?"

Julian stopped chewing and reached for the wine, used a mouthful to wash down his food. "Listen." The light in his eyes and smile faded some. "Don't tell him you saw me like that."

Niko folded his arms across his chest. "He doesn't care what I think."

"No, but I do. It's..."

"Complicated?"

"Yes."

"I'm not sure I can stay quiet. You were—"

"This isn't about you, Niko." Julian's tone hardened. "Pretend you didn't see a damn thing and enjoy the food. I have a day off, and I'd...I'd like to show you some more of the palace...to fill in your maps."

Niko wet his lips and unfolded his arms, startled by the

request and somewhat adrift considering how Julian was looking at him. He wanted to reach out and cover the gloved hand, maybe squeeze it softly, offering the same kind of comfort Julian had appeared to need last night. But something had changed, and in the daylight, that brief moment when he'd folded Julian into his arms seemed like a dream.

"All right," Niko agreed, professionally detached. "You can show me the parts of the palace I can't access alone."

Julian popped a grape in his mouth, crunched down, and grinned.

Niko wasn't sure what he'd expected of the day, but it hadn't been a grand tour of the palace's walled gardens, or the vast tropical orangeries full of strange, vibrant flowers from lands Niko had never heard of.

Julian relaxed more with every new room or sight they saw. The tension he'd always carried had all but vanished, turning him into a different man from Vasili's stiff guard. He showed Niko the stables and the enormous prancing horses that looked as vicious and wild as the princes they served.

The day came to a close on a grassy hill on the western side of the palace grounds, where the gardens were left to bloom of their own accord, full of wild flowers and sprawling grasses.

Niko had mapped the palace in his mind as much as possible and made a note of how many people came and went through the grounds. Considering the prince feared for his life, the palace was remarkably open.

Julian sat on a grassy bank with his knees drawn up, propping his wrists on them. "You can see the ocean from here."

Niko sat in the grass beside him and shielded his eyes from the setting sun. The glistening silver strip of ocean in the distance looked like the edge of a sword. "So you can."

"Have you ever seen it up close?"

"No. Mah's service to the manor and Pah's forge kept us close to Trenlake."

"You miss them?"

Astute of him. He hadn't realized he did, until now. "Yes. I do. I've almost forgotten their faces. Forgotten a lot of life before. The war makes things appear different, like those days happened to someone else." He stopped there, reining in the urge to tell Julian everything.

Julian sighed and leaned back on his elbows to watch the sunset-stained clouds. "Thank you."

"What for?"

"Being here."

Niko glanced down at the man, then promptly away to stare at how the palace grounds fell away beneath them, ending in a smooth white wall to keep the general Loreen population out. The glance had been quick, but enough to see how Julian's shirt had ridden up, revealing a hint of golden skin. Niko instantly imagined biting that tease of skin on his waist. He promptly wished he hadn't when lust heated his cock, making it stiffen uncomfortably. A good thing he was faced slightly away. By the three gods, he usually had more control than this.

The day had been marvelous. And strange. Seeing Julian out of his role was an unexpected delight. He laughed freely and often, making Niko fall into laughing with him. The day had done nothing to temper the urges Niko was experiencing. If anything, it had made them worse.

87

Julian continued. "And for not asking about what you saw last night."

"You made it clear it's none of my business."

"I..." He trailed off.

Niko looked back.

Julian twisted a sprig of grass between his fingers. He pinched his bottom lip between his teeth and let it spring free. What would it feel like to kiss him right now, Niko wondered, the both of them basking in the sun, alone, where the world couldn't reach them? Would he be soft or hard? Fast or slow? All of those things perhaps until Julian shoved him off and reported him to Vasili. The prince would probably take great joy in severing Niko's dick.

Yes, thinking of Vasili certainly dampened the desire to crawl up Julian's body, to press him into the grass, to make him murmur Niko's name between breaths. Dammit. Niko stood abruptly and stared at the city, keeping Julian behind him. "We should get back before your prince notices I've stolen you away all day."

"He's your prince too."

"No, Vasili is nothing to me."

"He—" Julian cut himself off.

Niko turned, his shadow falling over Julian, making his eyes widen. His pupils dilated. "Go on, finish what you were going to say."

"He had no hand in his father's actions," Julian said. "He no more wanted to surrender than you did."

"No? He's regent now, so why doesn't he fight back?"

"You know why. Our forces are scattered, exhausted, and broken. The peace is our last hope. If the kingdom rises up again, the elves will burn it all down."

Niko snorted. They'd burn it all down eventually

anyway. "That was Talos's doing. We were winning. His surrender devastated morale. I tried to keep the ranks together but what was the point? Two friends took blades to their own throats rather than return in shame."

"I'm... sorry."

Niko shook his head. "It's not for you to be sorry." Damn, this man was too good for this place. After the warmth of the day and seeing the softer, more open side to Julian, Niko wanted to take him away. The palace was sharp and cold and hollow, everything Julian was not. He lay there so open, his face so honest. Eyes wide, lips soft.

Julian blinked up at him. "What do you see?"

Fuck. Niko tore his gaze away and stared at the wall, grinding his teeth. The thoughts in his head were private. Voicing them would be a mistake. "I don't like that he hurt you."

Julian pushed to his feet and stood far too close for it to be anything but personal. Any closer and that small distance would be easily overcome with a kiss.

"You're a good man, Nikolas."

"I stopped being good the day I took a life."

Julian dropped his chin. His blond hair fell forward, masking blue eyes. "So did I."

No, Julian was still good. A miracle in this place. And it broke Niko's heart that Julian couldn't see it. "The sun's going down." He stared at that subdued red orb filtered behind clouds.

"Come, the prince has early morning plans for you." Julian sauntered up the hill toward the palace. His powerful strides carried him away until he was almost out of sight.

If Niko lived through this, maybe he'd ask Julian to

leave with him. Not *together*. He wasn't some love-struck fool wanting to elope. But someone had to free the man before Vasili's whip came down too hard and made the choice for him.

CHAPTER 10

"I assume you can ride. If not, this will be a short excursion for you." Vasili pulled the reins of his massive white charger, bringing the restless beast under control. Shod hooves struck the courtyard cobbles. It danced and chomped at its bit, half wild.

If that was the horse Carlo had been riding, then it was no wonder he'd fallen. The damn creature had probably killed him.

"I can ride," Niko confirmed stiffly from atop his own borrowed horse.

The prince smiled his reptile smile and chills ran down Niko's back. The horse Niko had mounted, by comparison, was a sedate chestnut creature. Slimmer and smaller than Vasili's, it was faster than it looked, or so Julian had assured him. A groom fussed at his side and his docile steed never wavered.

As Vasili's horse pawed the cobbles, Niko visually checked the saddle's straps for any loose buckles. He'd checked them by hand moments before Vasili had mounted, earning himself a scathing look from Vasili. The assassin would be a fool to try the same stunt a second time, but considering one Caville had already died on a ride-out, Niko hadn't wanted to be blamed for a second royal death.

Julian too was watching the number of stable hands bustling about while one finished adjusting his reins. The staff kept their heads down, going about their work without comment. Most shied from Vasili and his kicking horse. They obeyed him quickly enough, overeager to serve when he snapped at them, but beyond that, none met his eye.

"Ready?" Vasili asked in a rare show of something like concern. It didn't last. His icy gaze turned sharp, revealing cruelty. He dug his heels into his charger's flanks, and with a whiplike "yar!" he sent his horse rearing and screaming around the bit. Vasili gripped his mount with his thighs, and then the beast bolted forward like an arrow from a bow, galloping out the yard's arched gateway.

Niko spurred his horse into motion, startling his groom, and galloped through the gate after Vasili's retreating form.

Vasili's distinctive long white hair rippled like a flag. Niko sneered at the prince's foolishness. He knew he was being hunted, so why risk leaving the palace at all?

The charger's hooves clattered over the wooden bridge ahead. Niko's horse raced after it, thundering over the same bridge seconds later. Julian was likely cursing somewhere behind. A quick glance back revealed he was nowhere in sight.

Niko had wanted a chance to get the prince alone. When Vasili had summoned Julian at dawn and ordered a ride out, his heart had skipped at the idea. He'd been a natural with horses as a boy. In Pah's forge, the customers' horses had all been his responsibility. He'd learned to ride long before learning how to wield a blade.

Vasili would not beat him.

The winding road took them out of the palace grounds and around the outskirts of Loreen, quickly dipping into a valley. Vasili wasn't slowing.

The cold morning wind tore at Niko's face and clothes. His horse panted, nostrils flaring. Vasili's beast was fast, but Niko's was lighter, and gaining ground on the charger.

Vasili whipped around a sharp corner, slicing against a hedge. He knew the road and Niko did not. He lost time taking the corner wide and suddenly came upon a low stone wall. Niko's chestnut leaped. Its front hooves clipped stone and the animal almost tumbled, nearly throwing Niko from the saddle. Heart in his throat, he tightened his thighs, pitched with the beast and then they were racing forward again, the chestnut eager to catch its mate. They galloped faster, Niko's heart racing along too, the relentless pace pulling his mouth into a grin. The field opened up, stretching into the distance. Niko's heart hammered against his ribs. The ground rushed beneath, and Vasili grew closer.

Then the prince glanced over his shoulder, either smiling or sneering. One was more likely than the other. He spurred his beast on again, forcing a burst of speed, and impossibly, the animal had more to give.

This was insanity. This far from the palace, if one of them fell, there would be no aid.

Niko eyed the horizon, freedom whispering in his ear. He could ride and ride and not stop until he reached the seas to the south. But if he did that, Julian would suffer, and he'd never learn who was trying to kill the prince. Besides, he couldn't allow Vasili to outride him.

Vasili plunged his horse into a copse of trees, vanishing from sight. Riding at speed through the forest would ensure that one or both of them were thrown. There was risk, and then there was stupidity.

He reined his panting horse down to a trot and entered the cool, sun-dappled shade beneath the trees, half expecting to find Vasili on the ground. But the prince danced his horse ahead in a small clearing, patting its neck. Froth dripped from its mouth. It stamped the earth and snorted but had stopped trying to break. The prince was a good rider. He wasn't about to tell him that. Vasili clearly knew it.

Niko guided his horse into the clearing. "Is this wise?"

Vasili's sharp smile hooked into his cheek as he straightened in the saddle. His body had gained a casual fluidity since galloping out of the stables. He moved more, rocking with the motion of his horse instead of fighting against it. He teased the leather reins between his fingers, the gesture oddly tender. A competent rider, Niko thought, but not a daily one.

Niko might have gone so far as to say Vasili had enjoyed the bracing gallop. He'd begun to wonder if the prince even knew joy. But it was there in the smallest of movements and the flicker of his keen eye.

"What do you know of wise?" Vasili asked. His voice didn't lash like a whip, but it still held its cutting edge. "You've followed orders your whole life. Never had to think for yourself. You're a grunt. A tool. *My* tool."

Niko narrowed his eyes. His horse rocked its head, adjusting the bit in its mouth.

He was the same age as Vasili. Just because they'd been born into different families, that made the prince superior? Bullshit. With witnesses around he couldn't reveal his thoughts, but out here there was nobody to report on his words. The urge to speak his mind was strong. But being alone like this, Vasili could tell his aides anything had happened between them and have Niko flogged merely because he wanted it.

Vasili adjusted himself on his saddle, observing Niko as though waiting for comment. Color flushed his neck and face, and delight shimmered in his good eye. This was the most alive he'd looked since Niko had first met him in the pleasure house. "No comeback?" he asked. "I'm disappointed. I was hoping to hear some of that infamous honesty of you—"

"Why are we here?"

Vasili's smile faded. He turned his horse and nodded at a large rock jutting from the bushes. "Carlo was found there."

A long way from the palace. Vasili had said Carlo's horse had gotten spooked, but even so. This was an unusual place for it to bolt. "Was he a proficient rider?"

"He was."

"He rode the horse you're riding now?"

Vasili nodded and reined the animal in, gently nudging it with his heels to stroll forward to rein up alongside Niko's. Vasili's closer proximity made the small hairs rise on Niko's arms, like his body knew to ready itself for a fight.

"What are you thinking?" Vasili asked. He clasped the

reins in one hand and rested the other on his thigh. He wore black, still in mourning. The shirt clung to his chest in places where the heat of the morning and the ride had made him sweat. Black trousers hugged his thighs. Laced boots rode up to his knees. The clothing left little room for a blade, but he'd have one on him. The prince probably wouldn't have brought him out here only to attack him, but he was unpredictable.

Vasili's thin lips ticked and Niko switched his attention from the prince's physique to the granite rock lodged in the ground.

"He was alone?" Niko asked.

"That is a very astute question."

When he looked back, the prince's horse had shifted alongside his, putting the prince within touching distance. His attention was on the rock, not Niko, and his face was troubled and his jaw was set. A smattering of goosebumps tingled on Niko's arms. He gripped his own reins, wishing he had his sword.

"We're a long way from the palace," Niko said, glad his voice didn't betray his rattling nerves. "A spooked horse will generally return to paths it knows well. Did he often ride out here?"

"No. Carlo disliked riding."

Niko raised an eyebrow. "He disliked riding yet took your charger?"

Vasili patted the animal's neck again, showing an affection Niko hadn't thought he'd possessed.

"He had no horse of his own."

The drip-drip of information was infuriating, but at least it was flowing. Niko fell quiet and looked about them. The isolated copse, Carlo borrowing a horse he didn't know, but not any horse—his elder brother's. "He was meeting someone here."

A butterfly flounced through the trees and a bird startled from a branch above. Vasili's horse shied again, dancing away from Niko. He promptly pulled on its reins, drawing it in, turning it to face the rock. "Everyone assumes Carlo was the weak one. The small one. The runt." Vasili stared at the rock. His throat moved as he swallowed. "I once found him with a litter of kittens, all white, like Aura Herself had given them to him. He'd broken the neck of each one and lined them up at the end of his bed. His *dolls*, he'd said."

Disgust tried to pull Niko's lips into a grimace. He resisted, careful to school his face into a blank mask.

"He was not weak." Vasili turned his gaze back to Niko. The glare was cold again, all the warmth of the ride having fled.

"Do you suspect he had something to do with the attempts on your life and he was meeting someone here to further those plans against you?"

The prince's brow pinched. "I don't know. My brother did not plot so much as act. He was not subtle in his machinations against me. Perhaps someone thought to harness our rivalry, turning our jest against me."

"Jest? You and Amir strung your brother up and had him whipped. Almost killed him. You call that a jest?"

His lips turned down. "I see the rumors have found you at last. I did not think you were a man who listened to idle gossip."

"Gossip is all I have until you start giving me more to work with."

The prince's frown softened, the movement so small

Niko might have missed it if they'd been anywhere else. But here, alone, far outside the palace, it seemed the prince was less inclined to guard his expression. It might have been the first time Niko had seen a hint of the real Vasili. He was not as untouchable as he led everyone to believe. This place, his brother, the rumors—it pained him.

"Vasili!" Julian called from outside the trees. "Your Highness!"

Vasili's shutters slammed down, replacing the brief glimpse of emotion with cool, flat indifference. "Here," he called back, catching Niko's eye. A knowing look passed between them: a warning not to speak of this.

Julian walked his horse into the woods. "I was...I'm relieved you're here, my prince."

Vasili threw him a smile. "Where else would I be?" He kicked his horse and trotted out of the woods.

Julian's gaze lingered on Niko, full of unasked questions, before he followed Vasili's path.

Niko directed his horse toward the rock. It could also be that the most obvious explanation was correct: Vasili's horse, spooked, had dashed out here and thrown its rider. But there were no bloodstains on the rock, and in the shade, among the trees, protected from the weather, old blood would still be visible.

This did not feel right. But nothing about any of this felt right.

He walked his horse from the woods and saw Julian with Vasili several strides ahead of him. Niko had his horse fall into step behind the pair and let his thoughts drift. The princes clearly had a troubled relationship. With the youngest dead and Vasili controlling the flow of information, the only other source for answers was Amir.

He had to get closer to the middle prince somehow, without inviting his ire. Which meant finding something Amir wanted more than severing Niko's fingers.

Niko stared at the prince's back. His long, pale hair shone almost white under the sunlight. He rode with his back straight, chin up, just like the boys atop their steeds in the procession so long ago. The prince was back in his role again, but there had been a moment in the woods, right after they'd arrived, when he'd become someone else, someone a little more open, a little more honest. Clearly, Vasili hoarded secrets like thieves hoarded precious gems. It would be easier to get answers from elves.

Vasili wouldn't reveal his secrets, not without his own motives, but Amir would, if the right kind of pressure was applied. And Amir liked nothing more than attention.

Niko had to get to Amir, and Julian would know how.

CHAPTER 11

"*W*hat is that?"

Julian looked sheepish. "It's required."

Niko tilted his head and folded his arms. The clothing Julian had laid out for him covered less than undergarments. He arched an eyebrow at the painful-looking straps and laces. He wasn't even sure how to wear it. Did one wrap it around oneself or step into it or...

"Vasili's joke?" Niko asked.

"The prince rarely jokes."

Niko snorted. He'd never worn such a thing, although he did recall the men at the Stag and Horn wearing something similar. It was designed to exhibit someone's best *features*. It did cover up the necessary, but left very little to the imagination.

By the three gods, was he really going to do this? According to Julian, Amir had certain tastes, and if Niko was going to get his attention, he had to reveal some of his better features. Apparently, those features were his ass and abs.

He'd already been flogged. Wearing a harness was hardly worse than that.

Julian regarded the clothing with a guard's well-practiced blank expression. "I hear it's actually quite comfortable."

Niko had half a mind to tell Julian to wear it, and quickly veered his thoughts from that image before it took hold of his sense. "It looks like torture."

Julian half smiled. "I can help you—"

"No." The last thing he needed was Julian's fingers brushing his skin while he was climbing into *that*. He sighed. He'd slain countless elves, charged into battle and faced death every day. "I can do this."

Julian's warm hand landed on Niko's shoulder. "It's just for one evening. Amir will look, but won't touch you. He knows you belong to Vasili."

"Fucking wonderful."

Julian's laugh and his touch appeared to have a direct link to Niko's twitching cock. Or maybe it was the thought of the outfit that was stimulating.

Shrugging Julian's hand away, he snatched up the clothes and took them to the connecting room to dress. The room had become Niko's some time over the last few days. He'd made up a small cot, had his personal items beside it, and his sword nearby. He touched the weapon briefly—for luck, when he was nervous—and set about stripping off to buckle himself up in leather and laces.

Julian had thankfully provided a cloak. Doulos didn't have to parade themselves through the palace so exposed. Thank fuck for that. Niko tightened the straps and adjusted a few pinch points, then threw the cloak over his shoulders and tied it loosely at his neck. He briefly considered slinging the sword across his back, but if Vasili didn't punish him for that, Amir surely would, and the middle prince already had his eyes on Niko's fingers.

He asked himself again what he was doing here and was quickly reminded when he left his room to find Julian standing awkwardly at the end of his bed. He'd donned his palace armor and was ready to lead Niko to Amir's private entertaining chambers.

Julian cleared his throat, adjusted his belt, and fiddled with his two shortswords. Was he nervous too? Niko couldn't imagine why. Surely this was all routine to him.

"You look—"

"Save it," Niko snapped, more harshly than he'd intended. His heart raced, skin hot. His role tonight was to stand and be admired, to ignore Amir's taunts, of which there would surely be many, and play at being an obedient doulos. Vasili had apparently worded it as, *"Prove our Nikolas has been tamed. Amir must admire him, not despise him. Only then will my brother talk."*

All he had to do was nothing at all. Easy.

He unclenched his fists.

He'd thrown himself into an advancing force of vicious elves. He could certainly withstand whatever Amir could throw at him.

"This was your idea," Julian said, noticing Niko's frown.

"It's fine." His fingers twitched to pluck at the straps and pull them out from his crevices.

Julian was in front of him suddenly, filling Niko's vision. A small, telltale gasp escaped Niko. "For what it's worth," Julian said, his voice deep, "you have the perfect physique for this."

The words weren't personal. Just an observation. Niko swallowed.

"You'll have to tell me about the scars sometime."

More personal. Julian's gaze dropped to Niko's mouth, lingered, and flicked back up to his eyes. All right, this was different. More. Better. Now wasn't the time to grab Julian, pin him to the wall, and devour his soft mouth. Not when they were both trussed up like performers for a pair of princes who killed kittens to make new friends.

Yes, he should think of that, and not how Julian was so close, Niko could feel the heat radiating off him.

"Come along then, doulos." Julian's mouth slid into a smiling tilt. Niko's top lip lifted in a sneer and Julian laughed. "I didn't think you'd be submissive."

"Amir prefers his doulos slim, right?" Like the man Niko had punched in the face, the one whose throat Vasili had cut.

"He does. You are definitely not that." An appreciative glance. If it weren't for their roles, Niko would have kissed him already. Instead, he let Julian lead on, trailing behind in the corridor, as was his place as a doulos.

Each royal had their own area of the palace decorated as they wanted and staffed with their own personal attendants. Amir's palace wing was colorful, the furniture as loud as the man himself. Niko had to squint to see past the ostentatious reds and greens and golds. Like Vasili's bed, it was hideous.

He regretted the idea of getting closer to Amir as soon as he entered the private chamber. The smell of spice and potent wine tickled the back of Niko's throat. A woman lounged on one of numerous couches, a man on his knees between her legs as he serviced her. Niko quickly looked away, but his gaze found three men clearly a long way into their intimacy act. One of them, smaller and thinner than the other two, wore a similar outfit to Niko. At least he appeared to be enjoying himself.

It wasn't anything Niko hadn't seen before. It was just a lot of it in one room. All he had to do was ignore it and get through the next few hours, thus hopefully making a new friend in Amir.

"Good luck," Julian muttered. Then he bowed before Prince Amir, sprawled in a throne-like chair. "Your brother's doulos, Your Highness."

Amir waved him off without so much as a glance and Julian left, leaving Niko stranded like the last mare at an auction. Amir hadn't even looked over. He talked with a tall, stunning woman Niko had glimpsed at the banquets. Both of them were buttoned up to their necks in courtly clothing, clearly immune to the heat. The air was wet and sweet and tinged with sex, but neither of them seemed to care that half a dozen couples were getting off within reach.

"Disrobe," the prince said, his tone snapping Niko back into the present. His eyes were on him suddenly. *Roaming.* Taking in what he could beneath Niko's cloak.

"Shy?" the woman asked, a gleam in her eye.

Amir snorted. "I guarantee Vasili hasn't touched him." His lips parted. "What a waste." He leaned forward and rested both elbows on his knees. "If you were mine, you'd have been broken in long before now. You see in his eyes..." Amir jerked his head at his friend but didn't look away from Niko. "Defiance. Hatred. He despises us. This man is a lit firework waiting to go off." Amir wet his lips. "Well?"

Niko swallowed, having forgotten what was asked of him.

Amir stood, his height a match for Niko. He tugged on the cloak's ties and with one swift yank, the garment fell from Niko's shoulders and pooled around his boots.

The woman made a small appreciative noise and Amir stepped back. He poked his tongue into his cheek and assessed the sight. "He has a good eye, my brother." And then the prince barked a laugh at his own joke.

"Hm." Amir drifted around, admiring every exposed inch of Niko's skin.

Hate boiled through Niko's veins. But he could do this. Just stand and absorb it all like he'd absorbed the strikes of the whip. It would end. He'd get answers, hopefully get some evidence of the prince's plot against his brother, and be on his way to leaving this place forever.

"Muscles like yours... diminished somewhat by your stay in our cells. Hm... you must have been a sight in battle, no?"

Niko licked his dry lips.

"Well, speak, man. You do have a tongue, or did my brother take it?" He glanced at his companion, finally losing interest in Niko's body. "Now that would be interesting—"

"I was," Niko said. "A sight in battle, Your Highness."

The prince's attention snapped back to him. He stepped close, and to Niko's horror, the prince's warm finger ran up the scar on his thigh. Julian's assurances Amir wouldn't touch him had been wrong. A horrible fluttering started low in his belly. The prince's finger was clearly not an elven blade, but the touch cut the memories open all the same.

He could do this. Just stand still and ignore it all. It was simple, really. Easier than battle. Easier than killing. He just had to detach and let it happen.

"This one... you bled well from here." The touch trailed around the front of Niko's thigh, skipping to another scar. The attack had almost cleaved muscle from bone. He'd lain weak for weeks after. "And this one. Your enemy was aiming for the artery. Was it luck or skill that you survived?"

"Both."

"Hm, honest. I've heard that about you. I like it."

Yes, good. This was why Niko was here, to get inside the prince's head. And it was working. If he could just stay out of his own in return.

"You threatened Vasili, broke his wrist even, yet here you are." Amir stepped closer still, bringing himself chest to chest with Niko. He was slim. Niko saw how the man's eyes sparkled. Darker than Vasili's, but no less sharp. Niko imagined kicking his weight-bearing leg out from under him, and when the prince fell, he'd hold him down and thrust his knuckles into his face, making him bleed all over his fine clothes and garish furniture.

"What game is my brother playing with you, hm?" Amir asked, his breath brushing Niko's mouth. It would have been intimate if not for the desire to strangle the bastard. Although there wasn't much that was more intimate than wrapping fingers around a man's throat to throttle the life out of him.

The prince's touch vanished, earning Niko a brief reprieve, but then his thin fingers cupped Niko's cock. Heat flushed through the thin fabric covering him up.

Niko gasped, then caught the noise behind gritted

teeth and choked it off. He couldn't do much about his thudding heart, or how his breathing betrayed the rush of anger in his veins.

Amir's grin grew.

Niko hated this man, hated everything he stood for. Would gladly drive a blade through his heart. But as Amir's hand adjusted, molding close, Niko's cock warmed—shifting, hardening.

"Hate can be powerful. I feel that about you," Amir whispered. "While feeling a great deal of impressive other things. Such a shame my brother hasn't fucked you. You must be so desperate."

Niko hardened still. Anger and hate were indeed powerful, mixing with the effects of a man's touch. There was nothing to be done about the pounding erection, and in this scenario it worked. Let Amir think Niko desired him. He'd be more inclined to talk.

"All that lust," Amir whispered, lips brushing Niko's. "You're bottled up." The tip of his tongue flicked against Niko's lower lip. "Ready. To. Blow."

Niko fluttered his eyes closed. He did not desire Amir, but what he did desire was the thought of throwing this wretched prince down and fucking him as he screamed and writhed and begged. The startling image sent a pulse of heat through Niko's cock. Amir's grip tightened in response.

Niko opened his eyes to find the middle prince grinning. He stepped back, his hand gesturing away. "Stand over there, doulos."

Dry-throated and glistening with sweat, Niko passed in front of the woman, ignoring her downward glance, and turned his back to the wall. He clasped his hands over himself, covering the evidence of his arousal.

"Oh no." Amir laughed. "No hiding, or I'll take the fingers you owe me." He sauntered into the room, his gaze skimming those already lost in sexual acts. He drew a woman from between two men. She immediately ignored her partners and painted herself onto Amir's body.

Niko sighed, briefly relieved. Women were easier to ignore. He just might get through this after all. And then Amir gently eased her aside and, touching the chin of one of her male partners, drew the man to his mouth and kissed him long and deep, the kiss quickly turning hard and demanding.

Niko closed his eyes. But that was worse. Because now the scene was scorched into his mind and all he could see was the prince fully clothed, his scantily clad doulos subservient and pliable, so eager in his hands.

He clenched his jaw and thought of Vasili's cruel, snarling mouth, his vicious tongue, and the way he laughed like Niko was dirt beneath the heel of his boot. His cock pulsed harder, so fucking eager there was no hiding or calming it.

He opened his eyes, caught between the real world and the fantasy in his head. By the three, what was wrong with him? Maybe it was the spice in the air, making his body weak.

Amir had turned the doulos away from him and shoved him over the back of the couch. The prince fumbled with his own pant ties. One of the other doulos offered a pot of something Niko assumed to be lubricant and the prince scooped some out.

The doulos's back arched, his mouth opening wide, his

gaze far away. Amir looked up, one hand holding the man down, the other Niko presumed on his cock, the only part of him not wrapped in fine clothes. He thrust into the doulos, baring his teeth, and stared unblinking at Niko.

Niko's cock jumped. Amir saw that too, and thrust again. The doulos grunted. And Niko bared his own teeth in a snarl. Amir laughed and thrust and only took his eyes off Niko face to admire Niko's cock, now leaking its eagerness.

He ached to take himself in hand. His thighs trembled from restraint. It wouldn't take much to bring himself to completion. Amir hadn't forbidden it, but doing so seemed like surrender—and he'd never surrender to the Cavilles.

Amir threw his head back and fucked his doulos while the others in the room licked and thrust and bit and groaned and spent themselves inside each other.

"Oh, he *hates* you," Amir's female companion said, suddenly standing in front of Niko. A tumble of mahogany hair framed a beautiful face, mouth wide, eyes sultry, skin as black as a raven's wing. If he focused on *her,* he might regain some lost composure.

He still heard the rutting, heard Amir's grunting, but the woman looking at him had broken the prince's spell. His cock finally began to relent.

She smiled and leaned in to whisper, "Make yourself valuable to him or that fine body of yours will be swinging from the palace gates before the end of the week."

"Your name?" he growled, sounding more animal than man. That was beyond his control. Like everything else here.

"Lady Maria."

She lingered, blocking the room from Niko's view. He

almost thanked her, but to do so felt like admitting too much. "Why?" he asked instead. She'd helped him focus, and they both knew it.

"Vasili is important. And you are important to him."

Niko bit his tongue to keep from blurting how he despised the bastard and the rest of them. She seemed the sort to be able to see all that in his eyes anyway.

Amir growled out his release and Niko squeezed his eyes closed, then opened them again when his imagination painted the devastating picture of the prince losing his seed inside the doulos's ass.

Lady Maria leaned into him. "Imagine, if you will, you're the cuckoo in the nest. But the nest doesn't belong to kindly songbirds. It belongs to vicious raptors, the type who will shred you should they learn who and what you really are." She pulled back, fixed him with a long glare, and drifted toward Amir. The prince was shuddering out his final dregs of seed when Maria caught him by the chin and kissed him lightly on the forehead. She left, and Niko watched as Amir followed her every step from the room.

THE NIGHT PASSED BY SLOWLY, each hour feeling like a lifetime. Amir carelessly drank and snorted spice and fucked whomever he could get his hands on.

The terrible desires shredded Niko's mind. His body trembled, drenched in sweat and stinking of sex. He wasn't sure what was worse: when Amir ignored him, or when Amir looked at him. The middle prince's gaze carried promises, the kind that Niko wasn't sure he could resist.

He was sagging against the wall by the time Amir

approached. The prince's eyes were glassy from spice. His clothes hung open, his short hair was ruffled, and someone else's lip-paint marked his cheek and neck. He stopped in front of Niko and sipped his drink.

Niko eyed the goblet with envy. His head spun from warring with himself.

Amir lifted the goblet and, to his shame, Niko reached for it. The prince pulled the cup back and clicked his tongue. "Get on your knees, doulos."

He dropped to his knees, no longer caring. Amir tipped Niko's chin up, pressed the cool cup to his lips and tilted it upward. The wine was sweet with a dreaded, spicy kick. Too late, he turned his head away, refusing the drug. Wine sloshed over his cheek. Then Amir's thin fingers were around his neck, pulling him face to face with the prince. "Drink it!"

Niko bared his teeth again. "Fuck you."

"Oh, if only we could, but I know my brother's games, and there's something far better." His grip shifted to Niko's jaw, fingers digging in. He pressed the edge of the cup hard against Niko's mouth, crushing his lips against his teeth. Wine sloshed. Niko tried to yank away, but Amir's fingers dug deeper. "Hold him!" he shouted.

More hands held him down. Wine poured over his mouth. Amir's fingers dug deeper still into his cheeks, forcing his jaw apart. "*Drink!*"

Wine sloshed in, over his tongue, down his throat. He gasped, choked, and coughed half of it back up, splashing Amir's face, but the prince just grinned and poured more wine in.

"Hold his damned nose."

Someone did. Fingers pinched. Niko spluttered, the

overly-spiked liquid burning his throat. He gulped and gasped and choked, and then it was over. Amir staggered back, his face alight with glee. He threw the goblet away and with a flourish he announced, "Now take this piece of meat to my brother."

"My liege?" someone queried.

"Do as I say!" the prince roared. "Fucking question me again and I'll cut you." Amir's face was all Niko could see. "Tell that little bitch brother of mine I don't want his gifts if I can't fuck them, so I'm sending you back." He pushed Niko, causing him to stumble backward.

Niko barely registered whose hands were grabbing him and marching him away from the prince's sweltering chambers. Cold air licked his hot, wet skin, and gods, he was so fucking hard. He groaned, but the drug had already sunk into his veins. He was supposed to be somewhere else, with someone else, but he couldn't recall who, or when, or why. Maybe it was with Julian, whose ass Niko could ride for hours.

Voices mumbled, and then he saw the last person he needed to be near. Or rather, he saw his legs in black boots. And then he caught sight of his waist, so narrow and taut.

"What is this?" Vasili's voice, hard as it was, brought Niko's wayward thoughts back into the room.

He blinked, shaking his head to try and fix his mind back together, and found himself kneeling in a room he didn't recognize.

Vasili was here. His hair curtained half his face. He knelt, peering at Niko, looking down on him like always.

Niko had fought for these Caville bastards. He'd lost loved ones for them. Friends, family, Marcus. He sprang off his back foot and lunged toward Vasili. The prince dashed away, white hair swirling, allowing Niko to grab a fistful and yank.

The prince gasped, and the sound was so fucking satisfying Niko wanted to hear it again.

He flung him on the end of a bed and stilled. Vasili lay on his back, chest rising and falling, his shirt laces having spilled open, revealing a thin glimpse of a pale chest, and many smooth scars. Niko blinked again and staggered on the spot. He couldn't get his head straight. Scars. Cuts. Precise. Deliberate. All over Vasili.

He stumbled forward and braced an arm on the bed beside the prince. Vasili hissed each ragged breath through his teeth, but didn't move, didn't fight. Niko pinched the shirt and peeled it back, revealing an intricate patchwork of old scars. Niko frowned. He looked up into the prince's face and found it flushed with fury.

But Vasili didn't move.

Niko leaned closer still. The man's thigh was hard against his, just like it had been at the pleasure house bar. He could grab both wrists, flung back as they were, pin him down and make him gasp again.

The fury in Vasili's eye turned brittle. His top lip peeled back.

Suddenly, he brought his knee up, forcing space between them. The kick landed and threw Niko back. He hit a dresser and clutched its edge to keep from falling. A cool, slippery sense of dread tried to worm its way through the chaos in his head, but it was too late for that. He couldn't think, couldn't get anything straight. Gods, his ribs hurt. Vasili kicked like a horse.

A door slammed.

Niko sank to the floor. Alone. The dread turned to shame and the drug finally began to withdraw its claws, leaving him spent and shivering, stewing in guilt. He wanted to crawl back to Julian's room, into bed with him, and just lie there, but he didn't trust himself not to attack Julian.

Tucking himself against the wall, he pulled his knees close and buried his head between them. He might have cried if he hadn't used up all his tears long ago.

CHAPTER 12

*N*iko winced and closed his eyes. He'd somehow managed to stumble back to Julian's room in the early hours of the morning, stripped off the awful doulos outfit, and fallen into his cramped cot. He'd woken an hour later with a wretched headache and the need to toss his guts up, which he had done in a bucket, then promptly collapsed again.

Julian must have taken the bucket, because the next time he woke, the guard was gone and a fresh pile of clothes sat neatly on his bed.

While Julian was out tending to Vasili, Niko had somehow managed to dress himself without throwing up again and dragged his ass to the worktable to stare at the pieces of a puzzle that would probably be the death of him.

It was now mid-morning and Julian was back. Niko still wanted to crawl into a hole and stay there.

"What did you learn?" Julian asked.

"I learned..." His voice was wrecked too. "...that spice

is fucking nasty and Amir is a piece of shit."

Julian sighed and leaned against the table. "One of those things we knew already. A man like you has never tried spice?"

"Like me?" Niko arched an eyebrow.

Julian winced. "I merely meant *experienced*."

Niko rubbed his face. None of this was Julian's fault. "I'm sorry. I—I'm still coming down." The man's gentle smile almost tore Niko in two. He wouldn't have smiled like that if he'd seen Niko last night. "I've tried spice before. Once. Swore off the stuff when I woke up in a ditch east of Caemn. That shit will kill, or render a man unconscious for days. I've no idea why the fucking lords and ladies love it so much."

He had learned more last night, when bits of it came back to him. Lady Maria had been interesting, not least because Amir couldn't take his eyes off her. The prince was infatuated with her. There was leverage. And she knew a lot about Vasili, assuming he was the cuckoo she mentioned. Amir certainly wasn't.

"Anything else?" Julian asked.

"Only some surprises about my own fucked-up head. Things I'd prefer to beat out in training."

"That can be arranged," Julian said.

Niko pinched the bridge of his nose, trying to alleviate the headache. "Amir—the bastard—wound me up so tight and sent me back to his brother like that."

"Shit. What happened?"

"Nothing." A lot. The scars. The prince sprawled on the bed. Niko's startling realization that he'd desperately wanted to fuck him so hard, he'd make Vasili scream his name. Shit. That was the drug talking. And was it any surprise Vasili featured in his fantasies? The bastard had twisted Niko's screws so tightly, he was bound to blow. Amir had just picked up on that. The spice had heightened everything, made him think ridiculous things, and his body had gone along with it because that was what spice did: made fantasy reality.

Julian shifted, drawing Niko's gaze up. "Spice is potent—"

"Yes, thank you, I experienced that."

"And you did nothing with Vasili?"

A clear note of jealousy underlined Julian's less-than-subtle inquiry. The more Julian spoke about the prince, the more it was obvious they had a strong bond, perhaps a sexual one. As fragile as Niko was feeling, knowing Julian cared about Vasili soured Niko's mood even further. "If I had, do you think I'd still be here?"

Vasili clearly hadn't told Julian anything about their encounter. Niko had no desire to relive it. Julian didn't need to know. "I was so far gone. I could barely walk. I think he took one look at me and left. I don't really remember."

Vasili *had* left, but didn't call the guards or order him flogged. He just left. That seemed un-Vasili-like. It could have been much worse. The memory of leaning over Vasili, of seeing those scars, of wanting to pin down the prince's wrists and fuck him, and of how Vasili had briefly relented beneath him, like maybe he wouldn't fight—right before kicking him in the chest—that memory would haunt him.

He rubbed the spot over his heart. Bastard. No, Niko had been the bastard. He'd been about to rape the prince. There was no avoiding it. Vasili would have not reacted well and Niko probably would have lost his cock, then his head. Likely exactly as Amir had wanted. The middle prince had hoped Niko would rape his brother.

This fucking family. It would be easier to burn down the whole palace and walk away from the ashes.

"Hungry?" Julian beamed, trying his best to lighten the mood.

"No." The thought of food made his gut roll, but then there was Julian smiling down at him. "I'll sit with you if you are." And maybe, if he worded the questions correctly, he could find out why Vasili's chest had been cut up like a piece of meat. Not that he had any right to know. He really needed to think on something else, someone else. Like spending time with the only good man in the palace.

Julian's smile grew. "You'll need to regain your strength."

"By the three, why? I can't handle the princes again today." He wasn't sure he could look Vasili in the eye. "Don't make me go in again."

Julian's left eyebrow ticked upward at Niko's whine. "No rest for the wicked." He shoved off the table. "Bring your blade."

That sounded more promising. Niko snatched up his blade and followed Julian out of the room.

As they approached a walled courtyard and a line of dummy targets, Niko's muscles relaxed into the more familiar stance of carrying his blade. He'd rarely been without it on the front line, and having it back now centered him as nothing else could.

He squinted at the targets. A few other guards practiced their parries at the far end. A training yard. The loose-fitting clothes Julian had left for him made more sense now.

Julian shrugged off his outer light armor, dumped it on a dusty table, and rolled his shoulders, flexing his muscles. He carried two shortswords in his gloved hands. Clearly, missing a few fingers didn't worry him. He'd adapted, as soldiers did. They died if they didn't.

Niko tried to hide his smile and spotted Julian similarly trying to restrain his grin. They could make this professional. The illicit thrill buzzing through Niko's veins had nothing to do with the thought of finally clashing blades with the man whose body he'd meticulously studied.

"All right. Are you up to this?" Julian asked, circling around, weighing his blades.

"I'm not at my best, but I figure I can beat a man missing a few digits."

Julian's smile twitched. "Tough talk for a man who was throwing his guts up a few hours ago."

Niko swung the sword in his right hand, loosening up his wrist. He'd prefer to warm up but Julian didn't look as though he was going to wait. "Rules?"

"Do we need any?"

"Then I'll assume it's not to the death."

Julian grinned. "Best of three hits. Loser must serve the other dinner."

Well, that sounded delightful. Julian's grin was infectious and Niko found himself dampening his own. "Deal."

Julian sprang, whip-fast. Niko barely got his blade up in time to block the thin weapon, but even as he did, Julian's second blade slashed at his belly. Niko stumbled, tripped over his feet, and fell on his ass, jarring his spine. "Shit." Julian was damned fast for someone his size. Three seconds to get Niko on his backside. A record.

The guard chuckled and offered his hand. "We'll call that one mine, shall we?"

"Conceded."

Julian hauled Niko to his feet, his grip lingering. Niko flashed a grin and pulled the man close, making his eyes widen. "Will you serve me dinner on your knees?" Niko asked. He pushed off and rolled his shoulders, watching Julian stumble slightly. The thought had disarmed him. Good.

Julian's glare was suddenly full of passionate intent. Niko could have taken advantage of the man's small stumble, but he'd rather enjoyed seeing it, and enjoyed even more the way Julian was watching him now.

"You don't have the element of surprise anymore, soldier," he warned.

"No." Julian circled and Niko mirrored him, keeping him at a few paves length. "But there are other advantages."

Sunlight sliced through Niko's vision, reigniting his headache. Julian's twin blades flashed. Niko parried one, danced back, and brought the flat of his blade down hard on Julian's left hand. Julian barked a cry and dropped the sword. Niko kicked it aside and swung again, sweeping his blade in low. Julian barely blocked it. He staggered, losing his footing, retreating.

Hot blood pumped through Niko's veins. He struck again, blades singing between them, clash after clash. Julian parried each strike, but he couldn't withstand the weight of Niko's blows for long. The moment his back hit the wall Niko pinned him there, the blade under his throat, his firm, panting body trapped between Niko's and the wall.

Julian peered down his nose. "I concede."

Niko should have backed off. The point was his. But Julian's body was as hard as Niko had imagined, his skin hot beneath the thin layers of fabric. His mouth was softening from a sneer into something more forgiving, something desirable. Just a taste. A kiss. A test, to see if it was welcome, to see if there was something here, or if it was all in Niko's head.

A distant shout from the other guards shattered the moment. They weren't alone. The opportunity had slipped through Niko's fingers.

"The prince," Julian mumbled.

"What?"

"Behind you."

Niko sprang back from Julian so fast his head throbbed anew. Sure enough, Vasili had entered the yard. His head was turned away to observe the others, so maybe he hadn't seen Niko lingering too long with Julian beneath him. Because if he saw, he might think Niko made a habit of crowding men.

Shit, why did he care what Vasili thought?

"Final point for the win," Julian said, his words pulling Niko back to the match.

The prince being here didn't have to be distracting. There he was, in the corner of Niko's vision, crossing the yard, heading away. See. Vasili didn't even care.

Julian's blades flashed. "See something you like, doulos?"

Niko laughed and fixed Julian in his sights. "Now I do."

Julian licked his lips, probably knowing damn well how Niko absorbed that tiny gesture into every inch of his body. Julian thrust low. Niko parried, but the guard pivoted, so light-footed it put Niko's dancing strides to shame, and his second blade sliced in. Niko barely managed to lean back, saving his face from a new scar, but Julian wasn't done. His other blade flicked up, its deadly movement catching Niko's eye at the last second. Niko ducked and jabbed the pommel of his sword into Julian's unprotected middle. The man huffed and placed his hand on Niko's shoulder. Niko kicked his leg out and Julian fell hard onto his back, momentarily winded.

Niko pointed the tip of his blade at the man's throat.

They both breathed hard, sweating under the sun.

"Fuck." Julian spat.

"Later."

Niko glanced over his shoulder to see if Vasili had noticed. He'd noticed, all right. He stood in the middle of the yard, fine black clothes contrasted against the wall, his arms folded, hip cocked, watching.

A figure moved on the wall at the far end of the courtyard.

Niko squinted against the sun. Was it normal for people to be on that wall?

The figure reached over their shoulder. Niko's heart lodged like ice in his throat. He'd seen the same action a thousand times, and it meant only one thing: an arrow being pulled from a quiver.

"Down!" he yelled, bolting for Vasili. The prince unfolded his arms, but didn't move.

The figure on the wall slotted the notch of the arrow on the string and drew.

"Get down!"

The arrow sprang. Its spinning head zipped past Vasili's shoulder. The prince whirled. He should have run, or gotten under cover. Instead he clutched his shoulder, continued to stand in plain sight, and looked up the cloaked figure on the wall.

The figure bolted. Niko veered from Vasili toward the fleeing attacker. He dropped his sword, grabbed a ladder and raced up it, breaching the top in seconds to see the cloaked man—he assumed a male—running down the grassy hill toward the walled gardens. Niko dropped down the other side of the wall and chased the man through the grass, gaining on him.

The figure disappeared through a small, open gate and darted into the nearby city streets. Niko raced after him, but he was damned fast and clearly agile. He sprinted over a small rope bridge spanning a stream and a burst of speed took him down a cobbled street, upsetting the market traders.

"Out of the way!" Niko burst through the crowd, chasing the figure's rippling cloak.

Loreen's haphazard streets dipped and climbed. The figure leaped down a flight of steps, landing with inhuman grace. Niko launched himself down after him, stumbling over the last few steps but regaining enough to close the distance.

Strolling citizens blocked the would-be assassin's path to freedom. He shoved them aside, spotted a ladder and sprang up it, his bow and quiver bouncing on his back as he disappeared through a window. Niko clambered up the ladder seconds behind him and scrambled over the windowsill.

Inside a dark, small room, a dagger flashed toward him. Niko sidestepped and brought his left fist down on the assassin's face. He grunted. The dagger flashed again, this time finding its target. Pain burned across Niko's upper arm and he recoiled. The assassin lunged. Niko caught the man's wrist, blocking the thrust but the man shoved forward.

Niko's head slammed into the stone wall, his teeth jarring. A vicious punch to his side stole the breath from his lungs. Hands flung him back, pinning him to the wall.

The assassin grinned. Sharp teeth. Grey eyes. *Elf*, his mind screamed. Old fear plunged rods though his limbs, trying to freeze him rigid.

He grabbed the elf's face and shoved, then kicked, striking him in the chest. The elf stumbled back. Niko stepped forward, but the room spun out from under him. His knee hit the floorboards. *Wait*...

The dagger flashed again. Niko jerked back, grabbed the elf's wrist, and brought it down over his knee. Bones snapped. The elf howled, a familiar, blood-curdling sound. It hissed in his face, then sprang back, tearing from Niko's grip, and vanished in a whirl of cloak through a doorway.

Niko reached for a nearby table and heaved himself onto trembling, leaden legs. His legs slid out from under him, their weight all wrong.

Sticky wetness ran down his thigh. The punch—it hadn't been a punch at all. He groped at his side and his hand came away glistening scarlet.

The door. The window. If he could get to one, either, any... Gods, his head hurt. He collapsed against the doorframe, smearing blood onto it. Someone screamed—not an elf. Just someone nearby surprised at finding him.

He fell across a hallway, hit the wall, and slid to the floor.

"Vasili," he croaked before losing consciousness.

CHAPTER 13

*H*e was in Julian's bed, but not in the way he'd imagined. And Vasili was here, which definitely wasn't what he wanted. Or did he? Gods, no. He groaned, and a hand came down on his shoulder.

"Don't try and move," Julian said.

"Elf." They needed to know. If there was one, there might have been more.

"There are no elves here, brother," Julian said softly, mistaking Niko's words for delirium.

"No." He shoved Julian's touch away and rolled onto his side, panting with pain. He saw Vasili standing by the door, the prince's unblinking glare oddly comforting. Vasili was alive. And Niko was still currently alive. The assassin had failed. But Vasili didn't look surprised, like he hadn't looked at all surprised to see an elf in the courtyard.

"You son of a bitch," Niko slurred. Throbbing waves of unconsciousness threatened again.

Vasili's lips ticked. "Report to me when he's coherent."

Niko was fucking coherent, damn it, and he knew what

he'd seen. But the prince was gone, and Niko tasted blood on his tongue.

"Rest, Nikolas."

"Elf..." he mumbled again, but it was too late. Julian wasn't listening. The darkness swallowed him whole.

～

IT WAS a week before he could move without tearing open the wound. The cut was small but deep; the elf had meant to kill. The wound on his shoulder burned more, but he'd live. Julian must have been granted special leave to tend to Niko because he was in the room every time Niko opened his eyes. He fussed with clothes, fussed with a washcloth, fussed over Niko. He was endearing.

Vasili hadn't returned, but Niko hadn't expected him to. The prince was hiding secrets about elves, and Niko was going to get the answer out of him as soon as he could walk without gasping.

"I feel like an old man." He reached for the bedpost and steadied himself. He'd been trying to step into trousers but the damned wound kept stealing his breath. The wrapping around his waist restricted his movement, and he was tempted to remove the damn thing.

"You look like one too," Julian said, sliding in beside him to take his hand. "Will you let me help? Watching you struggle is painful for us both."

Niko grumbled, but sat on the bed to let Julian work the trousers over his feet. Julian ran his hands up Niko's shin in a way that had nothing to do with getting dressed and everything to do with stealing a feel. Niko arched an eyebrow, but didn't stop him.

Julian rose off his knees and pulled Niko to his feet, then leaned in to ease the trousers over his ass. The movement brought Julian's mouth temptingly close. Niko studied the concentration on the man's face. The way he bit his lip. How he desperately tried not to meet Niko's gaze.

Julian tightened the belt and looked down, fastening the ties. He managed well considering the limited movement. Niko still hadn't seen what was inside the gloves to know for certain he'd lost any digits.

Once the belt was fastened, Julian bit his lip and looked up. Niko searched his eyes for denial, for an excuse not to do this, but there was none of that. Just open acceptance, *want*, even. It was too late, anyway. Niko was already stroking his fingers along the man's jaw, brushing over rough stubble, making it hiss beneath his nails. When Julian didn't pull away, Niko nudged his mouth with his own, questioning. Julian's lips opened slightly. It wasn't much, but it was enough.

He'd fantasized about tasting Julian for what felt like forever. Niko kissed him deeper, feeling him give. He tasted soft, his response achingly gentle. This wasn't the passionate first kiss Niko imagined they'd share, but as Julian's lashes fluttered closed and he rested an arm over Niko's good shoulder, the kiss heated and quickened.

The kiss was better than Niko could have imagined, sensuous but growing harder, and now Niko couldn't think at all outside the feel of the man's mouth on his. Julian shifted, leaning in, pushing down. Niko dropped onto the bed and hissed at a sudden dart of pain.

"Shit, I...sorry." Julian blushed. "Damn, I shouldn't have."

"Don't." He winced. "It was me." He smiled up at the soldier who might have stolen the heart he believed was lost long ago. Niko wanted to kiss Julian again, to feel the heat of him beneath his hands and mouth, to feel him move and groan for more.

Julian grasped the bedpost beside Niko's head and bent down. His mouth hovered over Niko's close enough to share breaths. Then Julian sealed his lips against Niko's. Unlike the last time, this time Julian meant it. His hand came up to touch Niko's cheek and the kiss turned messy and ragged.

Niko pinched Julian's lip between his teeth. Julian repositioned closer, nudging Niko's thighs apart.

Julian's chin nudged Niko's, urging him on. His gloved hand slipped down Niko's bare back. Niko shuddered, a groan tearing free. He let his head fall, and Julian's mouth instantly went to his throat. He sucked and nipped, and slowly eased Niko down.

Niko winced again, hissing sharply. "Can't." He blinked up at the man trapped between his thighs, his blond hair a mop around his head, his freckles golden and eyes so blue. "Want to, though." Full sentences were apparently too much.

Julian's suggestive gaze dipped to Niko's crotch. "I can see that."

By the three, if Julian went down on Niko, he wouldn't last.

"This is new." Julian admitted, backing up. "Men, I mean."

"Oh." Shit. Niko had assumed Julian was experienced because he was probably screwing Vasili, or had in the past. "Is it a problem?" Niko asked, desperately hoping it wasn't.

"No." He puffed out a breath. "Definitely no. I just... I'm not sure how it goes."

Niko couldn't help but smile at his inexperienced soldier. Julian blushed, the color perfect on him. Niko wanted to follow that flush and see if it went all the way down.

He groaned and let his head fall back on the bed. "Give me another week, all right? And I'll show you exactly how this goes. Right now I'm... fragile."

"I've waited this long."

Niko raised a brow. "How long?"

Julian extracted himself from Niko's thighs, making Niko frown at the loss of his warmth. Julian grinned. "When the prince found you at the Stag and Horn. I was..." He chewed on his words.

"Tell me." Shy, too. Niko was doomed.

"I knew you were someone like me. An ex-soldier. And I'd thought about it on the front line, y'know? But never... gone there."

"Yeah." He knew. Killing alongside the same men every day made for some intimate, if rushed, moments of desperation. Not many of them were worth more than a frantic release. Perhaps it was good Julian had been spared the experience, especially if it would have been his first.

"I wanted you after you grabbed Vasili. I was sure he'd kill you for that. But he didn't, and you kept defying him—"

"Had me flogged." Niko smiled a little and Julian grinned back.

"It was that or execution. You surprise him."

"And that's good?" And why did this have anything to do with Vasili?

Julian fell over Niko and braced a hand on either side of his body, then lowered himself carefully so as not to upset the wounds. "It's more than good." He sealed his hot mouth over Niko's. His tongue thrust in.

Niko ached for so much more. He wanted to discover what Julian liked, how he tasted all over, and what noises he'd make beneath Niko's fingers and mouth. He wanted Julian writhing and begging, but also wanted Julian to look at him with eyes full of strength and understanding.

Julian withdrew, making Niko moan for more.

"Hm," the guard said. "I've watched you a great deal. Seen you furious, stoic, repulsed. I prefer you like this."

"Sprawled on my back, at your mercy?"

"Exactly."

He could switch that around once he was stronger. And then they'd explore each other during long, hot nights of pleasure. Niko wasn't particularly experienced, but that first encounter at the Stag and Horn and the stolen moments with Marcus had taught him much.

"You're clearly feeling better," Julian shuffled backward and climbed off the bed. "Vasili said you should see him as soon as you can."

Niko rolled his eyes. "Of course he did." But he did need to speak with the prince. "I doubt it's to thank me for saving him."

"He hasn't mentioned it, no."

He'd have been surprised if he had. Niko eyed his shirt, which was all the way across the room.

Julian tracked his gaze. "Would you like me to help you finish dressing?"

"Please don't," Niko smiled. "Or I fear we'll never leave."

VASILI WAS IN THE BATHHOUSE, which wasn't necessarily a problem, but he made it one by asking Niko to enter alone. Niko frowned and opened the door.

The baths were as empty as when he'd first visited weeks ago, but for one person.

Vasili sat in a huge sunken tub, facing the door. But his eye was closed, his head tilted back a little. The water was still, its surface broken only by pink rose petals. Niko had forgotten the subtle smell of roses and how it had clung to the prince the first time they'd met.

The door swung shut with a clunk, and Vasili opened his eye.

Vasili's stare landed, digging in like claws. A chill ran down Niko's back, but he'd be damned if he stood at the door like some timid deer.

He approached the edge of the bath, hands clasped behind his back. The wrappings around his waist constricted each breath, shortening them. Hopefully Vasili wouldn't notice and misconstrue his quickened breathing as fear—or something else.

"You have recovered well," Vasili said.

A compliment, or just a statement of fact? The latter, surely. "Julian is very attentive."

The prince's eyebrow arched. "He is, isn't he?"

Niko's gaze dropped guiltily. He set his body into motion, moving about the baths as though checking them for threats. Yes, that would be his answer if Vasili asked.

Checking for threats, and not moving because the prince might see exactly what Niko thought of Julian.

The prince was naked, his pale skin almost invisible beneath the milky water. A few pinkish scars showed through. Niko's thoughts unhelpfully flashed to having Vasili on his back and how he'd peeled open his shirt to inspect the marks. He'd tried not to think of that encounter at all, but the elf attack had left him with too much time and too many thoughts. He'd come to the conclusion that Vasili hadn't been afraid. He'd wanted Niko to see those scars. Why?

Niko's boots clicked solidly against the stone as he walked. It was a good sound, a strong one, though he wasn't feeling particularly strong. Steam and water soaked through his clothes, clinging to his skin. He made his way around the entire room before returning to his spot between Vasili and the door.

"The elf," Niko said, watching the prince's face closely for a reaction.

"Hm?" The prince shifted slightly, making the water ripple.

Niko's heart jumped into his throat at the thought of Vasili striding into the baths with Niko still present. A shocking thought. Vasili would never reveal himself so. Although if he did, Niko might be able to tell if the prince had a blade up his ass, which would explain how he was always armed and why he acted like a prick every hour of every day.

"The elf?" Vasili prompted.

"Yes." What had he been saying? He realigned his thoughts away from the prospect of seeing Vasili naked, and how terrible that would be. "You knew the assassin was an elf."

"I didn't know at the time. Only later, when you mentioned it while bleeding all over Julian's bed."

That felt like a lie, but Niko couldn't pin down why. The man was impossible to read. Vasili blinked back, lazily amused. Frustration heated Niko's blood. Vasili probably sensed that too, like he could sense small weakness in his prey.

"You have become close with Julian."

Not a question.

Niko's thoughts narrowed to a single point: Protect Julian. Whatever happened, however this ended, Niko still hoped to escape it all, but Julian might not want or be able to leave, and if Vasili didn't approve of their...whatever they had, Julian would suffer. He had to tread carefully.

"Friends, yes. He's a good man."

"He said the same of you. He's clearly wrong." Beads of water glistened on Vasili's lashes. He didn't look as though he were about to pounce or issue an order to have Julian killed, but he hadn't looked particularly murderous right before he'd cut a doulos's throat either. "You're both soldiers," Vasili added.

"Ex-soldiers."

"You have much in common."

Why had the conversation turned to Julian? "This isn't relevant."

"Isn't it?"

Niko swallowed and sighed, leveling his thoughts. "An elf made it through Loreen, breached the palace, and was able to fire an arrow at you from the training courtyard walls." A tiny cut marked the prince's shoulder where the arrow had skimmed him. It could have been much worse.

"I had noticed, yes." A tiny shimmer of—surely not humor?—brightened his eye. "Perhaps you should ask Julian what he saw."

"The same as I." Niko's brow pinched. "For a man being hunted by elves, you do not appear to be afraid."

"Fear is useless."

"I disagree."

"Then you have not experienced real fear."

"I'm..." Niko had been about to deny it, but stalled, wondering when the prince had experienced *real* fear. Vasili still rested against the edge of the bath, his arms spread, head tilted. But something had changed, like after the gallop through the field. It was too subtle for Niko to pin down. "I've experienced real fear. The useless fear you speak of is the kind that makes your body betray you. You freeze, unable to run, to fight, to do anything but listen to your own heart pounding and feel the cold sweat break out across your skin. You're a victim of it, not its master. I left real fear behind on the front line. If I hadn't, I'd be dead."

Vasili's mouth ticked. A tell. He recognized it now. A tiny imperfection in the perfect act. Some part of the real Vasili acknowledged his words, but he couldn't determine if it was good or bad.

"That fear is useless. I agree," Niko said. He knelt the way Vasili had knelt while Niko had bathed. The prince's gaze never left his face. Niko dangled his fingers into the bath water, again mimicking Vasili, and watched the prince's brow tighten. His cheek jumped.

Niko knew from rumors, as well as from Vasili's brother, that the prince didn't like to be touched. This wasn't touching, but it was something. And Vasili clearly felt he couldn't reprimand Niko without revealing too much of that fear.

"The elf..." Niko prompted again, bringing them back around to the topic at hand. "Someone left a small side gate open for him."

Vasili's lashes fluttered down. "Amir, probably. Or a servant, someone I insulted or a soldier who despises me? My aunt perhaps, she's been with Amir—"

"Your aunt?"

"Lady Maria."

Of course. Niko freed a short, sharp laugh. Maria—the woman who had helped him focus himself during Amir's orgy.

"My aunt is amusing to you, Niko?" Vasili pushed forward suddenly, cutting through the water, and then began to climb from the steps.

Niko straightened. He dared not move or look away, or look down, so he fixed the prince's eye with his glare. He wished he hadn't when a challenge lurked in the prince's glare, daring him to hold his gaze.

Absolutely naked, Vasili turned away, padded bare-assed along the side of the bath, and scooped up a gown. Rivulets of water ran from the long, wet hair plastered to his back and into the crack of his tight ass. The backs of his thighs weren't scarred like the fronts. All the princes were tall, but Vasili had a willowy elegance to him that belied toned muscle. He was a contradiction of a man.

Vasili threw the gown over his shoulders, disrupting the view.

Niko swallowed. Why was his throat dry?

Vasili turned—gown fully open—and gathered up his

hair, pulling it free from inside the gown's collar. The shifting musculature of his chest made the scars glisten. If he'd been afraid to reveal them before, he certainly wasn't now. They travelled all the way down to his hips.

A rose petal clung to his hip, and suddenly it was all Niko could see: a soft pink velvet kiss on the prince's pale skin.

"Did you believe the elves *had* taken my cock, mercenary?"

Niko closed his mouth. He could deny looking, but because Vasili had fucking said the word, Niko looked, and shit. Now heat rushed up Niko's neck and face. He had wondered about the cock thing, seeing as people in the palace liked to fuck anything that moved. Vasili didn't. Nobody touched him either. Except Niko at the pleasure house, and again on the prince's bed.

Vasili's cock was normal. Generous, even. Not a viper. Didn't have fangs.

"Look me in the eye, Nikolas."

Niko blinked. He'd been staring like a fucking fool. He looked down into the pool. "You're all fucking insane."

Vasili was suddenly close, the warm smell of wet skin and roses tickling Niko's nose. Steam rose off the prince; he tasted it on his lips.

"Look at me." An order.

Vasili's gaze drilled into him. The prince was intimately close now, his eye observing, reading Niko's face, studying him. Looking for the best place to thrust a blade, no doubt.

"Thank you," Vasili said.

Niko didn't know what to say. Vasili left, and the door clunked closed. Niko's heart thumped too damned hard, sending hot blood through his veins, as well as to other places.

"Sweet fucking gods." Niko ran a trembling hand through his wet hair. Why was it every time he spoke with Vasili he was left feeling like the bastard had rooted around in his soul and torn out his vulnerabilities?

It took too long to quench the way his body burned and slow his heart from its wild gallop. Yet again, he hadn't gotten the answers he needed.

He turned toward the door, but paused. Vasili wasn't going to answer his questions. Amir was a fucking bastard who Niko would attack on sight. But there was another Caville. One he'd recently met who might be more forthcoming.

Lady Maria.

$\mathcal{L}$ady Caville welcomed Niko into her receiving chambers with a breezy smile. "Darling," she purred. "Is it possible you look even more delectable *in* clothes?"

Her teasing appeared harmless, instantly making him breathe easier.

She waved him in, told him to sit, and poured wine without asking. "I hear you were stabbed? Gallantly chased my nephew's attacker across Loreen's rooftops. So heroic."

He sat in the offered chair at the window across a small table from her position. "Heroic? No. Just reactive. I lost the attacker and almost died for my efforts." He gestured at his chest.

"So modest. I see why he likes you." Niko would have asked who she referred to, but she had already moved on. He let her talk, accepted the wine, and casually scanned her room. There had been no mention of a Lord Caville but he assumed Maria must have married in to be living within the palace walls and in such fine chambers. He tried to recall his own attempt at recreating the Caville family tree.

"A thinker," she mused after his too long in silence. "Yes, it's all falling into place."

"I'm not sure what you mean."

"Vasili's attraction to you."

He laughed suddenly, caught off guard. "There isn't such a thing."

"Oh, attraction doesn't have to be physical. There's more to desire than sex."

Was there? Niko wasn't sure he could agree, but with Maria he felt open to being persuaded, especially as she appeared to understand his preference for men, and was unlikely to be a threat—at least in the bedroom. Unlike Amir. He instantly warmed to this woman's honesty. If she had married into the Cavilles, that surely made her formidable.

"So why are you here?" she asked, leaning back in her chair. She wore layers of colored silk draped around her. The color matched well with Amir's similar love of all things bright and beautiful. Did she know her nephew wanted to fuck her? "I assume it's something to do with the darling Vasili."

Darling was not a word he associated with Vasili. "Someone is trying to kill him."

"Yes, it does appear that way," she replied grimly. "Thankfully, he's not so easily killed." The glass in her hand shook a little.

"Tell me about him."

"About Vasili? By the time I arrived at the palace he was already missing."

"Missing?"

She waved. "Away. You know, *gone*."

"His absence wasn't planned?"

"Gods, no," she gasped. "Poor, dear."

"Then where was he?"

She sipped her wine and peered at him over her glass. So that question wasn't one she could or would answer. "I knew what everyone else knew," she continued. "He's the eldest, the most level, the leader of the three. Did you know he could sing, as a child? It was quite something, apparently."

Niko attempted to hide his disbelieving frown. Vasili's voice was indeed smooth and controlled, and another weapon in the man's varied arsenal, but singing? "You don't know where he was for the eight years he was missing?" Niko asked, steering her back toward the topic of his absence.

"Oh, I know." She sipped her wine and sent her gaze out the window. "He and Julian returned together."

"They did?" Three minutes with the woman and he already knew more than Julian or Vasili had revealed in weeks. The prince's years away hadn't been planned, and Julian had been with him?

"Vasili without an eye and Julian without his fingers. They're inseparable. I'm sure you've noticed. But it's not always..." She straightened her skirts. "Anyway, what do you want to know about our Vasili?"

He stopped short of saying *everything*. "I'm intrigued."

"Of course you are." She patted his knee. "Vasili is..."

"Complicated?" he offered, beginning to despise the word.

"Exactly. I see you understand. As his doulos, I imagine

you've spent a great deal of time with him." And now she was fishing for answers of her own.

"As you would expect."

"Hm, you're a slippery one as well. A soldier and a thinker. A dangerous combination. Vasili must be absolutely fascinated by you. I find myself similarly intrigued. No wonder Amir is jealous."

"Amir is jealous?"

"Well, yes. He doesn't see his brother for eight years and then Vasili returns with a guard nobody knows, demands control, and now you're here? And he isn't the same as he was. And it's not just the eye. Terrible, what was done to him. I hope they all rot, the butchering bastards." She clutched her skirts in her fists and sighed. "I know the Cavilles are difficult to love. But I loved mine."

"Your husband?"

"He died on the front line."

"A soldier."

"Yes, like you."

The king's brother. Niko didn't recall much of the man, just his name on the family tree. He probably kept himself out of public view.

"Those fucking elves took him," Maria seethed.

He fought the urge to hold her hand, unsure if she'd welcome the touch of her nephew's doulos.

His thoughts tripped on something she'd said moments ago. *Butchering bastards.* A great deal about Vasili suddenly fell into place. "Elves took Vasili's eye?"

"You did not hear it from me. I mean, the whole palace knows, but he's never confirmed it. He doesn't say much of anything at all anymore." She sighed, her tone distant. "The cuckoo in this nest."

"Is he so different from the others?"

"Can't you tell?"

"I…" He hesitated, not fully understanding the question. Vasili was different from anyone Niko had ever met, but all the Cavilles were. As a family, however, they were all the same.

"Ah." She stroked a crease on the tablecloth into smoothness. "I have perhaps said too much."

He was losing her. "No." He clasped her hand in his. "I… it's important I know. He's asked me to protect him"—that was mostly true—"and I need information to do that."

She looked at his hand and up into his eyes. "It's in their blood."

"What is?"

"The flame." She pulled her hand free. "It corrupts them. All of them. Makes them difficult. Vasili has… He has more of it, I think. But it's what the wretched elves wanted. They tried to cut it out of him but he kept it, because he's… he is Vasili and he'll always protect us even if the whole world hates him for it."

She finished her drink. "Terrible business. They were all just boys once." She trailed off, smoothing out the tablecloth once more. "Excuse me, talk of these things has put me in a foul mood. I'm afraid I'm not the best of company when melancholy. I'd ask you to stay and help me finish this bottle, but I do believe he'll want you back soon, and it's rather unseemly for his doulos to be in my chambers." She leaned forward suddenly and gripped Niko's chin. "You dear man. You will protect him, like he's asked of you?"

"If he'll allow me." Her passion and conviction made Niko almost want to believe his own words.

"Good." She let him go and turned toward the window. "Everyone else can burn, but he must survive. Loreen depends on it."

Niko had a thousand questions on his tongue, but she'd faced away and closed down. He'd get nothing more for the rest of the day. He left her alone, hoping she had someone to hold her hand—someone who wasn't Amir.

Niko walked the darkening corridors, mind whirring. He'd heard a reference to a flame before, but couldn't remember where. Something to do with the Caville name. He needed to find the palace library, but it was getting late and Julian would be looking for him.

A man carrying a messenger bag stepped from a side corridor into Niko's path. Niko narrowly avoided colliding with him and apologized before continuing on a few steps. The bag and clothing? They triggered a memory. He turned, frowning after the man. "Sir?"

"Excuse me." The man hurried on, unable to meet Niko's eye, clutching his bag to his side.

A light tingling tickled Niko's lips.

Spice.

The man carried spice. A spice dealer. And he'd been the same man who Julian denied had been inside Vasili's chambers. Perhaps that explained Julian's reluctance in admitting his presence. The squire wasn't so much a mystery as he was the prince's illicit drug habit. The Loreen people would certainly prefer their regent to be sober while running the country. Although, given the Cavilles' madness, spice might have improved their leadership abilities. It couldn't make them any worse.

Unless...

Niko followed the dealer's path down the hallway. Perhaps the man's lurking was nothing more than the nature of his business, but curiosity had its claws in him now. He followed the sound of retreating heeled boots, quickening his pace, and then found the man standing outside a door talking with another staff member. He ducked back behind a corner, out of sight.

"We agreed to a higher sum," the dealer argued.

"That's all he gave me."

"I won't be able to come back here. This isn't enough," the dealer said, his voice rising in pitch.

"Overdoses happen all the time. Give it a few weeks and the fuss will die down. He said that's more than enough. I can't give you any more. I don't have it."

The conversation ended and the dealer's heels tapped away at a brisk pace. The staff member's door was swinging closed.

Niko dashed out and rapped on the door. The woman yanked it open and froze when she saw Niko. She had tight curls and a young, rounded face. Spice made her eyes glassy, the pupils blown wide.

He smiled and opened his mouth to introduce himself.

She shoved the door in his face. He slammed a palm against it, bouncing it open, and bolted after the woman, who was already halfway across the chamber. She tripped on a rug and went sprawling onto a couch.

He narrowed his eyes and blocked her in by bracing an arm over the couch. "Overdose?"

She shrank into the cushions. "Shit, don't hurt me! He said it was just a game, something to make the prince's blood run hot. Spike it with too much spice, y'know?"

"Who, Amir?"

"Amir, what? No."

Ice gripped Niko's heart. "The spice was for Vasili?"

She nodded and bit her lip. "He takes it all the time for the pain."

"Did he just make a delivery to the prince?!" Niko growled.

"Y-yes?"

Shit. He pointed at the girl but backed off. "Stay here. I'm not done with you."

An overdose. Spiked spice. He ran from the girl's room, darting through corridors and up steps, cursing the wretched maze-like layout of the palace until he found familiar hallways. The last time he was here he'd been high, but as he came down he'd been able to map the route to Vasili's room.

He turned the handle to his chamber and shoved, but the door didn't give. "Dammit. Vasili?" He tried again, shoving it harder. Locked. "You in there?" A swift kick would break the lock. He backed up.

The door opened.

Vasili made an effort to straighten. His gaze drifted aimlessly, his mouth forming unspoken words. He slid down the door to his knees and, panting, slumped forward onto his hands.

He was too late. Spice overdoses could be lethal.

Niko knelt and reached out to support the prince, but the man turned his head and bared his teeth like a terrified animal. "You need help," he said softly. The prince's back heaved in time with his labored breaths. "The spice was tainted. You've been poisoned. Get to your feet."

"Don't...touch..."

Niko flexed his fingers. "All right, fine. Then I'll watch you die in a pool of your own bodily fluids. Is that what you want?"

Vasili reached up the door, grabbed the handle, and heaved himself onto his feet. "*Leave.*"

He was impossible. Spice was ravaging his body, burning his veins, shredding his mind, making him see and think things that didn't exist, just like it had with Niko. He could die, and still he stubbornly refused help. "Make me." He closed the door. He should find Julian, but he dared not leave the prince. If Vasili collapsed, his body might go into shock.

Vasili staggered to the bed and stumbled into a post. "I said...*leave*. Or..." He wet his lips, his pink tongue darting. "... have you whipped."

Niko prepared to catch the prince but kept his hands at his sides. "If you must, but I'm not leaving."

The prince bared his teeth again in answer. Sweat beaded at his hairline. He clutched at the post, his knuckles turning white as milk. But his glare was scathing. Niko glared back, unfazed.

Vasili's body let go, collapsing on itself. Niko grabbed him under the arms and pulled him into an awkward embrace, ignoring the hands shoving meekly at his chest.

"I have you." Maybe the words helped; maybe they didn't. But it was something.

Vasili sucked in a sharp hiss. Then with startling strength, his trembling fingers locked around the back of Niko's neck. His hard mouth crashed into Niko's. Vasili was sharp and bitter, all teeth and tongue. There was nothing sensual about it. The kiss was an attack. If the prince had held a blade, he would have stabbed Niko instead.

Niko grabbed the man's chin and forced him away. "You don't want to do that."

Vasili's mouth ticked. Then his lashes fluttered shut and his head lolled, and he was out cold, limp in Niko's arms.

At least Vasili couldn't argue while unconscious. Niko scooped him up and laid him on the bed, then quickly unlaced and unbuttoned his clothes. Spice overdoses had killed soldiers on the front. There, he'd known to keep victims cool. He had to do the same with Vasili before his body shut down.

Vasili's fingers twitched on the bed covers.

Niko peeled back Vasili's shirt, revealing the pattern of scars on his chest. It was no surprise the prince refused to be touched. The scars were likely numb, but the small islands of unharmed skin between them would ache. Niko tracked their path, going all the way down, stopping at Vasili's navel. Vasili breathed too fast. Sweat glistened on his face and neck, pooling at his navel.

No doubt this man's mind was formidable, but his body was just like everyone else's, and spice would kill him.

The chamber door opened. "Your Highness?"

"Julian! Get in here."

Julian would know how to handle Vasili. He immediately tore off his chest plate and weapons belt, dumping the armor on the floor and rushing to Vasili's bedside. "What happened?"

"Spice overdose. The man you denied comes here? He was paid to spike Vasili's dose."

"*What?*" Julian pressed a hand to Vasili's forehead.

"He's burning up." He grabbed the pillow from the other side of the bed and propped it under the prince's head. "Keep him elevated. If he starts to vomit, lift him."

Julian gathered up supplies from the room, knowing exactly where to find towels and ointments.

Vasili's torso heaved and Niko braced for the worst. "We should get a healer."

"Won't do any good." Julian placed a washbasin on the bedside table and used a wet cloth to dampen the prince's face and neck. "Need to keep him cool."

Niko undid the prince's boots and yanked them off, then pulled his trousers clear. The marks on his thighs stood out starkly against his skin. The scars were longer and deeper between his legs. Niko had known that, but seeing them so close made his gut roil. The scars weren't from battle wounds, like Niko's. Vasili's were meticulous and old. He'd been tortured, repeatedly, for years.

By elves.

He hadn't been hidden away, as Niko and most everyone outside the palace assumed. He'd been taken and tortured by monsters. It was a miracle he was coherent at all.

"He takes spice for the pain..." Julian said, noticing Niko's lingering gaze.

"I know."

"It's never a lot. He always has it under control. Not like this."

Julian genuinely cared for Vasili. It had always been there, but now it was obvious in the way he reverently stroked the cloth over his skin and defended him.

"You don't need to explain."

Where did that leave their relationship? Maybe they

didn't have one. There would be time to consider it all if the prince survived.

Niko helped tend Vasili into the night, until his breathing and heart rate stabilized. Then he left, telling Julian he had something to follow up on.

He returned to the girl's room to find her door ajar.

He shoved it open, tasted and smelled wet metal in the air. Blood. Then saw the body swinging from a beam. Her grey face suggested she'd been dead for hours, slung up by the neck, made to look as though she'd taken her own life.

Someone had guaranteed her silence.

CHAPTER 15

"I told them never to lock you up again," Julian explained.

Niko paced alongside him in the palace corridor. He'd spent the rest of the day in the dungeon after some well-meaning servant had seen him with the body and called the palace guards.

"How is Vasili?" Niko asked.

"Stable. Sleeping. The girl found dead... I assume she had something to do with the spice?"

He nodded. "She passed on the coin for whoever ordered his spice spiked. That person then tied up the loose end by killing her."

"You don't think she took her own life?"

Niko frowned at Julian's naivety.

"I just... I suppose you're right."

The girl had been caught up in the same mess that surrounded the prince's. It was a miracle Niko hadn't been targeted by the killer yet. He mulled over her death as they returned to Julian's chambers. Niko had planned to strip, removing the stench of the cells. But now that he was back in his room a restless energy rattled his nerves. He scooped up fresh clothes and strode past Julian. "I'm going to the baths."

"The guards won't let you in."

Niko paused at the door. Dammit. He'd forgotten he was still some doulos/squire pet for the prince.

"I'll come," Julian added.

The bathhouse was empty again. When Niko asked why, Julian confirmed they were for Vasili's use only, but Julian had *special* access.

Niko stripped, not caring if Julian watched. Warm water sloshed over the sides as Niko strode down the steps —ignoring the wrappings around the stab wound—and dunked his head, submerging himself completely. When he surfaced and turned, Julian was descending the steps, naked and flushed, his cock fully erect. Niko had hoped— was *hoped* the right word?—that Julian would join him. Perhaps *needed* was more accurate. The sight of him snatched the air from Niko's lungs.

Water lapped at Julian's chest. He strode forward, reached for Niko's cheek, and then his warm mouth was on Niko's, igniting the restless embers in Niko's veins.

He tasted divine, a little sweet from wine, but oh, so delicious. Niko threaded his fingers into his hair and claimed him, pulling Julian against his chest, deepening the kiss. He'd planned to ask about Vasili, about what they shared, and if Niko would get in the way of it. All of those questions vanished when Julian's ungloved hand slid down Niko's back towards his waist, where he spread his three fingers, and clamped Niko's hips against his.

Julian's cock brushed Niko's. Julian gasped. The sound

shot a dart of lust to the base of Niko's dick, fully hard-ened him, and made it pulse.

"I need this." Julian whispered, "I need you."

Niko drew him to the side of the bath and leaned against the edge, sinking both hands to Julian's ass and holding him tight, trapping their erections between them.

Vasili's name was still on Niko's lips. A question, a curse. He was afraid to ask, fearing the answer would screw this moment up.

Niko kissed him instead, hard and fast, forcing the prince's name to the back of his mind. Julian tilted his head and Niko nipped at his chin, his neck, his clavicle, making the soldier sigh and shudder.

By the fucking three, he wanted to undo this man, to take him apart kiss by kiss, and make him writhe. There would be time later for long, leisurely lovemaking. Maybe. Hopefully. If Vasili—

That wretched prince. He was in his head again.

"Kiss me," Niko ordered.

Julian immediately obeyed. His mouth was on Niko's and his hands roamed, sparking a fire in Niko's skin. Fuck, he'd never had sex in a bath before. The heat, flushing Julian all over, the wetness, smooth and soft. Julian's chest was slick under his hands, the water making his touch slide over firm muscle. He reached down between them and caught Julian's erect cock. Julian's breath stuttered while his cock pulsed, swelling in Niko's grip.

Julian wrapped his arms around Niko's neck and pressed his forehead to Niko. His eyes were brighter than ever, his skin flushed and hot from the bath—from the pleasure. His lips were plump and inviting. "Ah, gods, that feels... too good."

Niko smiled, took a breath, and dipped into the water-line, leaving Julian against the pool's edge. The rose-tinted water made his sight blur, but Niko didn't need to see clearly to find his prize. He gripped Julian's thigh, keeping himself braced beneath the surface, and with his free hand grasped the base of the man's cock. He closed his lips over the flushed crown and used his tongue to lick upward, skimming the slit, tasting the salty pre-cum. Julian bucked, briefly thrusting deeper into Niko's mouth. Under the water, Niko couldn't hear the soldier's groans, but he could feel their rumbles. He firmly circled his tongue around the head and consumed it, as deep as he could go, rubbing the tip across the top of his mouth and down his throat.

Julian grabbed Niko's jaw and yanked him upright. Niko gasped in air. Julian clasped Niko's wrists, spreading his arms wide, and kissed Niko on the mouth and neck. "You were sent to kill me with that mouth," Julian mumbled. "I know it."

"I'm not sure that's possible."

Julian kept Niko's arms spread against the pool's edge. He tilted his hips, grinding his dick against Niko's. "You feel so good. This is... new for me."

"You like it?" Niko asked, breathless.

"Fuck... I love it."

He was so fucking precious. It was a good thing he'd left the war at the Gap. Any longer in service and it would have ruined this bright, lovely soldier who looked at Niko with a sweet innocence.

"You've been with women?"

Julian's soft lashes fluttered. "It was average."

Thank the three for Julian having some sexual experience. Niko didn't want to be the man's first sexual encounter. It was pressure enough that it was Julian's first *male* encounter. "Have you fooled around with men?" he asked.

"When I was younger, there was a boy." His flush deepened and he turned his face away slightly. "We explored a little."

"Hey." Niko pulled his hand free from Julian's grip, then touched his chin, enough for their eyes to meet. "Don't be ashamed."

"I—" He bit his lip and Niko's cock pulsed. Niko liked when Julian worried his lip between his teeth, liked it a lot. Those lips, that mouth, he wanted to see him gasp and hear him moan Niko's name.

Julian smiled and wrapped his fingers around Niko's erection. "Like this?"

"Fuck, yes." Niko's voice hitched. Julian's fingers rode over the sensitive head a little clumsily, but then he found his confidence and stroked harder. Niko's eyes fluttered closed. He bit his own lip to keep from grunting like an animal. Julian's strokes strengthened—the man was clearly familiar with his own anatomy enough to know exactly how to get Niko off.

"Like this?" he asked again, his words brushing Niko's mouth while his hand pumped and fuck, if hearing him ask didn't spike Niko's lust even higher.

"Yes, fuck yes." Prettier words failed him. Julian looked at him like he wanted to flip him around and fuck him hard. Even if he didn't know how. Julian's raw, untested hunger made some small, sensitive part of Niko want to grab hold of him and never let him go. He wanted to pleasure the man first, to swallow his seed or feel it spurt across his hand, but Julian had an intensity about him that made it clear he wanted Niko to come for him now.

"Ah, fuck." Pleasure coiled tighter, the release so close it tingled Niko's lower spine.

Julian let go, pressed his dick against Niko's, and kissed him hard. Niko came, thrusting wildly against Julian's cock as Julian's tongue ravaged Niko's mouth.

"Touch me?" Julian pleaded, his voice as wrecked as Niko's.

Niko would do more than touch. He dropped beneath the water's surface again and took Julian into his mouth, licking and sucking the crown while pumping the shaft. He emerged once for a breath, and caught Julian's fraught, desperate expression.

"Is this... safe?" Julian asked. " I mean... can you breathe?"

"I'm fine." He teased his mouth over Julian's. "If I want up, I'll pinch your thigh." The man's breath hitched as Niko dove under for a second time. Julian's hips began to thrust. Niko let him fuck his mouth, ringing Julian's cock tight with his lips and tongue. His lungs ached for air. Julian gently held him down with a hand in Niko's hair, adding a jagged edge of uncertainty aligned with trust. Gods—this water play, walking the line—he needed to pleasure Julian so thoroughly that breathing was secondary.

Julian's rhythm stuttered. He pumped once, twice, three times. Hot seed soaked Niko's tongue. Niko swallowed, breaking the surface with a gasp. Julian was on him, teeth and tongue and mouth and hands, desperate and breathless with lust.

Dressing outside of the bath happened slowly, interrupted by Niko needing to stroke every part of Julian's skin.

The clothes came off as soon as they made it back to Julian's chambers, lace by lace, buckle by buckle, anticipation leaving Niko's mouth dry and his body alert all over again. Julian lay back, surrounded by quilts and cushions, naked and unashamed, a feast. And feast Niko did. He'd wanted Julian in this bed for weeks, months even, perhaps since he'd first seen the four-poster and Julian beside it. He had no intention of rushing it now.

Julian arched beneath him, grabbed the sheets, and twisted the fabric into fists as Niko tasted and teased the man's warm, trembling skin. It was divine, and more than Niko deserved.

As they lay in the dark, Julian snoring lightly, Vasili's words came back to him. Julian had called Niko a good man, and Vasili had known he was wrong. Niko wasn't a good man. He'd tried to be in the beginning, but somewhere amidst all the shit and blood and screams, that man had died. It was true they were soldiers, but they weren't alike. Niko had eight years of killing behind him. Such things did not leave a man right in the mind. Killing changed a man, and not for the better.

Niko was not good, but Julian was. And for the first time in a long time, Niko feared he'd drag another good man down into the dark with him.

CHAPTER 16

*N*iko watched Vasili sitting bolt upright in the smaller throne beside the king's more elaborate one. The king's was empty, naturally. Seeing it there, with all its curves and gold and velvet, Niko wondered if the king really was hidden somewhere or if he'd died long ago and the princes were waiting until there was just one left before announcing the heir. Amir was seated opposite in a throne identical to Vasili's. He slouched away from Vasili and wore an expression of absolute boredom.

Julian stood behind the prince, slightly offset from the other guards. He wore a helmet, but Niko recognized the man's solid stance, even from his position way back in the commoner's gallery.

A councilor was droning on about autumn supplies and Niko had no idea why he'd been ordered to attend the assembly when all he was going to do was sit at the back and daydream about how Julian had woken sleepy and soft in his arms. They'd kissed and Julian had turned into hot, writhing sweetness in Niko's hands, spilling his seed over his gorgeous belly, which Niko licked clean.

Niko adjusted his trousers. Hopefully, nobody nearby would notice his undue excitement at the dull events.

A murmur passed through the crowd and Niko stretched onto his toes to see Vasili standing. He came forward on the dais. Amir had straightened and leaned in, suddenly attentive. Whatever Vasili was about to say, it hadn't been planned.

"Thank you, councilors," Vasili began in a proud voice that carried regal weight to it few would be able to deny. "As always, I am humbled by your love and attention for our beloved country."

He didn't look like he'd spent the last day sweating out spice, but that was more to do with him always being as pale as milk. The grey patch of leather covering his damaged eye was new. A sudden attack of self-consciousness? He still wore black, but his jacket was studded with steel buttons, with decorative stitching far more becoming of a prince.

"It is with regret that I announce from the end of this assembly, after you have all left, that the palace and city gates will be closed and locked to those beyond our city limits."

The crowd's murmuring grew louder.

Niko frowned. He hadn't been informed of any changes, but then why would he be? Such things were far above his purview as Vasili's pet guard, or assassin, or captive—whatever he was supposed to be.

"Trade will of course continue, but all wagons will be checked. Even in times of peace, we must be vigilant. Now," he smiled like he knew everyone here loved him, and pressed a hand to his heart in a thoroughly convincing display of a caring prince, which was, of course, bullshit, "please allow me to address the many, many rumors circulating before that happens," Vasili went on, raising his voice. His tone carried far, and held a soothing confidence. Begrudgingly, Niko admitted the prince could hold a room. He'd expected him to sit on his throne and scowl at everyone present. This Vasili was different. And as he walked back and forth across the dais, one hand behind his back, the other gracefully gesturing, it was becoming apparent that this snake could change his skin.

"My father, your king, is recovering well. I hope you will all have a chance to greet him back to this very dais soon. He's certainly been asking after you. Your love for him, for Loreen, keeps him strong."

The people around Niko beamed, delighted by the news. Niko didn't believe a damned word of it.

"But let us not get complacent. Our enemies have not vanished. My father's negotiated peace with the elves is tentative and reliant on many factors, including their distance from us. Yet there have been some instances of foul play."

The crowd rustled and shifted, becoming restless, like anxious birds about to take flight.

"It is under control," he assured, "but until I can assure everyone is safe, the palace and the city gates must be closed for our protection. And yours."

Amir glared at his brother so aptly holding court.

The crowd stirred, voices rising. Vasili stood still, chin lifted, watching them all, waiting for them to settle. "I realize," he finally said, silencing them, "that you do not know me, not as you used to. And that is a deep regret of mine. But please, rest assured, I have always protected your homes and your families, and in every possible way, I continue to do so. The gates will be opened soon, and I hope it will be my father who opens them."

Niko found himself wanting to believe the words, wanting to believe in him. But these people hadn't seen their prince cut a man's throat for insulting him. They hadn't seen him slither about the palace halls, poised to bite anyone who dared get close. This Vasili was a lie, but the people loved it.

The prince bowed his head and left the dais, signaling the end of proceedings. Amir lingered, apparently uncertain as to whether he should follow, but then quickly departed, heels striking the dais.

Vasili continued to surprise him. Niko had thought he'd seen every side of the prince, but now he wondered if he'd merely scratched the surface of who the prince really was.

Julian had vanished as well.

Niko pushed through the stream of people to arrive at the dais, where he caught the sound of raised voices. One voice in particular. Amir's.

He climbed the steps and spotted the princes in the wings. Vasili was turning to leave when Amir grabbed his arm. The look Amir received was as cutting as any blade. The middle prince promptly let go but from Vasili's wide-eye the damage was done.

"You cannot make these decisions without consulting me!" Amir snapped, hastily throwing accusations.

"Of course I can."

"Eight years!" Amir exclaimed, pushing closer.

A ring of guards stood back, stoic and mostly invisible,

although Julian had broken from the ranks to approach, always so ready to protect his prince.

Niko started forward to draw the guards' attention. Several homed in on him.

"Eight fucking years, brother. I held this city together!"

"No," Vasili said. "Father did that."

"*Father is a fucking lunatic. Or had you forgotten?*" Amir roared, inches from Vasili's face. "He's already dead. Let him die. It's all he deserves."

"Careful, brother." There was more in Vasili's voice than a mere warning.

"Careful?"

A guard grabbed Niko's arm. He shook him off and picked up his pace, Amir in his sights.

"He's dead!" Amir pointed a finger at Vasili's face. "Like Carlo, and like you should be."

Vasili's backhand was a thing of beauty, which Niko could appreciate now that it wasn't directed at him. The thwack cracked so loudly that everyone surely felt it. Amir stumbled back and would have fallen if Niko hadn't caught him.

"Get off me, whore!" Amir fought Niko's grip. Vasili gave an almost imperceptible nod. Niko reluctantly freed him. Amir whirled and threw a disgusted grimace at Niko. "You're so fucking weak, brother, you have your bitch fight your battles for you."

Vasili tugged on his jacket cuff. "Only the battles you see."

"You're poison," Amir pointed. "They fucked you up and sent you back to rot in the heart of this palace. Everything has been wrong since you got back. Everything! You're not my brother and I'll not fucking stand for it."

The change from the reserved, cool, calm prince to a rabid, sharp, lethal killer snapped through Vasili in an instant. He grabbed his brother's face by the jaw and flung him into the wall of guards, who quickly recoiled, fearful of getting involved. Amir sprawled onto his back. Vasili bent over him, hand drawn back, ready to strike. Amir lay still, panting, looking up at his brother, his face white with terror.

"Touch me again and I'll take your fingers," Vasili warned him.

"You're more elf than man!" Amir spat.

Vasili lunged. Julian was on him in an instant, yanking him back, and Vasili twisted, throwing Julian off with a single devastating glare. He looked at everyone encircling him, all of them staring, watching, waiting. His throat moved. Niko saw it only because he knew to look for it, as well as the tiny twitch at the corner of his mouth. The real Vasili within, and he was hurting.

Vasili straightened, withdrawing into the stoic shell, sighed hard, and left, the guards quickly separating to avoid blocking his path.

Niko started after him, but Julian's gauntleted hand came down on his chest. "No, not you. I'll go."

"Or don't, and just leave him?"

"He won't hurt me, but he might..." He lowered his voice. "He might hurt himself."

Niko wanted to remind Julian that Vasili already *had* hurt him. He'd seen the whip marks.

Amir grabbed Niko's arm. "You have no idea—"

Niko's knuckles met the prince's face with a delightful crack of bone. Amir fell back, this time against a wall. He cupped his nose, then spat blood on the floor and grinned.

Blood quickly ran between his teeth. "Oh, you'll be sorry for that, Nikolas Yazdan. *Arrest him.*"

All eight guards moved in.

"No." Julian lifted a hand and tore his helmet off with the other. "Stop. Nikolas is protected by the king's regent, the eldest son and heir to the throne. Lay a hand on him and Prince Vasili will punish you."

"That doulos is a criminal, a thief, a whore, and a *deserter.*"

Niko moved in and would have pummeled the brat into the floor if Julian hadn't slammed both hands into Niko's chest, leaning into Niko's lunge. Killing Amir would solve a lot of problems, his and the prince's. And maybe he'd suffer for it, but he was beginning to think it would be worth it just to see Amir's twitching carcass beneath him.

"I watched a thousand men die for your perverted luxury of a life," Niko yelled. "You sick fuck!"

"Watched! And did nothing."

Rage, bright and sharp and brilliant, grasped Niko's thoughts, and funneled them into one purpose. "I'm going to rip your limbs off and make you choke on them, *prince!*"

"Stop!" Julian flung his arms around Niko's waist and wrenched him back. "Stop, Niko, please. Don't. You can't…" He pushed in close and grasped his face, forcing Niko to see him and only him. Julian's fearful eyes shone ."I can't protect you if you do this."

"I don't need protecting." What he needed was to kill Amir. Pin him to the floor, strangle him, and fuck him up. The rage was so potent, so real, it blinded Niko to anything else.

"Gods, Niko…" Julian's thumb stroked Niko's twitching

cheek. "You're the only thing I've cared about in years. I can't lose you."

"A failed soldier whose regiment abandoned him. I know you, the Yazdan boy. Bastard of Bucland Manor," Amir sneered, back on his feet. "Your mother was a lord's whore who couldn't keep her legs together and your father a second-rate blacksmith who drank his profits and sorrows away."

Shock staggered Niko. The things he'd said, ... they weren't true.

"Don't listen," Julian said. "Look at me. Don't listen. This is what he does. It's just words."

"Are you fucking him, Julian?" Amir wiped his hand across his nose and flicked the spilled blood across the floor. "Does Vasili know the bastard's had his cock up your precious ass, *Julian*?"

Julian slipped a hand around Niko's waist and encouraged him away.

"That's it, fucking run! Cowards, both of you! Wretched cowards. Our soldiers were all pathetic, that's why we surrendered, that's why we failed. It's your fault! Let the elves come and burn it all down. It's all because of you!"

Niko couldn't unhear the words. They lashed like a whip across his thoughts, again and again, pounding him with every step to Julian's chamber. Was his mah really Lord Bucland's whore? He'd have known, surely. Pah would have said. But when? There hadn't been time, and the war had taken them from him too soon with so much left unsaid.

"I have to check on Vasili," Julian said, entering his room after Niko. "Will you be all right?"

Niko waved him off, entered his chamber, and eyed all of the work spread across the table. Hours of study, pointless. What was he even doing here? These people, this place, they weren't his life. He'd lost battles, lost his men, lost his home, his family. There was nothing left but piles of paper trying to protect a prince from threats Niko barely understood and couldn't even see.

The screams were back inside his head. Visions of bodies swinging from trees. Friends. Lovers. Marcus. So much death. And it had turned him, made him different, made him broken inside. Made him *furious*.

He gripped the table and upended it. The contents flew, but it wasn't enough. He swept an arm across the sideboard, sweeping the ornaments to the floor. A wine bottle smashed. Still not enough. He grabbed his sword and brought it down with a roar across the cot. The blade lodged in the wood. Fury burned. Fury at the bed, the sword, the princes—both of them. Fury at Julian for stopping him from killing Amir. Fury at himself for being so fucking useless.

He left the chambers, sheathed the sword at his side, and strode toward Vasili's room. He'd be heard, if nothing else. Vasili would answer every damned question, even if Niko had to beat it out of him. About the elves, about the flame, about his scars and his brother's words. *You're more elf than man.*

He flung open Vasili's door and pulled up short, his own breath choking him.

Julian.

Shirtless.

Arms above his head, gripping the bed's canopy.

And Vasili. Holding a whip in both hands. Slim fingers stroking the leather tail.

Niko might have lunged for the prince, snatched the whip from him and beaten him with it, if not for one simple thing.

Julian's rapt expression, his lip pinched between his teeth.

Well, that and the erection tenting his trousers.

Julian groaned, so lost to whatever this was that he didn't know they were no longer alone.

But Vasili knew, and the prince raked his penetrating glare over Niko, the whip still in his hands, his chest heaving from exertion. At least *he* wasn't erect.

Niko turned on his heel and walked away, and kept on walking. Walked out of the palace, down the parade grounds and through the gates, hearing them slam closed for good behind him.

CHAPTER 17

*E*scaping the palace wasn't as simple as walking away. Thoughts of foul play, of the two princes at each other's throats, the absurd accusation of Vasili being part elf—they looped around and around his head. And none of it mattered to Niko. Not his life. Not his problem.

He stared at the ruined cottage, the chimney stack lying among piles of rubble and burned timber that had once been the attached forge. He'd walked all night around Loreen, until his feet had finally carried him home.

In another life, Pah's forge had been Niko's sanctuary. And now he was back, among the burned bricks, wondering how he'd survived to this day when so many others had not. The last few weeks seemed surreal, like maybe it had all been some spice-induced waking nightmare.

He picked up a brick and weighed it in his hands, then kicked aside a mound of debris and dirt, revealing the cottage foundations.

Sand, cement... He had both. All he had to do was put

one brick on top of the other. He didn't have to think of why he was here, or of the twisted tangle of snakes he'd left behind in the palace, or the war and how it had taken everything from him. Just one brick on another. Simple.

The days grew shorter as the weeks went by. The cottage slowly began to look like a structure again, but it would need a roof before winter. Niko was contemplating how best to make and fix the roof trusses in place when the heavy clop of hooves sounded down the old village road.

He knew by the gait of the lead horse who its rider might be. His damned heart raced, instincts readying to fight or run. A nearby bucket of water, pulled from the village well, caught his eye. Sweat-soaked and filthy, he scratched at his beard, listening to the horses trot closer. He considered dunking his head and then wondered why the fuck he cared if Vasili saw him caked in dirt.

He opened the door he'd made himself that very morning and leaned against the frame, drying his hands on a rag. The horses weren't draped in the griffin insignia and they didn't carry any banners, but the beasts were so perfectly groomed and powdered in chalk they could only have come from the palace.

The lead rider was cloaked in grey, his face hidden just like before.

Niko arched an eyebrow. He should probably kneel. Wasn't that what peasants did?

The rider dismounted with practiced ease and approached, his stride so confident he would have walked through Niko if he hadn't ducked back inside the cottage inside and let him pass. "Princes don't know how to knock?"

172

The figure turned in the middle of the room, his cloak swirling. *Room* was a stretch. There were only three walls and no roof. But the fireplace was lit, which was something.

Vasili reached up with bejeweled fingers and lowered his hood. The eyepatch was still in place—a permanent feature, then. "You will return to the palace immediately."

Niko had almost forgotten how that voice always held an edge. "More threats on your life? Or are you just bored with picking the wings off flies?"

The tick. Niko smiled to see it. It meant the prince wasn't infallible. He stepped up to him, no doubt making his guards outside nervous. Since a wall was missing, Vasili's guards could see inside, and hear much of what was said. "No."

Vasili lifted his chin. Icy Caville defiance burned in his blue eye.

Any second now, Vasili would order his guards to arrest him, and the whole thing would start all over again. He'd been expecting it. Every day he'd waited for the sound of hooves to come up the road and for the guards to drag him back until the task was done, and here Vasili was. Predictable in one thing at least.

Niko drifted toward the fireplace and used a stick to poke the logs, stirring up the hungry flames.

"He doesn't know you saw," Vasili said.

Niko breathed in, filling his lungs, and cleared his throat. Of all the sights that haunted him, seeing Vasili whip Julian was the one he couldn't shake or explain away. He stood, leaned against the old mantlepiece, and regarded the prince. "I don't know what that was, but it had nothing to do with me."

"True."

That one little word twisted like a knife in Niko's heart. He'd sworn off love, vowed never to let it touch him again, but Julian had been easy to fall in love with, so easy that Niko hadn't known it was happening. And now here was the prince, telling him whatever Niko had with the man meant nothing. Maybe the prince was right. That palace twisted everything around, made the bad good, made Niko want things.

"I'm not going back," he said firmly. "Order me and we'll have a problem."

Vasili wet his lips with the tip of his tongue. He looked around at the rubble-strewn floor, the hand-crafted bowls, the half-built walls. "Is this the life you want?"

"Only royals are free to choose how they live."

"You can't be so naïve as to believe I chose my life?" Vasili asked, his tone flat, a sign he was holding back.

Niko held the prince's glare. Vasili had not chosen the world he was in, and he hadn't chosen to be taken by elves and tortured. He hadn't chosen to be born royal, to have that responsibility on his shoulders from the moment he came screaming out of his mother's body. But every day he got to choose how to live it, and chose to fuck it up instead of using his position for good.

That life, that palace, would poison Niko's soul. It already had. Whereas here in the cottage with no roof, he had something. It might not have been much, especially compared to the prince's world, but it was enough. Some walls, a fireplace, and a door. Meager by any standards, but it was his.

"He knows only that you left," Vasili continued.

"I left because if I didn't, I'd have killed your brother

and probably you, eventually." He shoved off the mantle and met the prince eye to eye. "You were right. I'm not a good man. I will kill Amir, and get myself executed and maybe Julian too, because he'd get tangled up in it all. I can't... I don't want that. I just want to rebuild this forge."

That damn tick again. Was it a smile trying to break through the ice? "And make horseshoes for the rest of your life?"

"They'll be the best fucking horseshoes. Probably the only ones that damned devil horse of yours won't throw."

"You will return—"

"No."

"I'll pay you."

He pointed a finger at the prince's perfectly blank face. "Fuck. You."

"Sir?" one of the guards piped up, clearly upset Niko was getting in His Royal Highness's face.

Vasili raised a hand to his men, silencing them. "I've whipped people for less, Nikolas."

Mention of the whip made Niko's back stiffen, but he was not backing down, not surrendering. "Then whip me. You clearly enjoy it."

The prince swallowed. His brilliant blue eye narrowed. "I do."

And now Niko's heart began to pound. Vasili could end this in an instant. He'd haul Niko away, whip him, maybe hand him over to Amir to do with as he pleased. Or maybe he wouldn't because they'd passed the insults stage and Niko hadn't felt the sting of the prince's backhand yet. Why hadn't he forced him to his knees, made him kiss the ring, thrown orders, and had him roughed up by the guards? What even was this?

"You might be the most honest man I know," Vasili said, level tone lifting.

Niko laughed. "That's hardly a compliment coming from a Caville."

"You're afraid."

He huffed and gestured at the door. "You may leave, Your Highness. Our discussion is over."

"Afraid of me."

"Yes, I'm afraid of you, and that prison you call a palace. How's that for honesty? You fucking terrify me. I'd rather face an elf than look you in the eye sometimes because there's something in you, Vasili. Something dark. Something you keep bottled up and hidden, but it's waiting, and I do not want to be nearby when you lose control of it."

The prince tilted his head. "Why?"

Niko stared back at the prince, standing so coolly in his royal blues and greys. But there really was something inside all those layers of lies, and it was horrible. Niko knew it because he saw the same in his own reflection. "Because you and I both know what has to be done when that happens." Vasili was a killer, and one day he'd need to be stopped by someone. Nobody in the palace had the balls.

Vasili conceded with a single, soft nod. "And that is why I'm here, standing inside a house with no roof, Nikolas, asking you to return."

Asking. Not ordering. That must have been hard for him to admit. All of this was probably hard for him. He shouldn't even be outside the city walls. Princes did not visit unemployed, dirt-covered blacksmiths. He wouldn't be here unless he was desperate, which meant things inside the palace walls were dire, and Julian was in there. He'd always be in there, because he'd never leave Vasili's side. Julian was the only good thing inside those walls; certainly the only good thing in Niko's life. Julian had once told Niko to leave, opened the door to his cell to let him go. But who was going to free Julian?

"Gods dammit..."

Vasili's lips twitched.

No matter what he saw between Vasili and Julian, Niko couldn't leave him there, alone. "If I come back, things change. I'm not your doulos, *prince*. I'm your advisor."

"Impossible."

"And you need to start answering questions without the vague shit." Vasili's eye twitched and Niko hastily added, "Your Highness."

"No."

"And don't give me some line about doulos being the only people allowed in your chambers. You don't care what anyone else thinks of you. So advisor it is."

"Wrong."

"Just spin it," Niko waved a hand, "like you do so well."

"An escort?" the prince asked.

"A paid whore?" Niko laughed. "Is there any profession in your palace that doesn't involve bending over backward and getting fucked up the ass by a royal?"

"Sir," the uppity guard piped up, "his insolence is an insult to yo—"

Vasili jerked his hand up again but kept his stare firmly pinned to Niko's. "I do not recall asking your opinion, sergeant."

"Your Highness, I—"

"Silence."

Niko raised both eyebrows, waited to see if the guard had anything else to add, and said to Vasili, "An advisor, or not at all."

The prince's cheek flickered. "Agreed."

Shit, he hadn't expected him to actually agree. If he left the cottage standing and not in cuffs, it would have been a victory. Niko stepped back, needing a moment to shuffle his thoughts under control. He'd just agreed to return to the viper's nest, and he was looking at the most slippery predator of them all.

"Collect your things."

Niko grabbed the sword by the door as he passed through it, pausing a moment to admire his own handwork. He'd return and finish the roof—if he survived.

The chestnut horse waited for him at the back of the line. The animal bowed its head and snuffled at Niko's hair. He probably did reek of sweat and dirt, to be fair. He swung himself into the saddle, turned the horse and dug his heels in. The chestnut sprang forward, its rolling strides eating up the winding village road. Vasili's charger thundered past moments later. Niko couldn't see the prince's face, but knew the bastard was smiling.

CHAPTER 18

*N*iko saw Julian's pace stutter as he entered the prince's chamber. "*Niko?*" He made a valiant effort to hide all of the feelings from his face, and failed. His expression glowed, eyes wide. He was adorable. If Vasili hadn't been looming like an executioner's axe, Niko would have taken him into his arms and kissed him. "You're back."

"I sent him away on an errand." So smooth, the prince's lies.

"Julian," Niko said in acknowledgment, tasting his heart in his throat. He'd had time to shave and clean up, donning a smart pair of trousers and jacket more befitting an *advisor*.

"Nikolas was initially here under the guise of my doulos, as you know." Vasili explained, each word clipped for efficiency. "The ruse is over. He is to be treated with respect and decency befitting his station as my personal advisor."

Julian blinked. "Advisor?"

"Is there a problem?"

Whenever Vasili asked that question, it usually meant someone was about to have their throat cut.

"No, of c-course not." Julian stammered. "Just unexpected."

"Yes," Vasili said, with a half-hearted wave, "Nikolas is very good at deception. Make sure his status is well known among the staff and my family, especially Amir. He won't take kindly to the news, so perhaps send a note so he can burn it instead of you."

"Of course, yes," Julian said again, stumbling over the words. His gaze bounced between the prince and Niko.

"Now leave. Both of you. I must take my seat at the council. Julian, I will require your presence this afternoon. Until then, you are dismissed."

Julian walked beside Niko as they left the prince's chambers, armor clanking. Tension made his strides long and sharp, and Niko wasn't sure if it was anger or antici-pation winding him up. He had every right to be angry. Niko had abandoned him for three weeks without a word.

Whatever he had with Vasili was none of his concern. Julian had never said Niko meant anything more than a convenient fuck. His relationship with Vasili was clearly complicated and enduring. Looking back, the signs were there. Julian's wounds, his insistence they didn't matter, his devotion to the prince. He loved Vasili. Niko wasn't sure where he fit into all of that.

Julian passed through his chamber door, held it open for Niko, and lunged into a kiss the moment they were both inside. Desperation made his mouth clumsy. Julian's gloved hands were on Niko's face, then his ass. Niko's back hit the wall with a thud and Julian pulled back.

"Gods... I missed you."

"I gathered." Niko grinned. He touched Julian's face, committing to memory the brush of golden stubble and the softness of his lips. He drew him close, brushed his open mouth with his own, and teased his tongue in, gently this time. There was no need to rush.

Julian sighed, withdrew a little, and brushed his cheek against Niko's. "Undress me?"

Pale blue eyes flicked over Niko's face. Concern knotted Julian's brows, like he truly believed Niko might not want to.

Niko eased his fingers around Julian's waist and worked the buckles free. Julian's quick breaths warmed Niko's neck, then his jaw, and skimmed his lips on a kiss waiting to happen. The breastplate came loose and Niko set to work on the pauldrons, every piece of Julian's armor a puzzle coming undone, revealing the prize inside. The placard came away, and Niko made sure to stroke Julian's lower abs with his knuckles, making Julian shudder. The tasset went next, and more, until Niko had stripped his soldier of his armor. His erect cock trapped inside his undergarments revealed his obvious desire. Niko absently brushed it a few times, making Julian's breath hitch.

By the time Niko straightened in front of him, Julian breathed hard, his gaze fixed on Niko's face. "You left."

Niko winced. He couldn't talk about that just yet. "I'm back."

Julian pulled off his gloves and dropped them. His fingers mapped Niko's face, his jaw, his lips. "He refused to tell me where."

Because Vasili didn't know, or because he was protecting Julian? Niko grabbed Julian's hands and kissed each of his fingers. "Doesn't matter," he mumbled.

"It matters to me. I thought—"

Niko pressed his finger to Julian's lips. "Hush." He dragged it over the man's chin, past his neck and his chest, then down further, twisting his hand around to sink his grip over Julian's restrained erection. He sucked one of Julian's fingers into his mouth and cupped Julian's balls through the fabric, tugging gently.

"Oh gods."

Niko groaned low in his throat and Julian arched, angling his cock deeper into Niko's grip. Niko ran his teeth down Julian's finger, then grabbed the man by the back of the head and savaged his mouth, feeling Julian loosen and submit. Niko backed him into a wall and braced his hand on either side of him, trapping him. Julian's plump lips lifted, his eyes widening. He was a golden fruit ripe for the picking. Niko yanked the man's undergarments down, freeing his cock, and captured its warm, thick length in his fist.

Julian twisted his fingers in Niko's shirt. He tried to drop his hand to touch where Niko's cock strained inside his trousers, but Niko knocked the advancing touch aside. "This is for you." He pinned Julian's wrist to the wall and the man relented, his body a devastating display of soft and hard all at once.

Julian's back arched, his mouth open, his eyes closed. Niko gritted his teeth to keep from rubbing himself against Julian's hip. His neglected cock throbbed and leaked and ached to be seated deep inside something hot and tight. But Niko had left him, he'd hurt him, just like Julian feared, and so this moment belonged to Julian.

"Ugh... oh gods... can't..."

"Yes," Niko hissed against his cheek, getting him off hard and fast. Julian's cock twitched and pulsed, its tip slick. Julian panted harder, his small, beautiful moans becoming desperate. "*Come for me.*"

Julian flung his head back, arching, then held still as he crested. Spurts of wet seed dashed against Niko's wrist. Julian slumped into Niko's arms, his head falling onto his shoulder. "Definitely sent to kill me," he whispered.

Niko laughed and scooped his man up, wrapping him tightly in his arms. Julian clutched at Niko's shoulder.

"I'm not done with you," Niko growled. He pulled him by the hand to the bed, then let go to tear off his own shirt.

Julian's lazy gaze roamed, devouring, watching Niko undress and quickly reveal himself. They both stood naked, facing each other. Julian reached out and brushed the new, thin scar on Niko's side from the elf's blade. His touch skipped higher, danced over Niko's abs, and then higher, circling a nipple.

Niko caught his wrist and pulled him in, but Julian laughed and broke free, then crawled onto the bed and lay sprawled like a feast, head propped on his hand, hard cock nestled among golden hair. Niko absently took his own cock in hand and gave himself a few eager strokes. Julian watched, lips parted, fingers moving over his hip.

"Will you fuck me, Nikolas?" Julian purred.

Niko needed no more encouragement to straddle the man's thighs and plant his hands either side of his shoulders, pinning Julian beneath him.

Julian looked up at him, his face warm, his smile gentle. Niko was something dark towering over him, something hungry and insatiable. Gods, he wanted to fuck him, to bury himself so deep that Julian would think of him even when Vasili's whip lashes landed.

"What is it?" Fine lines appeared at Julian's pinched brow.

"Nothing." Niko's smile ticked. Damn. "It's nothing." He sucked on Julian's lip, trying not to think about Vasili, or the whip, or how Julian had been stretched in front of the prince like a canvas waiting for its artist's brushstrokes.

Julian's hand trailed down his chest and around his waist to spread Niko's ass. His fingers hooked in. Delicious pain thumped desire though Niko's body, making his cock leak pearly pre-cum.

"I need...," Niko mumbled into his mouth, "to fuck you." His cock ached, hot and hard and demanding.

Julian's throat moved as he swallowed. "Do it."

"You want that? You're sure?" Niko's mouth had dried, making his voice rough.

"I wouldn't ask otherwise," the man replied coyly. "Side drawer."

Niko reached out, tugged open the drawer, and spotted the pot of cream.

"I asked some... friends," Julian said, heat flushing his cheeks, "what I might need if we did this."

Niko groaned and buried his face in Julian's neck. So fucking accommodating. So thoughtful. But in Niko's current maddened state, he might hurt Julian. The first time was special, often strange. Niko was not in the right mind to go slow. He wanted a hard fuck, wanted to erase Vasili and his whip from Julian's head.

"I want you in me," Julian growled, then hooked his leg around Niko's and added a soft, moaning, "*Please.*"

"Julian... It's..." If he begged again, Niko would surrender. "I don't want to hurt you."

Julian's three fingers stroked down the shaft of Niko's cock, sending pleasurable sparks deep into Niko, and he bit his lip.

The lip biting. Like he'd done under Vasili's whip.

Fucking Vasili.

Didn't matter.

"You won't hurt me." Julian swept pre-cum down Niko's shaft. "You want this inside me, don't you?"

Niko thrust a little, seeking more. "Harder." Julian's fingers tightened. "*Fuck.*"

Julian's touch vanished.

Niko peered down at the smiling, wicked tease of an ex-soldier. "Fuck me, Nikolas." Filthy words from a beautiful mouth.

Niko tore open the pot of cream and stroked himself off a few times, lashes fluttering at the tight contact of his familiar hand. Better to put an end to that before he tipped himself over the edge. Bracing himself over Julian, he eased one well-oiled finger beneath the man's balls and stroked around the circle of tight muscles.

Julian gasped. He swallowed audibly. His hard, leaking cock jumped, interested in the way this was going.

"Relax." Niko eased his finger in, going slow, keeping control.

Julian gripped the sheets. His cock was flushed, head pink and sensitive. Niko fought the urge to go down on him again. He needed this to end with him seated deep in

Julian's ass, or Vasili and his whip would forever be in Niko's head.

Two fingers.

Julian let out a sigh. "Tight."

"Relax," Niko said again. "Trust me."

Julian's lashes fluttered. "I do."

Niko removed his fingers and stroked Julian's cock, then his own. "Touch yourself." Julian immediately clasped his cock in his hand. Niko positioned himself between Julian's knees, grasped his own cock and pushed the head against Julian's tight ring of muscles. He eased in bone-achingly slow, eyes closed, teeth gritted, barely holding back the urge to thrust. The slick tightness enveloped him whole.

"Ah... Gods...," Julian moaned.

"All right?" Beads of sweat rolled down Niko's back and chest.

"Good... good." He squirmed.

"Bear down. Breathe. Trust me."

Julian nodded and pumped his cock, throwing his head back, and Niko seated himself deep, freeing ragged breaths from them both.

"Yes...," Julian hissed. "Fuck yes. There. So good."

The noises; the talking; the smiles; the dilated pupils in deep blue eyes. Fuck, Julian was *everything*. Niko grabbed Julian's hips and tilted his ass, shifting the angle slightly. Taking the hint, Julian lifted his legs to rest them over Niko's shoulders. And Niko thrust, watching Julian's mouth drop open, his eyes blow wide. "Fuck! Yes! There..." He pumped his cock faster, writhing and groaning.

Need overrode control. Niko thrust again, deeper,

harder. Julian gasped and locked his gaze with Niko's. So fucking beautiful. Face flushed. Mouth open and inviting.

And then there was nothing but the tight feel of Julian's ass gripping Niko's cock buried deep, thrusting and grunting and losing his gods-damned mind to sweet ecstasy. He heard himself groaning, chasing down the pinch of pleasure that sent darts of lightning down his back and into his balls. Gods, he was close.

Julian cried out. His hand-pumping juddered. Cum wet his chest. It was too much. Niko dug his fingers into the man's hips and growled into the next three powerful thrusts. Sharp pleasure snapped up his back. He came so damn hard he forgot to breathe. He flew, cock releasing its seed, and then he was back in the room, a panting, shuddering mess of a man.

Julian's smile broke open whatever remaining doubts he had, making his heart swell.

Fuck Vasili.

Niko kissed him long and slow and careful, not wanting to break him. "I don't deserve you."

Julian brushed his chin against Niko's nose and looped his arms around Niko's neck, locking him close. "No, you don't. But fuck me like that some more and we'll call it even."

THERE WAS no time to sprawl in bed all day. After washing up and dressing, Julian left to perform his role for Vasili.

Niko watched him go, desperate to ask all the things he couldn't.

That was Vasili and Julian's relationship. Not Niko's.

Instead of dwelling on what he couldn't control, Niko sought out the palace library and found Vasili's library wing, and with the help of a grizzled old librarian, he dug out all the books on the Cavilles and spread them over a table. His head was buried so deeply in the massive tomes that he missed Amir's approach until the man was almost beside him. Thoughts of spice and sex and violence tried to worm their way into Niko's head.

"Advisor Yazdan?" the middle prince inquired.

"I'm working." Niko stared at the words on the open page, not reading a single one. He half expected a dagger in his back.

"Maybe I was wrong and you *are* fucking him. How else does a blacksmith's boy become palace advisor to the prince regent?"

He didn't have to respond, didn't have to rise to the bait. He was a grown man. Amir was a bratty prince, younger than Niko. A strutting peacock. Nothing more.

"Look at me, doulos."

Niko looked up. Amir wore a bright blue jacket stitched with silver and trousers to match. His white-blond hair had been cut since Niko had last seen him. Impossibly, the short hair made him look sharper.

Amir jerked his chin at the book. "Studying how best to screw your way into the Caville bloodline?"

"What do you want, Amir?"

"You. On your knees. Sucking my cock."

"Is that all?"

Amir blinked, revealing a moment's hesitation, before a smile slashed across his face.

"I thought it might be something important."

"What?" Amir asked, losing his footing and his words.

Niko resisted a smile, but a little of it slipped through. "There are some books around here on how to sexually satisfy your partner. If you're struggling."

Amir spat a laugh. "I'm surprised you can read, mongrel that you are."

"Oh, I meant to say I met your aunt. Delightful woman. She'll never let a prick like you fuck her."

The change was instant. The prince lunged. Niko kicked his chair aside, letting Amir sprawl past, then grabbed him by the back of the head and slammed him face-first into the table. It would have hurt him more if there hadn't been books in the way.

Amir grunted, startled more than hurt, but Niko predicted the rage would kick in immediately. Niko held him down by the neck, squashing Amir's face into an open book. "We know you want him dead. One mistake, and Vasili will take your head, *prince*."

"Get off me! Guards!"

Niko glanced up, but the guards nearby didn't approach any further. Interesting. It wasn't him they were frightened of, so it had to be the mention of Vasili. They must have known Niko's new standing, as well as all the palace gossip. Amir had no friends here.

"Little bitches like you got eaten by elves on the front line," Niko hissed against the prince's smooth cheek. "Had their faces torn off and hung from trees. Their balls too. Although I doubt they'd find yours." He yanked the prince off the table and shoved him back the way he'd come.

Amir stumbled over a chair, then spun and righted himself. Oh, the look on his face. It was a shame Vasili couldn't see it. Pure, unfiltered hate.

"You'll pay for this!" Amir snapped, tugging at his

clothes, trying to straighten himself up. He straightened his hair too, sweeping the short locks back into place.

Niko leaned against the table and smiled. "You looked me up? You know where the *"Yazdan boy"* is from. Then you must know what they called me on the front line?"

Amir's thin brows pinched. He sniffed and jerked away.

"Good riddance," Niko murmured. He'd made a powerful enemy in Amir. But as Vasili had said, it was better to have the enemy in front of you than at your back.

He scooped up some books and carried them back to Julian's chambers to copy notes. Julian had righted Niko's desk and documents, stacking everything in neat piles. So domesticated. Niko spread the books on the table, absently wondering if Julian might one day visit the forge. Help him rebuild it, even...

But he was clearly getting ahead of himself.

He skimmed the pages of the Caville family tomes and began to note down snippets of information. The Cavilles' name meant "guardians of the dark flame." The books revealed how many generations ago, in a different time, the Caville family protected the flame, keeping it safe from nefarious creatures, most notably the elves. Information about that time was more myth than fact, muddled up with fantastical talk of flying horses and snakes the size of houses, all obviously ridiculous. But elves weren't ridiculous. They'd long been present in the eastlands bordering the kingdom of Loreen, even when Loreen City had been no more than a few houses huddled at the base of an ancient, weather-beaten mountain. They'd occasionally attack, but their presence faded from history several hundred years ago. Until recently it had been believed they were simply gone, like everything else unnatural.

Not the case.

Vasili's grandfather, Neros, was the first Caville king to fend off a substantial elven force, losing several hundred soldiers to them. He bolstered the crown's military and saw several more attacks until his untimely death from mental illness. Talos, Vasili's father, was crowned king after. Curiously, it was from then on that the records grew thin.

Books regarding the newer generations were brief sketches of Talos's life and the three male heirs he produced. No mention of the daughter, if she'd existed. There were instead many torn and missing pages, as though someone really didn't want Talos's story told.

Maria had mentioned the flame, whatever it was, indicating it was hereditary. Some kind of mental ailment, perhaps? Inherited madness? Such things were common, made worse by the Caville tendency to marry their cousins, keeping their royal blood undiluted. They did not practice the more traditional method of royals marrying royals from different kingdoms. Any such kingdoms were across the seas and had little to do with Loreen. Niko didn't blame them. They were all probably grateful for the miles of ocean keeping the Cavilles at a considerable distance.

Besides, Vasili didn't seem the sort to marry. Niko pitied anyone trapped in *that* unfortunate arrangement. As for Amir, he would probably marry his aunt, given the chance. Poor woman.

He could try speaking with her again. Take the books to her, try another angle. As Vasili's advisor, he'd be allowed to visit without tongues spewing rumors that might damage her reputation.

Niko tapped his pencil over a faded paragraph about the dark flame. He hadn't found anything definitive about it. But the Cavilles and their griffin insignia were always cited as its guardians. Protectors. He stared at a sketch depicting a dark fire consuming howling souls with the Caville griffin standing over it, wings flared. Niko couldn't tell whether it was controlling the flames, or being consumed by them.

Interesting, but not particularly helpful.

Julian knocked on the connecting door and ducked inside, carrying a set of smartly pressed clothes over one arm.

"Going somewhere?" Niko asked.

"Hm." Julian laid the jacket and trousers on the dresser and drifted closer. Niko watched him approach and when Julian leaned down for a kiss, he happily obliged, heart quickening.

"You are," Julian said, clasping Niko's face in his gloved hands.

"Not in those clothes," he said, dismissing Julian with a laugh.

"Vasili's orders."

"Vasili can go fuck himself."

Julian kissed him again, fast and hard, then withdrew.

There was time, Niko thought. Julian could stay. Niko considered the desk with Julian bent over it. "When?"

"Dinner."

"*Family* dinner?"

"I think so."

Niko rubbed at his face and Julian frowned.

"What did you do?"

"Earlier today I shoved Amir's face into a book and told him his dick was too small for elves to find."

Julian's beautiful eyes widened. A beat passed. Then he burst into laughter so bright and free it summoned the same from Niko. It almost shocked Niko. He'd been expecting Julian to lay into him about speaking his mind around the Cavilles, not free laughter.

Julian's laughter faded and he looked at Niko like he was a lost cause, but one worth trying to save. "At least you didn't kill him."

"The day's not over yet." He couldn't sit among the Cavilles at dinner. "It's a terrible idea."

"Vasili doesn't think so."

"Vasili has a sadistic streak a mile wide."

And there it was, right in the room with them. Vasili, caressing his whip, Julian stretched against the bed, obviously aroused. What had happened before Niko had witnessed that? Had Julian been begging him? Was Vasili taunting him? He couldn't imagine Vasili saying much of anything. He always kept his words to a minimum, making sure those he did speak cut as precisely as a surgeon's knife. The prince hadn't been aroused, not like Julian, but Lady Maria had mentioned something about arousal—or was it desire? Something about there being different kinds. He couldn't remember. Maybe Vasili didn't get off on violence.

"What happened? Where did you go?" Julian leaned against the table beside Niko, close enough for Niko to reach out and brush his thigh. But thoughts of Vasili stopped him.

"Nowhere. It's nothing." He threw his pencil down and

scowled at the clothes on the dresser. "First he puts me in a doulos costume and now a peacock's?"

"Actually, it's a lord's dinner attire," Julian corrected him, half smiling. "Worth as much as I'm paid in a year."

"He's painting a target on my back. Amir will throw a fit if he sees me in it. In fact, that's probably exactly what he wants to happen, so he can watch me snap at his brother and get myself strung up in the courtyard again."

"Wear it." Heat flushed Julian's cheeks. "So I can watch you take it off."

Niko stood, pushed between Julian's thighs, and cupped his face. "All right. For you. But you can take it off me later, with your teeth..."

Laughter still danced in his eyes. "You always know the right thing to say."

Niko's racing heart swelled. "Will you be there?"

"Family dinners are always private. They don't allow guards."

Niko rolled his eyes. "You're not helping. Someone is going to die. It'll probably be me."

"Just don't kill Amir with a steak knife."

"A butter knife?"

Julian laughed. "Is that possible? No, don't answer. You're so wicked—"

Niko kissed him and nuzzled his neck, feeling the moment Julian surrendered all of himself into his arms. It was such a fucking turn-on how he just knew when to push back and when to give. "Wicked is the way you like me," he whispered.

"The way I love you." A word. A moment. A glance. His fingers on Niko's lips, the touch of a blush on his face. Niko's own heart skipped and his breath caught. Love.

Such a small word for something so heavy. Julian thwacked him on the ass, startling the moment from the room, and shoved him away. "Now go! Get dressed, *Lord Yazdan*. And fuck me hard when you return. I'll be waiting."

Lord Yazdan. Gods, the words on Julian's lips. Niko adjusted his pants to accommodate his arousal. "Or I can fuck you hard now *and* when I return?" Niko peered through his lashes, saw Julian's eyes light up, and swooped in, claiming him with a devastating kiss.

CHAPTER 19

The suit chafed and choked him, but it wasn't all bad. The trousers, tight around the waist and ass, were comfortable enough. Of course, there wasn't anywhere to attach a sword, but everyone here had fangs, anyway. At least he looked the part among the similarly dressed Cavilles and their extended family. Inbreeding certainly didn't fuck with their beauty, just their minds.

"What a wonderful wallflower you make, Nikolas." Lady Maria offered her hand and Niko dutifully brushed a kiss across the Caville ring. "I did not expect to see you here."

"Neither did I," he said softly. At least he had one potential ally here.

Vasili hadn't arrived. Neither had Amir. But there were plenty of minor Cavilles to fill the small, intimate space. They weren't yet all fucking or killing each other. Maybe that came later. Niko hoped to be gone by then, tangled in Julian's sheets with the man nestled close.

"You look well. The attire suits you. Clearly, you were

meant for better things than a blacksmith's forge, hm?" She scanned the crowd too, carefully watching whom to avoid and whom to dance with.

"Horses must have shoes, my lady."

"Indeed they must. And they must be broken in too, no doubt." She smiled thinly at him. "Be careful, dear. Remember the cuckoo?"

He cleared his throat. "How can I forget?"

"The raptors are circling." She drifted off and found a relative to laugh with.

As if he weren't nervous enough, she just had to go and twist the screws. Maybe she was more Caville than he'd realized.

Finally, an attendant announced Vasili and Amir. They strode in one after the other. No apology for their tardiness. Vasili had a look on his face that could cut a man's soul at ten paces. Amir's steps wavered a little, hinting at either spice or alcohol. The normal, then. The brothers took up their seats with Vasili at the head of the table, and that was apparently the signal for everyone to sit.

Niko had a brief moment of startled hesitation, looking for a seat, fearing there wasn't one, and he'd be dismissed like a fool. But Vasili caught his eye, frowned, and flicked his gaze to the chair on his right. Wonderful. The head of the table. His seat there would surely result in some etiquette crime.

There was obviously a reason he was torturing Niko, but he'd never reveal it. Niko unbuttoned his jacket and gracefully sat, feeling almost thirty pairs of eyes shift to him.

"This is thoroughly delightful, Your Highness," Niko

mumbled, forcing a smile when his gaze mistakenly snagged some older gentleman's scowling glare.

"Yes, I thought you'd appreciate it."

Sarcasm from the prince. Maybe? Niko couldn't tell.

Amir struck his glass with the edge of a silver knife, making it chime. Vasili's long-suffering sigh was rather telling from a prince who rarely let anything slip through his mask.

"Welcome, my dear family. And the doulos."

"Advisor," Niko corrected, smiling as politely as he knew how, hoping it didn't come off as a sneer.

"That's what we're calling it now?" Amir beamed.

His audience tittered. Niko grinned and contemplated stabbing Amir in the thigh with a fork. Amir went on to thank the people with a lot of nothing words. They all applauded and fell into chatting among themselves. All but Vasili, who sat as still as a block of ice. Amir quickly began his third glass of wine, laughing merrily with the woman to his left when he wasn't glancing at Niko.

Dinner was delivered by a train of staff. A bowl of soup and a chunk of bread would have been adequate enough, but adequate for the Cavilles meant half the city's geese and a seasonal supply of vegetables. And they hardly ate, probably fearing poison from the other guests.

"Why did you invite me?" Niko asked under his breath.

"I didn't invite you anywhere," Vasili replied. "I ordered you here. To observe."

All Niko had observed so far was a lesson in gluttony and high society bullshit.

"So..." The young woman to Niko's left smiled. "You're the Nikolas that has the palace all a-titter?" She wore her Caville-blond hair looped into elaborate curls and pinned atop her head. Glittering lip paint reminded Niko of the whores in the Stag and Horn advertising fuckable mouths. He doubted the same applied here. Or maybe it did, just with more frills and fancy words.

"That depends on what the titter details, my lady." Niko dipped his chin.

"Oh, I don't think the details of those rumors are polite talk over dinner. Do you?" She smiled slyly and glanced at Vasili, who'd turned away to watch his brother.

"You mean, am I the Nikolas who protects the prince from half the vipers in this room? Then yes."

She blinked and sucked in a breath.

A boot hit Niko's shin hard enough to make him wince. He glanced at Vasili, but the prince was still listening to Amir.

"You're not suggesting Vasili's life—"

"I'm not suggesting anything, my lady." Niko said, hopefully smoothing the way. "I'm just here to observe."

"Oh." She blinked. "I see. And what have you observed so far, Nikolas?"

Gods, he was no good at this courtly talk. Put a sword in his hand and he'd dance. But this? "How beautiful you are, naturally."

She blushed. "Well, aren't you smooth? Isn't he smooth, Vasili?"

Niko turned to the prince who, at the sound of his own name, had been startled out of watching his brother. Vasili blinked. "What?"

"Aren't I smooth, Your Highness?" Niko asked.

"Smooth?" He frowned. "No. You, Nikolas, aren't remotely smooth."

The wince on his face revealed he hated this situation

as much as Niko. Gods, he'd dragged him here to suffer alongside him so he didn't have to suffer alone. Well, that was interesting.

The young Lady Caville laid her hand over Niko's on the table and stroked down his fingers. "Vasili, would you consider lending—"

"No." Vasili threw back his entire glass of wine. A server quickly rushed in to refill it. "I do not share, as you well know, Nadia."

She huffed. "But I hear he's so well proportioned and it's not as though you're into co—"

"Where did you hear that?" Vasili asked, his glass now full and back at his lips. Perhaps he should ease off the wine if he was planning on staying sober. Or maybe he wanted to have the alcohol steal his reason for the evening, in which case Niko wasn't sure whether he should be terrified or intrigued.

"Amir, of course." She laughed. "He said your doulos was erect for hours before he sent him back to you, unspent." Nadia had a voice that rang like a bell when she wanted it to, and now everyone had hushed. Even Amir appeared surprised by that little gem of gossip she'd thrown into the ring.

Nadia balked at the sudden attention. "What? It's true."

Vasili downed his second glass and lifted it for another refill.

A sudden, bitterly cold silence fell over the table. The chill spilled down Niko's back. The fear in the room—he could smell it, taste it. And every single person was looking at Vasili.

Niko looked too, fearing the assassin had somehow

struck again, but Vasili was fine. He shakily held the glass up for a server to pour more wine. Nothing seemed amiss except Vasili's smile. A terrible, broad grin, full of teeth and madness.

The glass was now full and Vasili brought it down to his smiling mouth to drink. When the glass came away, the smile was gone, and his usual disposition returned. He frowned, waved a hand, and the titter continued like it had never stopped.

Only now everyone leaned away. It would have been comical if it weren't so damn disturbing.

"What was that?" Niko whispered. The prince's fingers trembled against the lace tablecloth. He saw Niko looking and withdrew his hand from the table, tucking it out of sight. "Are you well?" Niko asked.

"Observe them, not me, *Nik*."

Niko eased closer and lowered his voice. "As much as I despise being here, and being with you, you're not yourself, Your Highness. This feels like a mistake."

Vasili jolted from the chair and marched from the room, stopping short of running. The family stared open-mouthed, too afraid to say or do anything.

Niko followed fast on his heels, tracked him down among flickering lamps and billowing silk drapes. Vasili faced away, a shoulder propped against the wall, his body oddly slumped. Was it the wine?

"Vasili?"

He didn't move, didn't react at all.

Niko slowed his pace. A cool, sharp breeze sailed through the drapes, making them ripple. Niko heard only his own pounding heart. The palace was quiet, the night still. And Vasili lingered like a ghost, so quiet he might vanish in the moonlight.

"Vasili?"

"Stay back." His voice, always so level, was now torn at its edges. He no longer sounded like a hard prince, but something brittle and broken.

"How can I help?"

Vasili's shoulders shook, and he laughed. "My father... is awake."

It was not what Niko expected him to say. "That's good?"

Vasili collapsed.

CHAPTER 20

*T*he prince mumbled incoherently as Niko got an arm under his and managed to hitch him to his feet. He was semiconscious, mumbling nonsense on the route back to his chambers.

Niko guided him to the bed and laid him down. Vasili braced himself on an arm, shuddered, and dropped onto his side on top of the sheets.

"Shit." This wasn't just wine. Vasili's gaze was fogged, his mind elsewhere. "I'll get Julian."

Vasili blinked, his stare suddenly sharpening. "No."

"He's better at this than I—"

"No!" Vasili snapped and curled in on himself, teeth clenched. "Not... Julian."

"A healer, then. Someone." Anyone but Niko.

Vasili groaned in agony. "*Leave.*"

"Leave?!" Niko almost did. It was all the prince deserved, but if Vasili fucking died, Julian would never forgive him.

He grabbed a chair, dumped it beside the bed, then sat.

It got worse. Vasili's back arched, hands clawing at the covers. He cried out in pain. A dribble of blood escaped the prince's pale mouth.

"Dammit." Niko searched the room and found a wooden shoehorn. He pried the prince's jaw apart and rammed it in. The prince's eyes flashed with recognition and hate. "So you don't lose your tongue. Hate me in the morning."

When Niko couldn't stand to watch him writhe, buck, and groan any longer, he folded the prince's cold, clammy hand in his. The prince was probably beyond noticing. Vasili's fingers tightened and twitched. His muscles contracted, his body were rebelling against some unknown force. Niko had seen something like it in one of his soldiers. The man had convulsed, screeching and panting. But it hadn't lasted like this.

The prince hissed air through his gritted teeth, his chest heaving. Then, suddenly, he fell still. Vasili blinked. His startling blue eye had been completely consumed by inky blackness.

"What the...?" Niko leaned closer. Vasili bucked again and thrashed hard. Niko grabbed the prince's other flailing hand and pinned it down. Pinned, Vasili finally relented. The prince fell limp again, his eye closed, and his breaths slowing.

Niko gently plucked the bit from between his teeth and dropped back into the chair, shaking. He wanted Julian here. He'd have known what to do. But Vasili, even in his madness, had been adamant, fearful even. He clearly did not want his episode revealed to anyone.

Niko let his head fall back against the chair and closed his eyes. Amir had mentioned their father was a lunatic.

The princes weren't pillars of sanity. Their grandfather had died from a mental affliction. If this dark flame was hereditary, perhaps Niko had just witnessed it. There was nothing fantastical about madness, but the family had made it part of their mythos to protect their reign.

NIKO STARTLED awake to find Vasili in a black silk robe, standing at the washbasin. The room was cold despite the morning sunlight. An open window invited the late autumn air inside. The prince didn't seem to care.

Niko sat up and groaned, muscles aching. Vasili's thrashing had been violent. He would have certainly hurt himself had he been alone. Niko didn't expect any thanks for helping him. This moment was already awkward, and growing more awkward by the second. He glanced at the door. Would it be unreasonable to just slip out?

Vasili's long hair, always so smooth and perfect, lay in knots down his back. His face was so pale he almost glowed. His thin lips were a flash of pink but the blue eye was bright and as piercing as always. That gaze suddenly fixed on Niko, pinning him to the chair.

Vasili wrung out a cloth and ran it over his face, then lifted his chin and stroked it down his neck.

"I'll see myself out," Niko grumbled, levering himself of the chair. The lord's suit had twisted and creased around his body, and tightened at his neck. He tore a few jacket buttons open and yanked on the collar, needing air.

"Nikolas."

His name on the prince's lips brought him to a stop.

"No word of this," he said into the mirror. "To anyone."

"Julian—"

"Especially your lover."

He already lied to Julian about where he'd been while on the prince's errand, and lied about not seeing the *scene* in this very room. But Julian clearly had his own secrets, all of them involving Vasili. Niko nodded sharply and left.

Niko crept into Julian's room, but woke him anyway. "Long night?" he croaked, blinking his sleepy eyes.

Niko pulled off the jacket and unlaced his shirt, then crawled onto the bed, still half-dressed, and kissed Julian's accepting mouth. "No talk." He kissed down the man's shoulder and nipped hard. Exhausted, Niko wasn't even sure he could do this now, but he needed to feel, to ground himself in comfort.

"Hm. You smell like rosewater," Julian mumbled.

Niko paused.

"I waited." Julian's hand came around the back of his neck and pulled him down to eye level. "Where were you?"

Niko kissed him gently and lay on his side, tucking Julian in close. "Dinner. Don't ask. Exhausted."

Julian's leg hooked over his thigh. The man burrowed closer, resting his head on Niko's chest like a pillow. "Tell me later."

"I will." Niko listened to his soft breaths, soaked up Julian's warmth, and soon drifted off to sleep.

MORE CLOTHES WERE LEFT outside Julian's door, all perfectly tailored to fit. The prince had a good eye for measurements. The clothes were ridiculous, with courtly frills and lace, but if Niko was to continue to appear in public beside the prince, he apparently had to look like he belonged.

He'd woken alone, and an unpleasant knot of jealousy tightened inside. Julian was with Vasili. Getting whipped and getting off, no doubt. No, that thought wasn't fair. Julian was the prince's personal guard first and foremost. Whatever they did together in private was between them, and had nothing to do with Niko. Vasili had made this clear.

He shaved and dressed, applying all the layers of high society that didn't belong and, frankly, made him feel like a courtly performer. But he'd worn armor with the griffin on his chest, and it helped to think of the clothes as a different kind of role.

Julian returned after midday, his face etched with worry. He pulled off his light armor and hung the equipment on its stand. "The prince is sick."

"Something he ate, maybe." Gods, the lies tasted bitter.

Julian looked up, torn from his thoughts. "Yes. Probably. At dinner, was there any word of the king's recovery?" He ran a hand through his sandy hair and shook out his fingers, working out their aches.

Vasili had mentioned it, but not at the dinner. Was the encounter in the hallway part of his promise to remain silent? Gods, he couldn't do this. "Julian... Last night—"

"The staff are twittering about the king's recovery. He might even be seen today, and I'm surprised Vasili hasn't said anything."

"He mentioned it, remember? Told the people the king was recovering." Niko approached him.

Julian worried his lip between his teeth, not in a sexual

way, but out of concern. "It's just—Vasili won't see me right now."

Julian obviously cared for Vasili, and to keep the man's condition from him felt cruel. "Last night, Vasili had an—I don't know what you'd call it? An episode? It was after dinner. Nobody saw. I happened to be there and—"

Julian's gaze hardened. "An *episode?*"

"He's fine. I left him at his washbasin issuing orders, but I doubt he'll be attending any public gatherings for a few days."

"You didn't say anything." Deep lines appeared in his brow. "This morning, when you returned. You didn't say a damned thing, Niko."

"He ordered my silence."

"Even to me?" Not a whine, but close.

"Yes." *Especially to you.* Vasili, in his strange, icy way, probably didn't want to worry Julian. "I'm sure he's just embarrassed. But these fits, has he had them before?"

"No, I—when did he mention the king?"

"Briefly," Niko replied. Why did the king's recovery matter so much now? "He said the king was awake right before he collapsed."

"He collapsed too?!"

Julian's stricken face plucked at Niko's heart. He looked about ready to weep from anxiety. "He's all right." Niko reached for him, but Julian backed away.

"I have to go."

"Julian, wait. We need to talk."

The man's frown deepened. "We do, but not now. Later. I'll—I'll see you this evening. We'll talk then."

"Where are you going?"

Julian opened the door and left without answering.

He'd upset him and something in all of those words had pushed Julian away. He'd known he shouldn't have lied or kept it from him. If anything happened to Julian like that, Niko would want to know. Damn Vasili for driving a wedge between them.

At a loss, Niko walked the palace to speak with the staff and harvest what news he could. All were eager to speak with him now that he was dressed as a lord. Vasili wasn't at breakfast, or lunch. He hadn't been seen at all, but that wasn't the only news rattling around the palace. King Talos was awake and well enough to order staff back and forth from his day chambers. So he was alive, after all. Niko had been convinced the princes had killed him. Would he get to meet the king? Probably not. Vasili promoting a former soldier and blacksmith to pseudo-lord likely wouldn't go over well with the king.

One thing was clear: the dynamics of the palace would change. Vasili was no longer in control. That would please Amir, but it also unsettled everything Niko had learned.

Later in the day, word reached Niko of an assembly to be hosted by Talos himself. Niko breezed through the guards outside the grand hall and took a standing place alongside the main aisle. He hadn't been invited, but nobody had stopped him. So long as he kept his head down, he doubted anyone would notice him.

The hall gradually filled with people. Excitement buzzed in the air. Talos hadn't been seen in months. Most people in attendance had probably thought the next time they would see the king would be in a casket. His awakening was quite the story.

Amir took to the dais first, positively glowing, but he soon grew bored of being on display when the seconds ticked into minutes. "My brother does like to keep us waiting," he announced, playing to the crowd.

The gathered people chuckled lightly. Most here probably didn't care about the rumors of their royals being cruel or mad, they just cared they had someone to admire, someone to protect them, to order soldiers into battle. To most, the Cavilles appeared to do that.

Then Vasili arrived. He wore a red velvet doublet that accentuated his height. The sharp heels of his black leather boots clipped the dais. He almost pulled off an air of supremacy, but Niko saw his trembling hand immediately as he took his throne beside the king. He sat gingerly and lifted his chin. The pose was one of regal defiance and he always masterfully made it work, but not this time. His lips were grey, his skin sickly white. He looked as though he might collapse. Niko had seen healthier dead bodies.

A sense of unease trickled down Niko's spine.

King Talos arrived without fanfare. The sharp impact of the king's cane on the floor rang across the room, curbing the crowd's chatter. Vasili had clearly gotten his height from his father. The king's dark hair—as dark as Niko's—had been clipped short, framing a long, hard face alongside dazzling blue eyes. Niko had expected a frail old man, not a middle-aged man who appeared to be in his prime.

Talos reached the front of the dais, smiled, and the crowd erupted in cheers. The smile was like Vasili's too—the flat, shallow slice of the lips—but instead of being cold, the smile thawed the king's icy glare.

Gods, it was like looking at an older, more powerful Vasili.

Talos leaned on his cane and scanned the audience, soaking up their applause and appreciation.

Niko's gaze slid to Vasili. The prince stared ahead, frail and silent. If he collapsed in public, his reputation as a strong and capable regent would be destroyed. If Vasili became incapacitated, Niko's task would be far more difficult.

The king lowered himself into the throne as the people's cheers turned rapturous. Their king was back, the king who had stopped the war. All hail the fucking Cavilles.

He lifted a hand and gestured for them to calm. "My family." The king swept a hand, encompassing everyone standing in the front of the hall. "My people." He gestured to the crowd. "Thank you." He paused dramatically, a combination of Vasili's confidence and Amir's flair for theatrics. "Let it be known that the city gates have been reopened."

Vasili's shoulders sagged.

"There was no need for them to be closed. We are no longer at war with the elves. The peace I brokered remains in place."

The crowd grew enthusiastic again, and he lapped it up. He stood—clearly unexpected, by Vasili's flinch— and came forward, his cane striking the floor. "While I was unwell, it appears my hard-fought peace agreement was tested, and so I am going further to protect the fine kingdom of Loreen. From this day on, I will personally guarantee the safety of every soul here." More cheers. Niko's unease grew. "And I can do that because of my brave son, Vasili." The king swept a hand back, gesturing at his sickly looking son. The frenzied crowd whooped.

Vasili dragged a small smile from the depths of his hollow soul to his lips.

"It is because of my son that we will rest well in our beds on this night."

Vasili leaned back on the throne, allowing it to hold him up.

"He leaves for the border tonight. A gift to our new allies, the elves."

Niko's gut dropped. Gods, no. Was Talos mad? Elves didn't accept gifts. Anything sent to them, they'd rip to pieces, including Vasili.

Talos gestured downward to settle his people. "The elven king has agreed to withdraw any remaining forces from our lands and our borders, all because of my brave son. Vasili, your ever-faithful guardian."

Riotous applause. Oh, how they loved their royals.

Vasili's eye glistened, bright and glassy. This time with fear, not spice. The elves would kill the prince. The peace agreement was a sham. They'd string him up as they had before, take his other eye, cut his skin from his muscle, and carve off his face. They'd send him back to Talos, spill into Loreen, and burn it to the ground. Elves could not be reasoned with. How did Talos not know this?

It occurred to Niko that Julian would go with him. Because Julian would never leave Vasili's side, especially for something like this.

Niko clenched his hands into fists. This was absurd. Where were the king's advisors, the ones who told him elves could not be trusted? Why was no one challenging him? This fool had surrendered, and now he'd given up his heir. For what?

Amir's creeping smile said it all. Perhaps Amir had

planned this to finally rid the palace of his biggest threat. Sending Vasili beyond the front was as good as a death sentence.

Niko stepped into the aisle and strode toward the dais. Vasili's eye widened. He gave his head a quick shake, but it was too late for that.

The king's attention dropped to Niko, his mild surprise becoming curiosity.

Niko lowered himself to one knee and bowed his head. "My king."

The crowd settled at Talos's command and Niko looked up.

"Negotiating with the elves is a—" He desperately searched for the right word. One that wouldn't be an insult, but courtly talk was not his forte. All that was left was honesty. "—mistake."

Talos stepped back and leaned on his cane. "And what lord are you? I don't recognize you."

"He isn't a lord, Father." Amir grinned. "He's a doulos."

Niko shot the middle prince a glare. "Your Highness, I'm a soldier. I fought for you—"

"Why is there a doulos dressed as a lord in my court?" Talos laughed humorlessly.

Niko slowly rose to his full height. His heart pounded. "The elves will kill your son and send him back to you in pieces."

Talos's face was expressionless. Unconcerned by Niko's warning, the king commanded, "Get this slave out of my sight!"

Niko squeezed his fists tighter. "My king. I have served you since the war began, bled for you, and lost those I've loved for you. I know the enemy. I've looked into their eyes and witnessed the vileness of their souls. They will never surrender."

Talos straightened and jabbed the sharp tip of his cane against Niko's chest. "Get out of my court."

The palace guards began marching toward Niko. It felt surreally familiar, as though he were stuck in a perpetual loop of trying to reveal the truth in this horrible place, only to be punished every time. Niko met Vasili's unblinking gaze. The prince stared back. A forced mask of acceptance remained locked on his face, but the fingers on the arm of the throne trembled.

The guards grabbed Niko and pulled him backward. He held Vasili's stare, wishing he could have said or done more. Nobody deserved to be handed over to the elves like an animal to the slaughter.

Vasili closed his eye and turned his face away.

"Wait!" Amir stood, then quickly bowed to his king. "The doulos is Vasili's. As my brother is leaving us, it would be a waste to have his property *discarded*. I'll take him."

Talos eyed Niko with increasing interest. If the king relented, Niko would have to submit to that wretched fiend and he wasn't capable. He'd rather die.

"*Halt*," Talos barked.

Niko yanked himself free of the guards, if only for a show of defiance. They'd surely gather him up and drag him out again soon. He stared back at the king, understanding now where Amir's delightful personality came from. Anger bubbled over, and he wished he'd let the elves overrun this foul place instead of fighting for it. "The Cavilles are not worth the thousands of men and women who bled for you."

Talos smiled. "Have him prepared and sent to my chambers."

"Father—" Vasili.

"Silence!" the king snapped. Vasili shrank back. "You have no voice here, my darling, treacherous son. What is yours is mine by right. Now, get ready for your departure and fulfill your wretched destiny by *dying for our beloved people.*"

His last words were lost among the crowd's murmuring, but Niko heard them. There was no doubt Talos was sentencing Vasili to death.

"Come along," a nearby guard urged, his tone almost reverent. He reached for Niko's arm. Niko jerked back and walked ahead of them, maintaining his dignity. What was left of it would surely be stripped from him soon.

CHAPTER 21

*N*iko was shoved into a room he assumed to be Talos's chamber, although this chamber was like no other he'd seen in the palace. A few chairs, a dresser, a cracked mirror, and a musty, cobweb-draped four-poster bed were in it. The bed was stripped of all its sheets. The fireplace was cold, and the open window let in freezing air. The room was up too high for escape.

Niko stood shivering in the middle of the room, observed by two guards, their faces hidden behind their helmets with only their eyes showing through slits. They hadn't restrained him, but would given a single wrong move. Niko contemplated that move now, but the odds of taking out two heavily armored guards without a weapon were slim.

He'd been a fool. He should never have approached the dais. Had he stayed quiet, he could have travelled with Vasili and Julian to the front line. He knew the land. There would have been opportunities to keep Vasili from reaching the elves. Now he'd be lucky to feel a whip instead of a noose.

This fucking palace. The fucking Cavilles. Why had he returned?

For Julian.

Because saving one good man might go a long way to saving his own dark soul.

And now he'd let him down.

He tried to rub some warmth back into his skin, and began to pace.

Talos was exactly what Niko should have expected after having the misfortune of meeting his sons. The man was cruel, vicious, and ruthless. He'd sent his son to die for nothing. Did he hate Vasili that much?

He'd called him treacherous, so Vasili had done something to him, something bad enough to earn his father's ire. The cuckoo in the nest, the "stable" brother, the city's guardian and protector. The heir. What if he'd kept his father ill to protect the city?

Now there was an interesting thought.

But something had gone wrong. Vasili's plan had failed, and Talos had recovered. The king knew Vasili had tried to incapacitate him. Amir would tell him for certain. Vasili's actions could be construed as attempted regicide. And that was why Talos was sending Vasili to the elves. Amir had finally succeeded in removing Vasili from power, and Talos had banished a threat from the palace.

"Shit, shit, shit..."

This all would have been so much easier if Vasili had just answered his damned questions.

The door rattled.

Niko whirled, heart leaping into his throat. The king

would ask things of him. Niko would refuse, and the pain would begin. He'd braced for it. Mostly. He'd taken the flogger before. His body was no stranger to pain and hardship. He'd heal, or die.

A guard in full armor walked in, plates rattling. "You're relieved," he told the guards already present.

Niko froze.

He'd know Julian's voice anywhere.

"The king said—"

"The king has been waylaid." Julian added weight to his words. "You're to report to the barracks immediately. Do not keep him waiting. I'll watch the doulos."

"Sir."

The guards left. The door closed. Julian pulled his helmet free, tucking it under his arm, and gave one of his small, shy smiles. It soon died, replaced by a firm frown. "We don't have long." He didn't look Niko in the eyes.

Niko could kiss him, but Julian's sour expression made it clear now was not the time. He was furious. Because Niko was a fucking idiot—again.

"Come." Julian unclipped the sword at his waist and thrust it into Niko's hands. "You'll need it."

"Where are we going?"

"We're running."

"Vasili—"

"Him too." Julian finally met his gaze.

"Good." He swallowed. There was more to say, but it would have to be later.

They'd made it halfway through the royal wing when alarm bells began to chime.

Julian cursed and pulled his helmet back on. "Keep your head up. Act like a lord."

The words had barely left Julian's lips when a shout boomed down the corridor behind them. "You there!"

Niko twisted on his heel, saw the guard free his sword, and pulled his own blade free in response. He preferred to fight than hide, anyway. The guard thundered in and brought his blade down in a mighty swing. Niko blocked, both hands on the grip of his sword. The sudden impact jarred his bones, but also rattled free all his lethargy.

He shoved forward, rocking the guard back. Malice flashed in the guard's eyes, briefly visible through the slit in his helmet. The guard lunged. Unhindered by metal plate, Niko twisted away and cracked the pommel of his sword against the weak point of the armor at the back of the neck. The guard grunted. Niko kicked his weight-bearing leg out and pushed, sending the man sprawling.

"Go!" he urged Julian.

There would be no stealthy retreat from the palace. Adrenaline surged through his veins, summoning a bitter grin.

They skidded around a corner and pulled up short in front of an approaching line of guards. Niko grabbed Julian by the arm and dragged him down a narrow spiraling stone staircase.

"Where's Vasili?"

"Stables." Julian stumbled down a few steps, almost falling.

"Lose the armor," Niko said, already tearing Julian's buckles open. He discarded the breastplate behind them and tore off more pieces with every step, leaving the pieces strewn in their wake.

The stables were across the gardens at the rear of the palace. The gardens were the quickest route, taking them outside and away from the cramped, maze-like palace corridors.

They burst through a door and sprinted across the quiet, shadow-shrouded training yard.

"Stop!" The sound of marching boots echoed about the grounds behind them.

Niko tucked his sword under his arm and grabbed the courtyard ladder he'd used during the elf chase, then bolted up it. Julian stayed close, moving freer now. If they could just get ahead of the guards' line of sight, the darkened gardens would swallow them up. They might just get out of the palace alive.

Arrows pinged off the wall. "Down!" Niko grabbed Julian's head and shoved him to his knees. Arrows twanged left and right. There was a brief reprieve as the archers reloaded and Niko dropped down a hatch into the grassy, wild garden. Instead of heading for the gate that would probably be locked, Niko veered right, plunging through a hedge, into the manicured gardens, and dashed across the open space.

Guards appeared on an arched section of hedge ahead. Niko couldn't go back. There was only one way out: through them.

Niko's legs pumped and with a roar he launched himself at the first guard, tackling him onto his back. In the corner of his vision he saw Julian take on the second and third guards, his dual swords flashing, steel crashing against steel, ringing through the quiet.

A gauntleted punch landed on Niko's side. Bone buckled, and for a second he was blinded with pain. He funneled the pain into his fist, jerked the man's helmet back, exposing his neck, and punched him in the throat. The guard dropped, choking.

Julian's fingers dug into his arm as he pulled Niko into a wild sprint. Pain danced and snapped as he clutched his side. He spotted the stable's archway ahead and took cover behind a bush.

"Looks clear," Julian said, but he hesitated.

It was too open. As soon as they broke from cover, they'd be exposed.

The clomping sound of restless hooves suggested the horses were active. But if it wasn't Vasili, they'd be walking into a killing zone.

"Of all the stupid," Julian began, staring back the way they'd come, checking for more guards. He flung a look over his shoulder to Niko. "Did you honestly think the king would listen to you?"

Niko yanked him into a hard, breathless kiss. Julian's mouth stubbornly resisted, but not for long. His fingers gripped Niko's shirt and he returned the kiss like he could devour Niko whole.

Julian pulled back, licking his lips, eyes wide and frantic. "If we don't survive—if this is—"

Niko grabbed the man's face. "Hush. Stay down, stay quiet. Worry later." Niko freed him, gripped his sword, and stepped from cover.

No alarms shrieked. No arrows flew. He waved Julian on and jogged through the arch into the stable yard.

Vasili's huge charger shied at Niko's sudden approach, shaking its head and snorting. The cloaked Vasili pulled the reins. His sneer was all that was visible beneath his hood. "*Hurry*."

"Trying." Niko sheathed his blade, got his foot in his

chestnut's stirrup, and mounted up. Julian rode a white horse, its tail high and demeanor flighty. That one would be a handful. He hoped Julian could handle it. Falling was not an option.

Vasili caught Niko's eye. The prince's expression was cracked and brittle, his eye searching for an answer to an unknown question. There was much to say, but none of it would help them now. Niko nodded his readiness. Vasili whirled his horse around, dug his heels in, and spurred the beast into a gallop. Niko followed, Julian behind him. The sound of hooves was too loud, and sure enough, bells and shouts rang out again, upsetting the night.

Niko glanced behind him and grimaced at the sight of the mounted guards spilling from the stable yard. "Cavalry!"

All three horses surged into rolling, moonlit fields. Julian stayed close, his white stallion breathing hard, its nostrils flared, but it had plenty of stamina. Vasili's heavy horse would tire before the others.

Niko urged his mount on, the animal dipping and rising as it galloped across uneven ground. Hedges sailed past them. Vasili's hood had fallen back. His long platinum hair waved like a flag caught in a gale. Niko spurred his horse faster, drawing up alongside Vasili. The prince stared ahead, transfixed on the horizon. Foam flew from the charger's mouth. He'd ride the damn thing into a grave. If they escaped, they'd need the horses in the coming days.

"Follow," Niko shouted, leading the others toward an old road. Niko veered onto the overgrown track. Thick trees lined both sides blocking the moonlight and slowing their pace.

"Where are we going?" Vasili demanded.

"We can't outrun them," Niko said, and Vasili flashed him an impatient look. The prince didn't like having his question ignored. Niko smiled, taking the spike of triumph where he could.

Jagged ruins loomed out of the dark ahead.

Niko slowed his horse and guided into the abandoned village, between gutted homes and an old stone-well. Moonlight made the ruins glisten. He'd often visited Palcombe village as a boy to buy supplies from the market, his belt lopsided with a heavy coin pouch. Elves had since burned most of it to the ground.

His horse trotted into the thicker trees, approaching what looked like a wall of brush and ivy. Then the straight line of a timber-clad wall emerged, and in it, an overgrown door. Dismounting, he tore off the ivy and tugged on the door. Julian joined him moments later, helping rip the ropes of ivy free until the door gave, opening enough to lead the horses inside an old barn.

Niko heaved the door closed behind them and pressed his face to the slit, watching the quiet ruins for movement. The cavalry arrived just as Niko's heart slowed, kicking its pace up again.

Vasili's horse stamped its hooves and snorted. "Hush that thing," Niko hissed.

Vasili's gentle whispers eventually soothed the animal.

"Search every ruin!" a voice commanded.

Niko tightened his grip on his sword and waited.

CHAPTER 22

*T*he guards passed the barn and continued their search through the night, but they missed the barn. By the time Niko and the prince emerged into the morning sunlight, the horses were well-rested. Vasili looked healthier too, a little pale, but seated confidently on his horse.

"Do you have a plan?" Niko asked.

"Head south," the prince answered, offering no further explanation.

"All right." Niko steered his horse toward the village ruins. "We'll cross farmland, stay off the roads. They'll be looking for you." He kicked his horse on and glanced back to check Vasili was following. The prince nodded, then urged his horse into a trot while Julian tagged behind, scouting their rear.

A day of riding brought the industrial town of Tinken into sight. Surrounded by mining stacks spewing black smoke into the air, the town was full of bedraggled, hard people. But it also hosted one of the largest trading networks outside of Loreen. The people here were familiar with traders passing through. Vasili in his cloak wouldn't be too conspicuous.

Niko led the way toward a familiar inn and handed his horse over to an eager young stable hand. He'd stayed here a few times after the war while looking for work. They'd be relatively safe inside.

"Keep the cloak on," he mumbled to Vasili as Julian helped the stable boy with the three horses. "Hide your face. Nobody here knows what you look like, but we don't need word getting back to the guards."

Vasili pulled the hood further over his face. Niko noticed the prince's rings. "Lose the Caville ring."

The prince plucked it from his fingers and dropped it into a pocket without complaint. He seemed content to let Niko lead. It probably wouldn't last.

"Give me your other rings." Niko held out his hand.

Vasili lifted his chin. Orange light from inside the inn illuminated the sharp press of his lips.

"We can sleep on the road and eat rabbit if you wish, or we can use your jewelry to pay for a bed and a bath."

Julian returned, and noticed Niko with his hand out. "Won't rings such as those raise suspicion?"

Vasili began to pluck them, one by one, from his fingers.

"Not here." Niko smiled, perhaps enjoying the prince's obedience more than he should. "Tinken accepts anything valuable as currency."

Vasili lifted his gaze at the inn's filthy windows. "I should have known you've frequented these *rooms* before."

Niko stowed the rings away in a pocket. "I'll book us a room."

"Just the one?" Vasili asked, probably horrified he'd have to share.

"I can rent three if you wish, but we don't know how long we'll need these rings to pay our way or bribe anyone showing too much of an interest."

"Fine," the prince conceded. "Do as you see fit."

Inside, a lounge was packed wall-to-wall with miners. After leaving Julian and Vasili at a window, Niko shoved through the crowd toward the bar and eventually caught the eye of Adrian, the proprietor who took the rings without question. "Not seen you around for a while, Niko. Heading south?"

"East," he lied.

"Surely not to the front? Didn't you get enough of the elves?"

He laughed. "Gods, no, not that far. Won't ever go back there."

Adrian chuckled. "I'll see to it your bath is drawn. Won't stay hot for long, mind you."

"I'll be happy if it's wet." He scooped up three tankards of mead and forced his way back through the crowds. It was the end of the week. The miners, many of them ex-soldiers, were celebrating getting paid by pissing it all away at the inn. They wouldn't care about the three strangers at the window. "Don't drink the water here," Niko said, setting the tankards down. "It's drawn from the well out back, next to the shithouses."

"Delightful," Vasili grumbled, his mouth finding a grimace.

"I've asked for a bath. No offense, but we need it." Both Julian and Vasili appeared mildly surprised at Niko's thoughtfulness, or the fact they'd have to bathe in one room. "We'll wash separately, obviously," Niko added. "Vasili's lily-white ass can wash up first."

"I appreciate that," he said, his dry tone making it clear he didn't appreciate any of it.

Niko reached for his drink and flinched, his broken rib grating against his insides.

"You're hurt," Julian reached for Niko's hand, but stopped halfway and swept up his drink instead. Maybe he hadn't been reaching for Niko's hand at all, or maybe the quick glance in Vasili's direction had reminded him they weren't alone.

"Just a rib. I'll live."

The prince knew about their relationship, Niko mused, drinking the mead. Vasili wouldn't have cared had Julian taken Niko's hand. Niko couldn't help but remember Julian tied up with Vasili standing behind him, whip in-hand. Maybe the prince did mind, but kept it to himself.

None of that mattered now while fleeing the palace, but the secrecy grated at his soul like the broken rib inside his body. If they were going to be on the road together for an extended length of time, the truth of it all would soon shake free. It always did.

"We need to rest well," Niko said, "Tomorrow will be a hard ride if we're to keep ahead of the palace cavalry."

They drank in an awkward silence. Vasili stared out of the window and Julian watched him with concern on his face that was more than professional. After a boy came and told them the bath was ready, Julian stayed at the table while Niko and Vasili went ahead to check the room. It was a good size with a roaring fireplace and a steaming copper bath. One bed, large enough to accommodate two, had enough blankets and pillows to make up a third on the floor. Safe, dry, warm. They couldn't ask for more.

Niko drew the curtains closed, thanked the boy, and sent him on his way.

Vasili pulled off his cloak and laid it over a chair, then rested his hand on the back of the chair, gripping it tightly. Mud had splashed his trousers and his face. His long hair was ridiculously tangled, with a few errant waves. It would be sensible to cut it all off, but Niko would broach that subject later, when he'd settled. All of this would be difficult for a man like him—someone used to luxuries.

"Enjoy your bath, Your Highness."

Vasili met Niko's gaze briefly. "Nikolas...?"

"Yes?"

The prince hesitated, regarding the room warily. "Be careful. Watch Julian... Keep him safe."

Niko frowned. He did not need to be told to protect those he cared for. "Of course."

He rejoined Julian at the table and immediately slipped his hand over his as he took the seat beside him. Startled, Julian yanked his hand back, pulling his lips into a sneer before recognizing Niko. "Sorry. Tired." He sheepishly smiled and ran his hand through his hair in an automatic gesture to resettle himself. "Do you think they're close?" he asked, glancing again at the window.

"Perhaps. But we made good time today. Without a lead, they've probably returned to the palace."

He smiled again to humor Niko, but chewed at his lip. Thin lines gathered around his eyes and between his brows. Exhaustion had washed the color from his eyes, making them look grey in the inn's awful light.

"Thank you for coming to get me," Niko said. "I was

prepared to—I wasn't about to let the king do whatever he had planned. Whatever happened, it would not have ended well."

"Why did you speak up?" Julian blurted, then winced, lowering his voice. "Why couldn't you just leave? Just walk away. You didn't have to stay. You didn't have to protect him or speak up for him. What was all that, Niko?" he hissed. "Telling the king those things—you don't even like Vasili!"

Niko gripped his hand, and this time Julian didn't pull away. Instead he looked at Niko, eyes wide. "I wasn't protecting him," Niko whispered. "I was protecting you. You'd have gone with him to the front and beyond, into—"

"You don't know that."

Niko frowned. "I'm not an idiot. I know you and Vasili... I know there's more to it."

Julian's brows pinched. "There's nothing more to it, Niko."

A blatant lie, right to his face too, without so much as a twitch or a glance away. It hurt more than seeing them together. Niko lifted his hand off Julian's and picked up his drink.

"You should have just left the palace when you had the chance," Julian mumbled.

"Well, I didn't."

"No, you knelt in front of the king and told him to his face that he was making a mistake."

"That wasn't the worst thing I said either."

"It's not a joke, Niko. It would have been worse than any whipping and there was nothing I could do. He would have killed you right after humiliating you. I had to hear about it from others—how the prince was being sent to the elves and his fucking doulos tried to *protect* him."

Niko swallowed any attempt to argue. He did not want to increase the divide Vasili had caused. "I'm sorry."

"But you're not."

"No. I'm not." He replayed the moment in the assembly hall in his mind, standing in front of the king. "I couldn't let that bastard send Vasili back to the elves after everything he's clearly been through under them. I don't like the prince, but that doesn't mean I want to see him tortured again—"

"Tortured? What?"

"Oh c'mon, the whole palace talks about it." Niko leaned closer so their shoulders touched, feeling his anger rising. "Don't try and lie to me and tell me he was just *away*. You brought him back to Loreen. You escaped the elves together." Niko glanced pointedly at Julian's gloved hand.

Julian curled it into his chest, his eyes haunted. "I can't talk about that."

"I'd never ask you to. But the least you can do is not lie to my face, Julian."

Julian's lips pursed. He sighed and faced the window, his gloved fist still pressed to his chest. Was he remembering all the things he and Vasili had faced at the hands of the elves? "I don't want to fight."

Niko wished he could take that pain away. Eventually the trauma would fade, but it would forever stay a part of him. And sometimes, it would be right in the room with him, like yesterday, causing him to wake at night, heart racing, screams in his ears.

Niko rested a hand on Julian's thigh, soaking up its warmth. "Neither do I."

"Vasili said you'd been taken. Had he not told me where to find you, you'd be gone now."

Niko slipped his hand around Julian's waist and placed a soft, gentle kiss at the corner of his mouth. "I'm here now, thanks to you."

"You make everything sound effortless." Julian sighed and leaned into Niko's touch. "You speak to a king like he should listen. Like anything is possible. Like a blacksmith can command kings."

"Anything is possible," he whispered against Julian's lips. There had to be a shadowy corner somewhere nearby, away from prying eyes, where he could distract Julian's haunted thoughts with more pleasant ones. "We both survived impossible odds, and here we are." Niko pushed Julian against the wall. "I call that a fucking miracle, don't you?"

"We can't do this here. Vasili—"

"Fuck Vasili." Niko kissed him hard on the lips and Julian opened his mouth, tongue thrusting back. Julian's hands rested on Niko's chest and gently pushed.

"Not right now." Julian winced. "With everything that's happened, and..." He didn't say it, but Niko heard Vasili's name implied. "We're filthy and tired and—"

Niko smiled and kept a comment about *being filthy* on his tongue. "It's fine, go take your bath." Vasili would be up there. They could both get each other off. It wasn't like Niko could stop them. And he wouldn't, if that was what Julian needed.

Julian left the table, the crowd swallowed him, and Niko leaned against the wall, his body aching to have

Julian nearby. He'd fallen hard for the soft-hearted soldier, even if Julian hadn't felt the same way. He couldn't stop caring, especially when the man had come to his rescue, proving himself the hero Niko hadn't known he needed. He'd saved Vasili from the elves too, that much becoming clear. Why was it always the soft ones? Marcus, and now Julian? Heartbreakers, both of them, and far too good for Niko.

Maybe he should cut him loose.

The next few days would probably bring an end to things, either way.

Niko finished his drink and drifted outside into the quiet, night air. He wandered around to the stables to check the horses and found the stable boy hard at work grooming Vasili's beast of a horse. The young lad could barely reach the animal's back.

"Here." Niko took up a brush and started on the animal's neck. "Allow me to help."

"Thanks, mister. He's a big one. Looks scarier than he is though, I reckon. I dare say he can be mean." The boy prattled on. "He had a loose shoe. I took it off but the farrier won't be here 'til the mornin'."

"Good job." Niko hid his alarm. They couldn't wait for the farrier to fix the shoe. "It's late. Why don't you head off to bed? I'll finish up here."

"You sure?" The lad looked hopeful. "You're all paid up. I don't wanna get in trouble..."

"Go on. I've got this."

The boy scurried off, almost colliding with a tall, imposing figure loitering just outside the door. Niko glanced twice before seeing the eye-patch obscured by the damp bangs. The smooth, silvery hair was shoulder length, curling at its tips, making him look less regal and more... human. He still wore the same clothes, although he appeared to have borrowed a jacket from somewhere so he didn't glitter and shine like a fucking peacock.

Niko focused on the horse's flank instead of the prince. "You're not wearing your cloak."

"It's dark. I won't be seen." Vasili stroked his horse's neck and moved down its flank. The animal huffed, scenting his owner, and stomped on the spot. "I heard Adamo has thrown a shoe." He emerged from behind the horse's hindquarters. His shirt was slightly unlaced, displaying a v of skin but not enough to reveal any scars.

So Adamo was the beast's name, huh. Niko dropped the brush into the bucket. "Is that your way of asking 'May you assist me, Nikolas?'"

"You do want to leave early, don't you?"

Still, he hadn't asked for help and clearly wasn't going to, but he was right. They did need to leave before dawn. "You have the shoe?"

Vasili lifted the dinner-plate-sized shoe. So very accommodating.

Niko snatched the shoe and appraised Adamo's hooves. "It's been a while and this horse of yours is a back-breaker." He patted Adamo on the shoulder, then stroked his hand down his foreleg and gripped the fetlock, lifting the massive hoof off the ground. "There's a good lad..." The hoof wall was sound. It would take the shoe back on without a problem. "You have any nails, Your Highness?" He straightened again to find Vasili on his left. The prince held out a bunch of steel nails.

Niko took them, spread them in his palm and popped

one between his lips. "Hammer?" he mumbled around the nail.

Vasili found one hanging on the stable wall and handed it over.

Niko lifted the hoof again, seated it between his legs, and lined up the shoe. It had been years since he'd shod a horse. The last time had been right before the war, when Pah had been training him as an apprentice.

He hammered the first nail in and Adamo thankfully behaved, reassuring Niko that he wasn't about to get kicked from the stable, seeing as the horse had enough presence to cause a problem. Much like the owner.

Niko's neck and back tingled beneath what could only be Vasili's stare. "The king called you treacherous," Niko said, glancing over his shoulder as he popped another nail between his teeth. Sure enough, the prince was watching closely. "Did you try and kill him?" he mumbled.

Vasili leaned against the stable-wall and folded his arms. "What makes you think I'll answer such a loaded question?"

"Honestly, I'd be surprised if you did."

"But you ask anyway?"

Niko hammered in another nail. Adamo fidgeted, bored with the man between his legs. Vasili was suddenly in front of Niko, his hand on the horse's neck. Adamo snorted and settled.

From his doubled-over position under the horse, Niko saw only the prince's fine boots, scuffed and muddy from the ride.

"My father agreed to a peace with the elves after I—in exchange for my return."

Niko absorbed that information and hammered the

final nails home. He dropped the hoof and straightened, wincing around the angry rib.

Vasili watched him, like he always did, waiting for something. Judgment from Niko perhaps?

Vasili's words had made it clear his return had been the reason for the ill-timed surrender, the reason countless soldiers died for nothing. The prince was the whole reason the war was lost. Or that's what Vasili likely wanted him to think. But sons were not responsible for the actions of their fathers.

"Looks like your father doesn't want you around any longer, huh?" He replaced the hammer in its socket on the wall and brushed dried mud from his hands. A bath was calling his name, but Vasili was talking, opening up, and that seemed like too good an opportunity to walk away from. "Maybe because you tried to kill him? Seems like a good enough reason to send you back east."

Vasili's pale hand stroked the horse's neck, showing more affection to that animal than anyone else in all the time Niko had known him.

"Elves cannot be reasoned with," the prince said, facing Adamo. "As you succinctly—if foolishly—attempted to explain to my father."

"Yes, that conversation went as well as everyone expected it might."

"You have a tendency to say exactly what you're think-ing." Vasili smiled, and it was a strange thing to see, because it warmed his face, even softened his sharp lips, etched so deeply by a lifetime of sneering.

"It's called honesty." Niko smiled. "You should try it sometime."

"Unfortunately, that approach is not the best in court."

"So I learned. But all your courtly games brought you here." He gestured at their meager surroundings.

"You can't play chess with a hammer, Nikolas."

Of course he'd say something superior like that. "Life isn't a game, Vasili."

"It is to me."

And that was perhaps a lie and the truth. This version of Vasili—stroking his horse, talking quietly and with absolute honesty—was the real Vasili. And it might have been the first time Niko had met him.

"You're good with animals," the prince said.

Compliments? This Vasili really was new. "So are you," Niko replied. Adamo had no complaints; in fact he appeared to be falling asleep, which was exactly what the rest of them should be doing.

The moment stretched on, growing thick. Niko cleared his throat. "I figured you'd be with Julian...I mean, you and him—"

"—are fucking?" Vasili interjected, straight-faced. "Only with his head."

The urge to lash out with words was a strong one, but this wasn't Niko's fight. "Just tell me one thing. What I saw? He wants that?"

Clearly, Julian had wanted it. But Niko struggled to reconcile his kind, gentle Julian with the man Vasili had whipped. His Julian was sweet and soft, and that made him truly strong. But what he'd seen with Vasili wasn't strength. A strong man did not submit to such things being done to him, and to thoroughly enjoy it, that wasn't strength. Or perhaps it was?

Vasili's eye shone but with what, Niko wasn't sure. "It's complicated."

239

"Right." Vasili knew which screws to tighten in Niko and was doing that now. The more Niko talked about what he'd witnessed, the more Vasili applied pressure to the damned wound. "Sleep well, prince. We ride all day tomorrow."

CHAPTER 23

*V*asili took the bed. Without a word Julian climbed in next to him, back-to-back, clothes still on, leaving the window seat for Niko. He wedged himself in and watched the street outside until all the miners had stumbled home drunk and the town fell quiet.

A soft succession of raps at the door woke him some time later. It was still dark out. He answered and found the stable boy looking up at him. "I's sorry to wake you, mister, but I seen riders come up the road and thought maybe you might wanna know."

Niko ruffled his hair. "Good boy."

Julian and Vasili woke quickly, threw on their jackets and hurried to the stables.

"I readied 'em for you." The boy beamed. "Fed and watered, maybe could do with some more rest, but they'll be good for a while."

Niko mounted his ride outside the stables, catching sight of Vasili dropping a ring into the boy's hand. "Your assistance shall not be forgotten," the prince said, cupping the boy's hand in his own with surprising tenderness. He didn't flinch from the touch either.

"Thank you, sirs."

"Run home, lad," Niko snapped. The sound of hooves thundered closer. The lad darted off and Vasili shot him a look. "If they know we were here, they'll question him, and they won't be kind." Niko's horse danced beneath him, chomping at its bit.

"I know somewhere..." Julian said, mounting up. "It's isolated. They won't find us. But stay close, the roads are old and treacherous."

They galloped out the mining town and deep into the lush countryside, leaving the cavalry far behind. Rain began as soon as dawn lightened the way and didn't let up until dusk. By then, the horses had slowed to a plodding walk. Julian guided them deep into the brush, some of it impenetrable, causing them to detour. Julian hadn't been wrong when he'd said their destination was isolated.

An old house loomed ahead in the moonlit scenery. Julian led the way into its overgrown garden, dismounted, and tied his horse loosely to a sapling sprouting in the middle of the garden. He tried the door, found it stuck, and gave it a shove, but the stubborn wood wasn't giving up.

Julian rummaged around the base of the old, overgrown rosebush which was climbing up the house's walls, retrieved a rusted key, and let himself in.

Niko checked Vasili for comment, but the prince had already tied his horse to a leaning gatepost and was making his way inside.

The abandoned house was impressive up close. Likely a farmstead before the war, it probably housed a large family and staff to work the land. Niko noted, as he wandered inside, it hadn't escaped some decay. Water dripped through the roof and stained the ceilings. Ivy crept through windows and along walls. But it was secure and well hidden.

Julian swept cobwebs from the fireplace and began collecting dry wood. He hadn't said a word since their arrival, and remained focused on his task. They'd spoken little since the inn. The rain and the ride had been grueling. Talking felt like too much of an effort, and there was nothing to say.

Niko cleared the old furniture from in front of the fireplace, creating a space, and Julian set the fire, using a flint and steel to nurse a flame into roaring blaze.

Firelight and warmth instantly soothed Niko's soul. Any longer on the road and they'd have gone into exhaustion. Julian had done right by leading them here.

Niko followed Julian's example and stripped off his soaked jacket and boots, laying them out around the fire to dry. His shirt went next. Then he sat on the floor in front of the hearth and propped himself against a chair to soak the heat into his skin.

Julian took up a similar position on the opposite side of the fireplace, which left Vasili between them. The prince hadn't been shy in taking off his jacket and shirt. He laid out his wet clothes, appearing unconcerned by how the firelight licked over his pale scars. His back was less cut up than his front, but it hadn't completely escaped the elves' attention.

Niko caught the frown Julian threw in his direction, but was too tired to care. He folded his arms and stared into the flames.

Running wasn't a plan. It had kept them alive, but they could not run forever.

The south, Niko had heard, was an each-man-for-himself land. It had open plains with big skies, and was too big an area for guards or sentries to manage. Towns had sprung up where the few rivers met. The coast was said to be a stunning sight, lapped at by turquoise seas, but also full of pirates who'd cut a man's throat for the contents of his pockets. Seran city was perhaps the perfect place to hide a prince.

Niko fell asleep thinking of hotter, drier worlds and the men who inhabited them, their smiles as sharp as Vasili's. He woke to the murmur of voices and the smell of roasted rabbit.

He hissed at his protesting rib as he unfolded himself from his position and stood on aching legs. There wasn't much to be done for a broken rib, except live with it. But the escape and the relentless pace had worn him down. He'd lived for this wilderness shit when he was nineteen and surviving each day on the front line. Now he was twenty-three, which wasn't old, but was beginning to feel like it should be. His time at the palace had aged him more than war.

Julian approached from an adjoining room and handed out a plate of rabbit to Niko. "I er... I do owe you dinner, so..." He smiled and Niko couldn't help but smile in return, but it quickly faded. "You're bruised pretty bad. Rib bothering you?"

Niko nodded, but when Julian reached for him, he moved away and propped himself against the wall. Julian's hands were a reminder of things he'd rather avoid thinking about. He focused on his food and consumed the rabbit in a few bites, easing the hunger pangs.

Julian stoked the fire and tossed on a few freshly cut logs. He must have dressed, chopped wood, hunted rabbit, and prepared breakfast all while Niko slept. To find cut logs, he'd have to have known where to find an axe, like he'd known where to find the house key.

"This is your home?" Niko asked the obvious, setting the plate on a dusty table.

"Was." He looked up from where he was crouching. "Feels like forever ago." Julian rose and reached out his gloved fingers, and as much as Niko should have said no, the word stalled on his lips when Julian gently probed the bruises around the sore rib. Pain throbbed, making him hiss. Julian looked up, and Niko could think of many other parts he wished those gloves would stroke.

Movement outside the room signaled Vasili's return. Julian snatched his hand back. "We should stay here a few days. We won't be found, and you need to rest that rib."

"The rib's fine, but I agree, a few days' rest will do us all some good."

Julian stepped back and acknowledged Vasili in the doorway with a nod. "How are you with an axe, Your Highness?"

No doubt as proficient as he is with a whip, Niko silently answered.

"Passable." He gestured at his patched eye in explanation. "What do you need?"

Julian's throat bobbed. Color crept up his face. He stared too hard at Vasili. *What do you need?* It had been those words that had triggered the arousal he was so desperate to hide.

And that was Niko's cue to leave.

He pulled on his shirt and retreated outside into bright sunshine. He tended the horses, fixed a few broken fences, and set the animals loose in an enclosed area at the back of the house to graze. If their group was staying a while, the roof would need fixing and the horses would need to be turned out somewhere larger.

Niko set himself to work, focusing on the simple tasks instead of the complicated mess waiting for him inside the house. But one thought kept creeping in when his guard was down. He wished he didn't love a man who loved another.

IT SHOULDN'T HAVE BEEN a surprise that Vasili wielded an axe with the same skill he wielded everything else. Niko spotted him as he was climbing down the ladder from the roof. The prince swung the axe back and brought it down with a thunk, efficiently splitting the logs as if they were the skulls of his enemies. Sweat painted Vasili's shirt to his back and chest, emphasizing the play of muscle.

Niko leaned a hip against the ladder and watched the prince chop wood. Missing an eye didn't appear to hinder him at all. Where had he learned to swing an axe, and why did he look so comfortable doing it? In fact, he appeared to be more comfortable here than at the palace. His fear and exhaustion, clearly on display on his throne, had vanished some time during the past few days at the farm.

Vasili split the final log and lowered the axe. Shielding his eye from the sun, he looked straight at Niko.

The same icy intensity simmered in the prince's gaze,

tangible even at this distance. Niko fought the urge to look away, to surrender. It was silly, perhaps, to stare back at the prince. But if Vasili was given an inch, he'd take a mile. So they stared, and although Niko couldn't be sure, it seemed the prince's mouth turned upward at one corner.

A door slammed.

Vasili dropped his gaze to Julian, who approached through the long grass to collect the wood. Julian bundled the logs in his arms and Vasili stacked more on top. Julian said something Niko couldn't catch, and the prince smiled. The scene was domestic.

Niko had wondered about Julian joining him at the forge. A fantasy, obviously. Especially since now he couldn't return to Loreen without the king taking his head. But he'd enjoyed the idea of it, of having someone live with him in a home of his own. A simple life without the Cavilles, the court, and its killers. It would be like this, perhaps. Chopping wood, hunting for game, just living. Maybe a week of it would drive him insane. Maybe not, if he had the right company.

Gods. He laughed at himself and descended the ladder. He really must be getting old.

IN TWO DAYS the debris in the house was cleared and the dwelling made watertight and comfortable. Niko spent much of the time outside. Despite the farmhouse's generous size, the prince's electric presence filled it, leaving no room for personal conversations between Niko and Julian.

To avoid the tension, Niko spent the evenings sitting

in the long, hot grass watching the sun set over distant forests. He didn't know this land, didn't know where the roads led. He wasn't well travelled, not before the war, and the front didn't count. Elves were rarer in the south, but not unheard of, and now Talos was opening the gates, they could travel down this far. Or had Vasili's disappearance put an end to the peace?

The king seemed the sort to spin everything to his advantage, the same as Vasili would.

He heard someone approach and barely had time to see who when Julian straddled his thighs, cupped his face, and kissed him hard on the mouth. Niko pulled back, but Julian's left hand dropped, clutched the back of Niko's neck, and claimed him so fiercely that a bolt of lust shot through him. Niko gasped and kissed him back. Julian planted his ass on Niko's lap, held him down, and shoved at his chest, pushing him to the ground.

The rib poked uncomfortably. "Julian..."

Instead of fighting with the laces of Nikos shirt, Julian rode the hem up, revealing Niko's abs. He nibbled them, teeth pinching hard. Niko braced an arm behind him, his mind falling fast into the idea of where this was going.

Gods, wherever this had come from, Niko was here for it. He thrust his hand into Julian's hair and not-so-gently urged his kisses downward. Julian yanked at Niko's trouser ties, grasped his erection, and plunged his hot, wet mouth over the crown.

"Fuck," Niko gasped. Too fast. *No, gods, faster*.

He kept his hand on Julian's head, feeling Julian's controlling pace. Julian took him deep, running the tip of Niko's cock over the top of his mouth and down his throat while his hand pumped, the strokes stuttering, devastating, and damned wonderful.

Niko growled, an incoherent sound. Julian didn't let up. His teeth grazed Niko's shaft, making his cock pulse in the man's mouth. Julian's tongue pushed and stroked and flicked, and Niko was losing control of himself. He thrust up to meet Julian's mouth. Julian's head bobbed, lips tight, and his hand working, causing Niko to come so hard he heard his own shout ringing across the empty field.

Julian's mouth slowed, his tongue pushing and milking Niko into a shuddering mess. Then he lifted off, licked his lips, and thrust his wet, salty tongue into Niko's mouth.

Niko groaned and reached down, seeking Julian's erection.

Julian caught his hand and pushed it aside, then eased Niko onto his back and pinned his wrists to the ground. "That was just for you." Julian grinned.

He kissed Niko again, each kiss a short, sharp attack on his mouth, chin, and neck.

Niko blinked at the darkening sky. He wanted to touch Julian, to kiss him. Needed it. But something about the man's sudden fervor stopped him from saying the words. Too much might push him away again, and this was the most they'd touched in days. Julian was in control, and Niko, pinned beneath him, welcomed it.

Julian rested his head on Niko's chest, which was rising and falling with each of his breaths.

"We could stay here," Julian mumbled. "Plant crops. Live out our days making love under the sunset. You and me."

Niko waited for Vasili's name to make an appearance. When it didn't, he looked down. Julian propped his chin on Niko's chest, his face flushed, blue eyes full of desire. It was a nice fantasy, but that was all it was. "Your home is lovely." He gently stroked Julian's hair from his cheek and tucked it behind his ear.

"There's land. It needs work, but we have the horses."

Niko smiled. He seemed so genuine, but the sex, and the daydreaming were too much, too soon for someone who'd never been this forward. "Where is this coming from?"

Julian pushed up to sitting. "I..." He bit his lip, making Niko's insides melt. "I just—is it foolish to hope for more?"

"Not at all. I may have been thinking the same." There was the small matter of Vasili, but this conversation, as sweet as it was, clearly wasn't real. So they could both dream, if only for a little while.

Julian rolled off him and lay adjacent in the grass, staring up at the sky. "I'm not prone to dreaming."

"*Man would stand still if he did not dream'.*" Niko quoted words he'd heard long ago.

His wistful tone must have alerted Julian to something. He frowned, clearly wanting to ask.

Niko allowed himself a smile at the fond memory. "The man who told me that was a poet. He was also an escort at the Stag and Horn, and my er...my first male encounter."

Julian's gaze lit up with silent laughter. "I can't imagine you inexperienced."

"Shocking, I know." Niko propped a hand under his head and recalled the flamboyant poet who wrapped his tongue around more than pretty words. He'd been worth every coin. "He died at the front."

"You looked for him?" Julian asked, brow raised in surprise.

"Ah, what can I say? I was young, and fell in love too easily."

"Were there others in your life?" Julian rested his hand on Niko's chest, over his heart.

"Marcus." The words lodged in his throat as soon as he'd summoned them. "He was a lot like you—"

A shout sounded from inside the farmhouse, followed by a crash, like furniture falling. Julian bolted. Niko scrabbled to his feet, tucked himself away, and sprinted through the grass after him. More yells and crashes sounded. Julian burst through the front door, almost stumbling over a fallen chair. Niko skidded in behind him.

Vasili was up against a wall, a thrashing fiend clawing at his face and neck.

Julian darted away, likely going for a weapon. Niko lunged in, got his fingers around the strange mass of smoky air and muscle, and heaved. Vasili helped by shoving, growling hard through gritted teeth. The fiend began to tremble, its body weakening, but then it found a last burst of speed and jerked in Niko's hands, snapping its teeth together inches from Vasili's chin.

Vasili let out a roar and finally the fiend let go. The sudden loss of grip sent Niko staggering back. The fiend darted up a wall and launched itself again at Vasili.

Niko reached for it.

Vasili snatched an old pan from the counter and smacked the creature out of the air, making the pan ring.

The fiend twisted and thrashed on a rug, righted itself, and bolted, howling at Vasili. The prince ducked and the fiend hit the wall, but recovered and leaped on Vasili's back, sinking its claws in. Vasili arched, crying out, and the creature crawled to his front to smother his mouth as though it intended to crawl *inside* him.

Niko buried his fingers in the creature's mouth from behind it and tried to pry it off the prince. Its strength was brutal, making Niko's muscles burn.

What had Julian used before... salt?

He saw a small bowl of old salt on the side, readied his stance, lunged for a handful and smashed it against the fiend's face.

It screamed, launched off Vasili, skittered through the open window, and was gone.

Vasili staggered against the table, gasping, and Niko stumbled with him, briefly tangled together. "You all right?" Niko touched his cheek with salty fingers, turning his face toward him. There were no signs of any wounds around the prince's gasping mouth, but he was clearly shaken. "Slowly..." Niko urged him, withdrawing his hand. "Breathe slowly. That pressure on your chest passes."

Vasili slumped back. His lashes fluttered closed and his breaths steadied. Niko stayed close, ready to reach for him should he collapse again. Vasili's panting eventually eased enough for him to wheeze, "*Fuck.*"

He'd be fine. Niko quickly extracted himself from being pressed against, hastily stepping back, giving him room. "How did it find him?" He directed the question at Julian, who was standing by the fireplace, having returned now the fiend was gone.

"How did you...?" Julian asked.

"Salt. You used it before..."

"Oh. Yes. Gods, yes." He leaned against the wall. "I don't know."

"How did it find him?" Niko asked again, glancing at Vasili who still wheezed. "Someone knows we're here. We've been seen."

Julian shook his head. "There's no road for miles. Smoke... from the chimney, maybe... but—"

"Why is the assassin still hunting him if he's out of the palace? And why use the damned *fiends*?"

"I don't know!" Julian snapped back.

Niko flexed his fingers and shook salt off them. He strode to the fireplace and righted a chair to give his hands something to do when what he really wanted was to find the wretched bastard who'd sent the fiend, and strangle the life out of him.

If Amir was behind these attacks, how could he have known where they were?

The prince held his head low, concentrating on breathing. His hair curtained his face, hiding it. He knew more than he was letting on. His damned secrets were going to get them all killed.

Niko started forward. "You need to start talking, or the next time that thing attacks, you're on your own."

"Niko!" Julian abruptly stood in Niko's way, protecting Vasili.

Vasili lifted his head and glared through his bangs. That glare did nothing to deter Niko from getting answers.

"You ordered me to find the assassin." Niko pointed past Julian at the prince's hard face. "You threw me in a cell, you made me a part of your life, and I hated you for it. I left because of this shit, and I only returned because you said you'd start answering questions. You know exactly who is sending the fiend. You know why the elves tried to assassinate you in that courtyard. You know why your brother died and you know why that girl was hung in the palace after feeding *your* spice habit."

Julian reached for the shortswords that weren't at his hips. "Niko, that's enough." Would he really have used the swords on Niko to protect his prince?

Anger, fear, resentment—it all came too fast, too hard. The words left his lips before he could stop them. "You're just as bad as he is. Did you fuck me just now because he won't let you fuck him?"

Julian's face fell.

"Did Vasili not have a whip to hand?"

"What...?" Julian's mouth dropped open and his eyes widened with horror.

"Nikolas." Vasili's voice was shredded but the warning still came through.

Niko backed away from them both. Vasili's glare was cold, but Julian's... Julian was wrecked.

Disgust boiled in Niko's guts. Disgust at himself for lashing out because he was scared to lose Julian. To lose Vasili. Shit. To lose this. Because without them, he had nothing. Was nothing. He was a shadow of a man who should have died at the front with everyone else.

"Start talking," he demanded, "or I'm out of that door and I'm never coming back."

"Niko, no." Julian moaned. "Gods, no—"

"Let him go, if he wishes it."

"Fuck you, Vasili." Niko spat. "These last few days, you almost made me think you were human under all that Caville bullshit, but I see I was wrong. Who wants you dead enough to send a fiend here, Vasili? Lie to me and I'll kill you myself."

Vasili held Niko's gaze for seconds, then looked away.

Niko hissed a laugh and strode outside. The sun had set but the heat of the day and dusklight lingered. He retrieved his saddle and set it on a bench, then went to the field to collect his horse.

Vasili was already there, whispering to Niko's horse and stroking its nose like nothing had changed.

"Get away from my horse," Niko growled.

"This horse is mine."

Niko stepped inside Vasili's personal space. The horse shied but Vasili held it by the mane.

"You are also mine," Vasili said. "Or had you forgotten?"

The audacity of the asshole. "I'm not some animal you can beat into submission, which I'm about to prove by taking your damned horse and leaving you and Julian to do whatever it is you do together until the guards arrive, or the fiends do. Have a terrible rest of your life, prince. I'm sure the elves will enjoy taking your other eye—"

The open-handed slap wasn't entirely undeserved. It rang in Niko's ear and set his cheek ablaze. Vasili raised his hand to land another blow but Niko caught him by the wrist. Vasili tugged and opened his mouth to issue some vicious punishment for touching him, but before he could speak, Niko kissed him. Quick. Sharp. Hard. Mostly to shut him up, or shock him, or for some other reason Niko couldn't fathom with the feel of the prince's bitter mouth against his own.

Vasili's hand thumped Niko in the chest, shoving him away. Absolute rage flushed Vasili's face. He recoiled, building for what would be a terrible lashing retort.

"Fuck." Niko hadn't meant that *at all*. He wasn't sure

where it had come from. He only knew the prince's cruel mouth needed to be silenced, and—

Vasili grabbed his shirt and smashed his mouth into Niko's. His tongue thrust in, demanding more, and Niko gave it.

Wild, jagged lust snatched all thought and reason out of Niko's head. He sank his free hand into the prince's hair and held him rigid, kissing back so hard that he thought he might have bruised his lips. Vasili added to it with sharp teeth and his clumsy tongue, but oh, by the three, the pain felt good.

Vasili kissed like he wanted to carve Niko open and devour him from the inside out. He tasted of citrus and bitterness. Of Caville poison. And Niko had never wanted so desperately to fuck a man raw as he did this prince. How could it be that he hated someone so passionately and yet wanted to ravish him?

Vasili punched hard against Niko's chest, pushing him off a second time. He wiped his mouth on his sleeve and shot Niko a look that seemed to demand, *How dare you kiss me?* Had Niko kissed him? No. Yes. The first time he had, but the second time it was all the prince, and fuck, Niko wanted to taste him again.

No, wait. He didn't want any of it. It shouldn't have happened.

Shit. Julian. What if he'd seen?

"I tried to kill my father because he holds the flame in his blood," Vasili said. "In his madness, he planned to surrender the flame to the elves. His actions will kill us all."

Niko stood motionless, staring at the prince with his tousled hair and plump lips and bright, penetrating gaze full of hatred and fear and lust. He blinked, trying to process the revelation in the words, but all the blood in his body had rushed to an aching erection, making his head thoughtless and splintered.

Niko stumbled on the spot. "The... what?" He knew about the flame, of course, or some of it, but aligning the important thoughts was taking more effort than it should have. His body and head were full of terrible ideas involving kissing Vasili again and not stopping until both of them were spent.

Vasili's blond brows pinched. "Do pay attention to my words, Nikolas."

"Excuse me for being distracted—"

"If my father dies, as the eldest heir, the flame ignites in me. I almost had it." He clenched his hand. "Felt it, but the spice stopped coming and I couldn't keep him under, and—"

Wait, what? "Vasili, shit. Slow down. Spice?"

"Yes, spice," he hissed. "How else could I keep him unconscious all this time?"

He was using spice to keep his father incapacitated? Someone must have discovered that along with Vasili's spice habit, and stopped the flow of spice, meaning the king would wake.

"Leave." Vasili threw the word like an accusation. "I can't stop you. But know that if my father succeeds, there will be nothing left of Loreen or its people, and I can't stand against him alone."

Vasili turned on his heel and strode toward the farm-house, white hair a flash in the dark. Niko was left alone in the field, feeling like he'd just been flogged without Vasili landing a single blow.

CHAPTER 24

*N*iko returned to the house under a starlit sky after standing in the field for what felt like hours. He'd weighed his choices and came to the conclusion he had no choice at all. Cavilles be damned, Loreen could not fall to the elves. He would never forgive himself if he walked away.

He ate the soup left for him and found Vasili and Julian in the kitchen discussing herbs, of all things. Niko's arrival cut their talk short. He tried not to notice the intimacy of the scene, with Julian at the basin and Vasili watching nearby, and set his bowl on the wooden countertop.

Niko had no right to judge Julian, especially after that kiss in the field—which *Niko* had started. Vasili wouldn't have told Julian. Niko wasn't about to tell him, either. It was just a horrible mistake. The prince was unavoidable. His very presence made Niko's skin burn. The first kiss had been a release of that tension. He'd hoped to shock Vasili, that was all. Despicable, yes, but he'd rather be despicable than experience actual desire for the viper.

"Tell me about the flame," he said, taking a seat at a small table.

Julian glanced at Vasili, questions in his eyes. Vasili stared back at Niko, his arms folded over his chest so tightly that they wrinkled his shirt. His hair, always straight, had gained some waves. Dirt smudged his cheek and chin, and his glare appeared to have softened, though it was likely a trick of the light. The glare was less dagger-like, and more reluctant resignation.

"Did you not read the books you stole from my library? Julian informed me you can, in fact, read."

"I borrowed the books," Niko corrected him. "And you know very well they're useless." This was familiar ground. He could handle Vasili being lofty and judgmental. Nothing had changed. Neither kiss had happened. He was back to hating Vasili, Julian was still looking at the prince like the sun shone out of his ass, and Vasili was looking at Niko like he wanted to scrape him off his boot.

Niko tapped his fingers on the tabletop. "I thought the flame might be a hereditary ailment. But there are signs it's more than that. Your...episode, right after you told me your father had regained consciousness. I saw something in you then." He felt foolish speaking the words. He still wasn't sure what he'd seen, but there had been something. "I believe it was the same darkness that terrified your family at dinner."

Julian took up a position against the basin, arms crossed, observing. Mention of the flame certainly hadn't surprised him; therefore he knew of it too. Probably knew a lot more than Niko.

"Carry on. You're doing so well," Vasili said with a patronizing roll of his hand. Niko recalled breaking that wrist, the same one he'd held and used to pull Vasili into a kiss that should never have happened.

He cleared his throat. "Your father, no longer under the influence of spice, regained consciousness, and the flame that had ignited in you while he was on his deathbed reverted to him, shocking your body into shutting down. How am I doing?"

Vasili's fingers tapped against his bicep. "I was raised to believe it was a curse. A burden. My father attempted to keep its existence from all of us, but Mother told me all she could before she died. It's made out to be a myth, but it's real."

Julian stared openly at Vasili now, riveted.

"An old curse, if the books are to be believed," Niko said.

"Seven hundred years old, yes."

"Your aunt. She called it a poison."

Vasili winced at the mention of his aunt, or maybe the word poison. "Some believe it to be powerful and have coveted it for generations, scheming their way into the Caville bloodline, believing their children will be blessed with it." Vasili thrust his hands into his slim pockets and lifted his gaze to the ceiling. "It is no blessing. It's a madness; you had that right. A poison with no antidote that infects Caville blood. The elves..."

His voice hitched. His throat moved as he swallowed, and he looked into Niko's eyes. "When I was fourteen, a band of elves took me from the palace gardens, threw me in a crate, and carried me across the border to their lands. They bled me from that day to the day Julian broke me free. Eight years. Every day." His one-eyed stare was fierce again, daring Niko to comment, to argue, to insult. "They were searching for the flame in my blood. That is why you were drafted into a war nobody wanted. Why you lost everything. Because the elves took a boy from his garden, cut him to the bone for power, and my father...

"Talos fought until he learned I was still alive, and then he surrendered. Julian and I...Julian brought me home. But what the king got back was not the son he remembered." Vasili drew in a breath, filling his lungs, then sighed it out. The truth had likely been difficult to speak.

Niko swallowed. Eight years their prisoner? "Did the elves get it? The flame?"

Vasili rubbed at his forehead. "I assume so, or they'd have killed me after a week. A hint of it, at least. They..." He closed his eye. "They cut me, bled me, and drank the blood, believing it would bring them closer to power." When he opened his eye, its icy blue almost glowed. "But I didn't have the flame then, not fully. They eventually learned that. And so the war continued. Father was adamant he could give up the flame to them and make the war simply go away. So I took matters into my own hands. But someone must have realized and began to hinder my efforts."

"You don't know who?" Niko asked. "Amir?"

"Amir thinks the flame is a myth. He's a jealous, short-sighted, self-centered fool. He's always tried to undermine me at every opportunity, but I'm not convinced he's completely behind this. It's too subtle for him."

"And Carlo? Why was he killed?"

Vasili straightened. His cheek fluttered. "I suspect someone was trying to coerce Carlo into acting against me. It's widely known we did not get along. Perhaps my brother resisted, or perhaps he aided them, and his services were no longer required."

"Where does the fiend fit into all of this?"

"That is..." He cocked his head. "Unexpected. I don't know its origin. I don't know nearly as much as you give me credit for."

It was a lot to take in. But this flame...the elves were clearly desperate to claim it, and probably had been for centuries, resulting in skirmishes over the years. It was only in this generation that they'd built up their forces enough to launch an outright war. "How does Talos plan on surrendering the flame if it's inside of him?"

"You may have noticed my father isn't entirely sane."

"A family trait."

Vasili's eye narrowed. "He saw what they did to me. I suspect he thinks he can bleed the flame out of him, hand it over in a jar, and they'll go away."

"Will that work?"

"I doubt it, but he's not particularly reasonable, as you saw. They'll capture him, torture him..."

"If they kill him, the flame ignites in you, yes?"

Vasili nodded. "Only if I'm nearby. If my father dies away from the Caville stronghold—the palace—the myth points to something else happening."

"Something else... like?"

"From the books, did you read about the reign of darkness before the Cavilles were cursed with the flame's protection? Etara and Aura said to Walla that *a griffin must forever hold the flame?*"

Niko had, but it had been fantastical nonsense. Anarchy. Chaos. Vicious creatures drawn as monsters upon the page. A time when preternatural power was said to be real and wild, and the people its slaves.

The elves clearly believed it. Talos would go to them, and they'd isolate him, bleed him, and eventually kill him, releasing whatever curse was in the royal bloodline. As they'd tried to do with Vasili.

"We can't go south," Niko said. "*You* can't run from this."

"I had come to the same conclusion, yes. But my resources are limited to a mercenary of questionable loyalty and a devoted but distracted palace guard."

Julian opened his mouth to argue when Niko plowed on. "No." He leaned back in the chair. "You have more than us. When you spoke in the hall that day, the people listened. There are guards inside the palace who will kneel to you. Your name has weight."

"Because they fear me."

"They fear Amir. What you have... it's more than fear, Vasili." Perhaps Vasili didn't see it because he was so close to the nightmare, but he did have people in the palace who would listen to him, perhaps even follow him. "There's loyalty but it needs to be forged into a purpose. Out of all the Cavilles in that vipers' nest, you are the only one whom the guards and the Loreen people trust."

"Then what do you suggest, Nikolas?" Vasili asked.

"You had it right all along. Kill the king, ignite the flame, rally an army and finish the elves. That was your plan from the beginning, yes?"

Vasili blinked. His gaze flicked to Julian, who shrugged and said, "Niko makes everything sound simple."

"Just... kill the king?" Vasili asked, smile ticking.

"Well, naturally, he's not going to allow you to merely walk back into the palace and take his head."

"We could lure him out?" Julian suggested.

Vasili shook his head. "He never leaves the palace unless it's to hand the elves his blood. They'll want to see him bleed. For them."

"We get to him first," Julian added. "Niko kills him, the flame passes to you."

Niko frowned. Why was he the one being volunteered to kill the king? Of course, Vasili's slash of a smile revealed the prince liked the idea.

"I'm not your assassin," Niko protested. "If you remember, I was quite clear in that distinction when we first met, right before I broke your wrist."

Vasili's smile twitched again. "You are what I order you to be." And there was Prince Vasili Caville, the viper, ready to crack his whip and have others bend for him in pleasure or pain.

It was a test of loyalty. Vasili had certainly given Niko enough information to see the prince hanged for treason in the Loreen town square. But he'd drag Niko down with him. Whatever Niko thought of the prince, there was no running from this. The three of them were all neck-deep in it together.

"We'll sleep on it," Niko announced, suddenly needing to get out from under the prince's glare. He retreated to the upstairs room he'd claimed as his own, but his mind was too full of the prince, plots, and elves to rest. He stood at the window instead, staring over the dark gardens.

They couldn't stay in the farmhouse. The fiend had found them, suggesting whoever controlled it knew where they were. Returning to the palace made the most sense, but it would also be the most dangerous choice. One mistake, and Niko would be back in cuffs, and Vasili on his way to the elves.

Eight years.

How had Vasili survived it?

Niko had seen men take their own lives just from witnessing the elves' vile work. Vasili had lived it, breathed it, for most of his adult life. Those vicious creatures cut him up for eight long years.

And Julian. He'd been there. Captured at the Gap early in the war when the elves had overrun the Loreen forces. He'd been imprisoned and tortured, but he'd broken Vasili out. That was a story Niko would love to hear, but he couldn't bring himself to ask. Julian would have to volunteer it.

As though his thoughts had summoned him, Julian came up behind Niko, slipping his arms around Niko's waist. "Forgive me?" he whispered against the back of Niko's neck. Shivers cascaded down Niko's back.

"What for?" He turned his head and Julian nuzzled his neck.

"You saw? The...me and him and the...with the whip?"

"I saw."

"When?"

"I was never sent away on an errand. I saw you both the night I left. Vasili found me three weeks later. We made a deal. He wanted me back to—I'm not sure why, considering everything he's just told us. But I returned to the palace for you. It's a prison and I couldn't stand to leave you there."

"I'm so sorry. I never meant to hurt you." Julian sucked Niko's earlobe between his teeth.

"It didn't—" It had. "It's fine." It wasn't.

Julian pulled Niko back against his chest. "Vasili and I are close in a different way."

Niko turned in Julian's embrace to peer into his shadowy eyes. In the darkness, it was impossible to read him. There was just the dusting of golden stubble across his chin.

"When I found Vasili," Julian began, "he was ruined—"

Niko kissed him, not wanting or needing to hear the words. The personal things that happened between two men in war were sacred. Niko had taken comfort in nameless soldiers when they'd needed it, men who had died, men who had just disappeared, presumed dead. Passionate and hungry one night, gone forever the next.

Julian gasped, freeing himself. "Wait. I need to say it, or I'll never say it, and you should know because of this... this thing we have. Together."

Niko lowered his hands to Julian's hips and bowed his head. He wanted to know, but also didn't, because his mind had already provided an idea, and all of it was horrible.

"Vasili is... We were together a long time with the elves. They kept him tied in a cage, Niko. Sometimes, I could reach his hand. At first he didn't respond. He didn't respond to anything. They came and cut him and took more and more of him, and sometimes they held him down and... He would just lie there and all I could do was watch."

Niko slumped down onto the window seat and pressed his cheek to Julian's shirt, listening to his steady heart.

"He never cried out. Maybe he had in the beginning,

but by the time I got to him, he didn't move. Didn't speak."

Niko closed his eyes, feeling too much wetness at their corners.

"I took his hand any time I could, for weeks, and then one night he squeezed back. I knew then I had to get him out. He was just a man. I didn't know his name or who he really was, but I think what happened to us made us close. I love him, Niko. I've always loved him. From the first time he held my hand in that place of nightmares, I've loved him."

Julian's gloved hands ran down Niko's back, pulling him close. Julian trembled, and it had nothing to do with desire.

"They took my fingers for touching him," Julian whispered, and Niko's heart broke open. Gods, he couldn't stand to hear any more of this.

"I got him out. We ran. Didn't even know where, just that we had to get away. I don't remember much from the first few days. Just Vasili shivering in my arms every time we hid in the dark, sure the elves would find us."

Julian clasped Niko's face and made him look up. He brushed the tears from Niko's cheeks while his own tears lay cold on his face. Julian, the soldier with a heart.

Niko loved him. It didn't matter how he loved another. He'd move mountains for Julian, protect him to the end because he was good and honorable and full of hope. And those things were rare in the world.

"We were on the road for weeks. We nearly died. Then the border guards found us and Vasili spoke for the first time, telling them his name."

Niko didn't deserve Julian, and he damn well shouldn't

get between him and Vasili. He dried his face with the ball of his thumb and eased out from the man's loose embrace. And to think Niko had forced a kiss on Vasili. Gods, he was disgusted with himself. He dropped on to the edge of the bed and ran a hand through his hair, wishing he wasn't such a selfish asshole.

"I understand." He sounded as broken as he felt.

"No, Niko, you don't." Julian crossed the room but stopped short of reaching for him again. "What I have with Vasili is from that nightmare place. The things we do..." He averted his gaze. "I'm ashamed of it, really."

Niko opened his mouth to beg him not to be, but Julian rushed on. "But you and I, Niko, what we have is light and wonderful and I'm selfish, I know it, because I want that too. I want *us,* too."

Julian tipped Niko's chin up with the crook of his finger. "Vasili doesn't love anything. I don't think he's capable after what he went through."

Niko had no right to argue, but he wasn't sure he agreed. Trauma like Vasili experienced—like they both experienced—made people push those they loved away.

He pulled his chin from Julian's finger. "You should go to him."

Julian gripped his jaw and stepped in, parting Niko's knees to slot his thighs between them. The angle made him look up, made him *see.* "You're brilliant, Niko. Stubborn, brave, strong, and honest. You talk before thinking, which I'd love about you if you didn't speak your mind in the palace."

Niko's reluctant smile grew.

"But I love you for it. I'm a long way from perfect, and I won't leave Vasili. I can't. I'm asking if you'll still have me, even with the horrible parts I can't ignore. It's who I am."

All soldiers carried ghosts, some darker than others. Niko caught Julian's hands and pulled him down. "Nothing about you is horrible. You're the brightest thing in my life." He hovered his mouth over Julian's. "I'm honored to have you."

Julian kissed him. Niko drew him across the room and down onto the bed to make him moan, make him bite his lip and cry Niko's name. It didn't matter that a part of Julian needed Vasili. The prince could have that side of him. Niko would relish the rest.

It was equal parts wonder and terror, because Niko wanted to save Julian from a life that would surely see him killed. But how could he save someone who didn't want to be saved?

Whatever happened with the flame and the king, it seemed the three of them were in it together. But there was still one thing between them. One thing Niko had put there. "Julian?"

"Hm?" He laid Niko back and straddled his thighs, concentrating on unlacing Niko's shirt.

"Something happened with Vasili. You should know."

With a careless grin, Julian fell forward, bracing an arm on either side of Niko's shoulders. "It's bothering you, so tell me."

It wasn't fair to keep the kiss from him. "In the field, earlier. I was about to leave but Vasili was waiting. I said some things—"

"There's a surprise." Julian grinned and lowered himself as though to kiss Niko's mouth. But if he did that, Niko would swallow the words again.

"I kissed him."

Julian's beautiful eyes flicked up.

"It meant nothing." Not strictly true. "He gets to me, somehow gets under my skin, and I wasn't thinking. It happened, he pushed me off, and..." *And then he pulled me back and gods, it was like he was a different man. A passionate, powerful, and furious man who needed to fuck like he needed to breathe.* But Niko couldn't speak those words, not with Julian searching his gaze. Maybe he saw the truth in Niko's eyes.

Julian's hot mouth brushed over Niko's. His tongue stroked in, asking, teasing. Niko answered. Maybe he'd said enough, but it didn't feel like it, because when Julian's kisses grew rougher, demanding more, Niko recalled Vasili's bitter sweetness and how his body had blazed, burning for a man he despised.

COLD STEEL NIPPED at his throat.

Niko snapped open his eyes and looked straight into an elf's vicious grey eyes. Fear for Julian gripped him, holding him down. Niko breathed through his nose, frozen beneath the male elf's blade, and swiveled his gaze around the room. More cloaked elves climbed in through the window, creeping like shadows.

This was no dream.

He couldn't fight so many. Where was his blade?

The bed beside him was empty. Julian was safe. He'd gotten Vasili out. He had to believe it.

The male elf grinned, baring serrated teeth.

The elf would kill him.

Niko yanked his knee up, striking the elf in the gut. It barked a cry. Others rushed forward. Niko clasped the elf by the head and slammed its skull against his own, then threw it backward. Niko tore from the bed. A thump struck the back of his neck, and the room spiraled. His cheek hit the floor. Hands grabbed his arms. Ropes tightened around his wrists, making them burn. The elves grunted and snarled and snapped their commands.

But Julian had escaped. Niko clung to that thought. He'd escaped with Vasili, and they were miles away. That was all that mattered.

Death had been chasing Niko since the war. If it was here for him now, he was ready. But damn these creatures, he wouldn't make it easy.

CHAPTER 25

*N*iko came to on the kitchen floor. The rag stuffed into his mouth tasted bitter and gritty against his tongue. His bound wrists ached in his lap. A dull pulsing heated the back of his head and neck. He could smell blood, probably his own.

He counted eight elves in the kitchen and guessed more were about the house.

They'd turned over Julian's furniture. Some came and went from the room, communicating in gestures, nods and expressions. They did speak, but preferred not to, at least not in front of Niko. The elf watching Niko from the chair across the kitchen stayed silent, and stared, occasionally tilting his head back and forth, as though trying to unravel a mystery. He was bigger than most and wrapped in various dark leathers. Niko didn't linger too long on the origin of those skins.

Niko shifted uncomfortably. They'd allowed him his shirt and left a pair of trousers beside him. They wouldn't have done that if they were planning on killing him.

Niko reached for the trousers with his bound hands, all the while watching the elf watch him, waiting for him to pounce. With trembling fingers, he eventually managed to pull the garment over his hips, and the elf continued to stare, eyeing him up for the best cuts of meat.

A horse whinnied outside, then abruptly fell silent.

Niko panted around the gag.

They'd kill him. But not before taking his fingers, ears, and tongue. Hopefully he'd pass out before they carved off his face.

Julian would be all right.

He wasn't here.

He must have gotten up in the night, seen them too late to rouse Niko and woken Vasili. They were out there, a long way away. Adamo was galloping, Vasili riding him hard.

A *thwack* across the head roused Niko from his distant thoughts. The big elf leered at him, pressed a fingernail into his cheek, and dragged it down toward the corner of his mouth. His grey skin was leathery too and pockmarked by small scars. Sharp teeth hinted at how they used them to tear flesh from their victims. The elf's nostrils flared. He sniffed at Niko's cheek and neck.

The metallic smell of old blood coated the back of Niko's throat.

Boots clipped floorboards.

Elves didn't wear boots. They covered their feet in soft leather made from the skins of anything they could find, making their steps silent.

A door latch rattled.

"Where is he?"

The big elf straightened and stepped back, revealing

Julian. Niko's heart swelled. He sobbed around the gag. No, he couldn't be here, he had to get away. *Run, Julian!*

"He was asleep," Julian continued, words grating. "The same as this one. I made sure of it." He flung a hand at Niko, not sparing him a glance. "How did you miss him?"

"*Julian,*" Niko tried to say, but the rag muffled the sound. "*Run!*"

Why wasn't he running? Why was the big elf baring his teeth at Julian in a look of pure hatred, but not attacking?

"Dammit, I told you Vasili was difficult." Julian dragged a hand through his hair. His gaze landed briefly on Niko.

Niko widened his eyes, trying to convey what his words could not. He mumbled through the rag, not even sure he was coherent. At any moment more elves would arrive and Julian would be outnumbered. He had to run now.

Julian crouched in front of him and pinched his lips together. "Elves." Julian sighed. "They can't be reasoned with." The smile he gave was more like Vasili's sharp slashes than his usual warm grins. It was out-of-place on Julian's face, like a stranger's smile.

What did he mean? Niko mumbled some more and tugged on his wrists. Julian was pretending to go along with the elves. As soon as they were alone, he'd get Niko free, like he had with the guards in the king's room. How he'd convinced the elves to allow him to walk freely, Niko had no idea, but his plan was working. Was Vasili free too? His words seemed to indicate he must be.

Julian sighed again and looked away. "Damn. The fiends were supposed to work." He stood, facing the elf who seemed to be watching all of this with mild curiosity. "Vasili is attached to this one. Bring him with us and the prince will follow."

What? No, if the elf took Niko outside with the others, there would be too many to fight.

"Julian, wait," Niko tried again, but the rag choked his words.

The elf grabbed Niko and pulled him to his feet. The sudden motion set his head spinning and his gut heaving. He couldn't make his feet work, or his thoughts. The elf shook him and grunted, shoving him stumbling out of the kitchen and down the hallway. Niko searched for any sign of Vasili, but saw only elves. So many. His chestnut horse lay in the garden, its guts steaming across the farmhouse path.

Niko choked out a sob.

"Hurry!" Julian barked. "We have a date with the king!"

THE FIENDS WERE SUPPOSED to work.

Bring him with us and the prince will follow.

Niko placed one boot in front of the other. He didn't look up.

The heat of the day felt like heavy hands pushing him down. Julian's hands. No, those were around his heart.

The fiends were supposed to work.

One shuffling step, then the next. Day and night.

His head throbbed and his chest burned, but his heart hurt the most.

He tried to reason with himself. Julian was under duress. They would hurt him if he didn't comply, torture him. But the more they walked, the more that rang false. Julian rode his horse far ahead, scouting, then returned with any reports of people to avoid. And the elves obeyed.

All but the big one, but he seemed content to go along with it. Julian wasn't a prisoner. He could gallop off at any second and not return.

The fiends were supposed to work...

It didn't make any sense.

The rag had dried and glued itself to his tongue and mouth. His throat was so tight every breath scratched it raw.

But Vasili wasn't here. The prince *had* gotten away, and it seemed Julian and these elves were searching for him.

Vasili would be halfway to the southern seas by now.

They stopped for water by a creek and made camp for a few hours. The big elf tied Niko's restraints to a tree, giving the rope a few good tugs to prove Niko wasn't getting away, and left him to his own devices.

Niko dozed fitfully and woke when Julian tugged the dried rag free, tearing Niko's lips.

"Drink." Julian crouched, upending a pouch of water into Niko's mouth. He drank too fast, almost choking, tasting his own blood, and was still parched when Julian took the pouch away and hooked it to his belt.

Gasping, he waited for the explanation, the excuses, but Julian straightened and was just going to walk away, to just leave, without a single word, as though Niko were nothing but his prisoner all over again.

"Wait," Niko croaked.

Julian pulled up short.

"Why?"

Julian's shoulders shifted, softening. He turned, trudged back and crouched in front of Niko. He stroked a finger down Niko's cheek, following the line of the raw cut the elf had given him. The smile on Julian's face was all wrong, changing him from the man Niko knew and loved to someone else entirely. Someone cruel.

Niko jerked his head away.

Julian suddenly clamped his hand on Niko's jaw and slammed Niko's head against the tree, jarring Niko's thoughts and making his head ache. He smiled and blinked slowly, lips parting. "You were the best fuck I've ever had." The man leering at Niko was not Julian. "I see your mind working. This must be difficult. Honest men like you—your weakness is your willingness to trust."

Julian didn't exist.

The gentle man Niko loved was a lie. But he couldn't let it go just yet. There still might be something Niko was missing, some element he didn't understand that made Julian work with them. "You don't have to do this. You can get away."

Julian ran his other hand down Niko's chest. "Those times you were in me, holding me down—I'll take those with me. There's nothing like the feel of a man like you against my back." His hand reached Niko's crotch and pinched. The sharp bite of pain jerked Niko's knees up and made him gasp. The light in Julian's gaze turned predatory. "With every lie, you fell harder. *Let's build a life together...*" he mocked. *"I love you."*

Niko swirled his tongue around his mouth, collected the small amount of liquid he could, and spat. Blood and spittle splashed Julian's cheek.

Slowly, he wiped it off and chuckled.

"You're no soldier," Niko said.

Julian's face warped into rage. He grabbed Niko by the throat, and pushed all his weight against it. Niko's lungs burned; he kicked out and thrashed, gagging for air. Tears leaked from his eyes.

"Neither are you, *Nikolas Yazdan*. Your own men feared you. Called you a butcher. Said you'd gone elf. I know you. You're a fucking animal, like me."

Then Julian rammed the rag back between his teeth, choking off Niko's gasps, tied it off, and left.

The next night, they tied Niko up to a new tree in a new camp, but this time nobody came.

CHAPTER 26

He'd given up trying to writhe free of the ropes binding his wrists. Tremors relentlessly assaulted his body. Each step was a mountain, like maybe it would be his last.

Too many days and nights. No food. No water. The trails they walked were never-ending.

He fell and cracked his knees on stones. Maybe he could rest a while. The big elf yanked him back to his feet and rattled him like a toy. Niko didn't care. Death could have him.

A necklace fell from inside the elf's collar and Niko's delirious mind focused on the strange, little talismans dangling in a row. He knew what they were, but his thoughts scurried from the terrible truth. Shades of pink and brown, tipped with tiny nails. Small, thin, delicate fingers.

Children's fingers.

The furious spark that had been simmering inside since the farmhouse blazed to life, bringing with it a growl.

He couldn't fight and win, but sometimes fighting was enough.

The line of elves was moving through the brush but the big elf hung back. "*Move.*" His horrible voice was more animal than man. He slammed both hands into Niko's shoulders. The forest tipped as Niko's back hit the ground, the air whooshing out of his lungs, stopped again by the gag.

The elf slammed a knee into Niko's middle, grinned maniacally, and produced a blade, its edge serrated like the elf's own teeth. A pinch at Niko's left ear warned him what was about to happen. Cold steel touched hot flesh. Pain burned through Niko's jaw and cheek. He shouted foul words around the rag and tried to buck and writhe, but the elf's knee dug deeper into his gut and the mounting pain in his ear thumped harder.

Thunder shook the ground, rolling on, coming closer. Niko tried to shove his bound hands at the elf, desperately seeking to lever him off.

A huge blade flashed behind the elf, arcing downward. It lodged in the back of the elf's neck. The elf jolted and swiped madly over his shoulder, trying to grab at the blade even as blood streamed down his neck and chest.

An enormous white horse reared. Its hooves punched the air, clipping the elf's head, knocking him down on top of Niko. The horse screamed and reared again. Through the blood and pain and chaos, fear surged through Niko's veins. He heaved himself out from under the elf a split second before the horse's massive hooves came down and smashed the elf's skull into the dirt.

"Wrists!" Vasili barked.

Niko stared up at the raging horse and its familiar white-haired rider.

"Nikolas," he said, softer now, using his name to organize Niko's shattered thoughts. "...your wrists."

Niko held out his bound wrists. The sword—*his* sword, he realized now his thoughts were beginning to catch up—carved down between his trembling hands and slit the ropes. He tore the filthy, blood-soaked gag free and almost sobbed with relief.

Vasili offered an arm. Niko grabbed it, swinging awkwardly onto Adamo. He flung his arms around Vasili's waist and clutched at the prince, plastering himself to his back. The thudding of his own ragged heart, the snorting, heaving horse and the blood in the air. It was too much.

"Hold on." Vasili yanked Adamo around and the tilt almost unseated Niko.

Adamo bolted through the brush, gathering speed as he veered around trees and jumped any that had fallen.

If the elves gave chase, Niko was too far lost to shock to know it. He listened to the horse's rhythmic hooves, to Vasili's pounding heart, and fought to hold on to Vasili. This was safer—not safe, far from that—but better. Vasili had come and Julian was...

He didn't know what Julian was anymore. He'd loved someone who didn't exist. The pain from that betrayal overshadowed the physical hurt. He must have been a fool not to see it. Julian had taken them to the farmhouse and gotten word to the elves, or he'd planned it all along to get the prince out of the palace.

But he'd mentioned the king, as though they were expected.

It didn't make any sense.

But mostly, it just hurt. Everywhere, all at once.

He hadn't grieved for Marcus because they'd known one of them would die first. But this wasn't war, and Niko had fallen for a lie. He had believed Julian so thoroughly, that what he felt now was worse than any physical pain.

Adamo slowed. The world had gone cold and distant. Niko's fingers slipped from Vasili's waist. Vasili shouted an alarm. The ground rushed up to meet him. But it wasn't so bad. It was quiet now. And the quiet didn't hurt.

THE BED WAS WARM, the room tiny. A small boy stared at him from the doorway. Niko blinked, and the lad had vanished.

He heard shoes shuffling outside along hallway floorboards.

"Mah! Mah! The mister is awake!"

"Shush, Ezio!" he heard a woman chide. "He don' need you screamin' the place down now, does he?"

Niko rolled his tongue around his mouth and wished he hadn't. Everything throbbed: his head, his back, his shoulders, but mostly his chest.

A woman appeared, her face wrinkled with smile lines and age. She dumped a hot mug of something sweet-smelling beside the bed, and wiped her hands on her apron. "S'all right," she said, "Rest up. You're safe here."

He tried to ask her where here was and who she was, but the pain was too much. It stole him away before the words could come.

The next time he woke, it wasn't a small boy watching him from the doorway, but Vasili, his tall, imposing figure leaned against the doorframe. His arms were crossed over his chest. His clothes were wrinkled and his wavy, tousled hair lay half over his face, covering his patch.

"Drink your medicine," Vasili said, and left.

"Yes, Your Highness," Niko muttered. He managed to keep the drink down despite the pungent herbs floating in it, and fell asleep again.

"HEY MISTER!" Ezio beamed at him from beside the bed. "How you feelin'?"

"Better," Niko croaked. The herbal drink, whatever it was, had cleared his head at least. He still ached and sweated and was in desperate need of relieving himself, but the boy stared at him, itching to ask his questions. The same boy from the stables in Tinken—so they'd reached the mining town. Niko remembered nothing of the journey and struggled to imagine himself slung across Adamo's rear as Vasili rode them to safety.

"Were you in a battle?" Ezio asked. "Did you fight elves? Mah says you're a soldier. I want to be a soldier but mah says I'm too young."

Vasili strolled into the room and ruffled the child's hair in such a startling display of relaxed normalcy that Niko could only blink at the easy-going prince.

"Off you go, Ezio." Vasili waited until the boy had left before perching on the edge of the bed. He pressed a finger to his lips, indicating they should be quiet. The boy likely hadn't gone far and was clearly a curious one. "You appear to be recovering well." The prince smiled. It wasn't a broad smile, or even a typical Vasili smile. But it was real, which was rare enough.

Niko reached around the back of his head and winced when his fingers brushed over a scabbed cut.

"When you fell from Adamo."

"Ah." He mostly remembered. The hitting the ground part, anyway. The rest was a blur, apart from Vasili almost taking off an elf's head and Adamo trampling him to death right after. "Thank you."

"It would have been sooner, but I had to wait for you to become separated from the rest."

Vasili had been stalking the elves all that time? Impressive. But why? Not for Niko, certainly. Probably for Julian. Did the prince know Julian had played and betrayed them both?

His chest ached. He rubbed the spot over his heart. "Where are the elves now?"

"They were heading for Loreen." He cast his gaze out of the small cottage window.

To the palace, to Vasili's father, but without the prince. In a rare moment of honesty, Vasili's gaze softened. His guard was down, and the ice within him had thawed. Here, on the edge of the bed, in a stranger's house, he seemed less distant and untouchable. It reminded him of the Vasili he'd observed chopping wood. Just a man unencumbered by the weight of the life he was trapped in.

Niko shifted higher against the headboard. "Julian..." How could he say it? Where to even begin?

"I saw." Vasili's cheek twitched. That was all the expression he allowed before the shutters came down again.

"He was taking me to the..." Niko trailed off, aware the

room wasn't private. "To your father. And there were some others things he said." Pain shot down Niko's neck. He gritted his teeth, fighting it off. The thudding eased, but the memories didn't.

Niko clenched his jaw until it ached.

"Rest. The Makibs are generous hosts," Vasili said. "They were more than happy to help after learning how we'd gotten lost on our ride and how your horse had thrown you." Vasili's gaze lingered. "We're safe," he whispered, leaning closer so only Niko could hear. A hesitation, a breath, a moment of knowing passed between them where it seemed Vasili would tell him everything. The weight in his gaze spoke of a terrible burden and a sadness Niko had not seen before. He knew Julian had lied to him too.

"We cannot stay for long." Vasili left the bed and headed for the door. "Dinner is at six. You will attend."

DINNER WAS PLEASANT, although Niko's appetite didn't stretch to much. The wine, which he'd drunk too quickly, had made his thoughts light and body numb. Vasili chatted with Diana Makibs, the lady of the house, and told Ezio a story about a prince who lived in a glass palace. Niko found himself staring more than once. Worse, Vasili caught the long looks too. The prince gave a small, private smile that would have been shy on anyone else but on him it looked like the edge of a blade, one he'd happily wield at any moment. This new prince unbalanced Niko more than any blow to the head.

He thanked Diana and Ezio for their generous help

and retired to his room, naturally gravitating toward the window to stand watch. The dark streets outside were quiet. A few citizens stumbled home from the bar. Someone smoked a pipe in the doorway of a terraced house opposite, the end glowing with his every draw.

The door gently clicked closed behind Niko.

When the prince didn't speak, Niko glanced over to find him bracing his forearm against the window frame, scanning the street for fiends, soldiers, and friends who were enemies.

"I had no idea," Niko whispered. "I didn't see any of his lies." And it was all lies, from the moment they'd met in the Stag and Horn, through every touch, every kiss and lazy smile.

"It is done."

For him, maybe. Niko had loved the man. Still did. And that pain in his chest, that feeling as though someone had ripped out his heart, that wasn't fading. If he thought about it too long, he'd fall to his knees and weep. He hated Julian, but he hated himself more, for being so thoroughly led along.

Clearing the knot in his throat, he asked, "How did you escape the farmhouse?"

"I don't sleep." Vasili kept his unblinking gaze on the street.

"He said something about the fiends," Niko whispered. "He said they were supposed to work. He knows who sent them."

Vasili slumped against the wall and released a breath. "Julian sent the fiends, Niko. Each time." His eye closed, and a frown cut deep lines into his pale face. "He sent the first in the palace, thinking I slept," Opening his eye he looked down, "hoping to render me helpless. He sent the second as a test to see how you would react—whether you'd let it kill me or not. And the one at the farmhouse. That one... That one almost succeeded while he distracted you."

Gods, the pain in his chest could choke him. While Julian had whispered about impossible dreams, he'd known the fiend was about to attack Vasili. His heart still refused to believe it. "But how can he control them? He's not a sorcerer."

Vasili cocked his head. "The elves harvested my blood and with it, whatever dregs of the flame it contains. Is it really such a stretch that they found a desperate prisoner to make their pawn and poured my blood down his throat?" He folded his arms, closing himself off. "He's always worked with them..." He trailed off and his frown cut deeper, gathering shadows on his face. He looked up, right at Niko. "I didn't escape the elves. Julian released me. I unwittingly brought a spy back to the court."

"How long have you known?" Ice constricted his heart, weighing it down with a terrible sense of dread.

"He is convincing and I was weak. Initially, I believed he was good. He went to great lengths to earn my trust. We were close. I thought I understood him."

Niko swallowed the knot in his throat. He had trusted Julian too, believing every lie. "How long have you known, Vasili?"

Vasili's lips turned down. "A few months. When I found you in the pleasure house, I suspected his motives weren't honest. I needed someone unbiased from outside the palace who could see through his lies. He'd get close to you, test you, try and understand why I'd brought you in. I needed him distracted and focused on someone else to give me room to think—"

Months. Through everything, Vasili had been watching, planning, maneuvering Niko. "You've known for a few months and you let me *fall in love with him*?"

Vasili looked over. His frown turned to contempt. "Who you love is not my concern."

A bright, sharp stab of rage made Niko gasp. He stepped up close to the prince, watching him lift his chin in defiance and give no ground. "You used me to get to him!" he hissed.

"I used you to get to the elves!" Vasili hissed back, punctuating the line with a fist at his side. "And I'll not hesitate to do the same again. If you're looking for compassion or empathy, you'll not find it in me."

"You have made that *perfectly* clear."

"This city, its people, I have to protect them from myself. From the cursed flame that drives Cavilles insane, and from the elves. It's all I am. So don't look at me like I disgust you, Nikolas. I've never pretended to be anything other than a Caville. I don't have time for your petty drama and emotional affairs with the enemy. I brought you in to distract Julian and to find out if he truly was the one trying to undermine my efforts to stop my father. Whatever you think of my methods, it worked. Julian has revealed exactly who he is."

Despite his treacherous actions, Julian had been right. Vasili didn't care about anyone, and he'd used Niko from the moment they'd met. It shouldn't have surprised Niko. Every time he thought the prince had a heart, Vasili proved him wrong.

"I'd like you to leave this room, Your Highness."

Vasili clenched his teeth. "I can't stop Julian and my father without you. And if I don't stop them, Loreen will fall to the elves. Hate me if you must, but think of the city you fought for and the people your soldiers died for. Elves are here, Niko. They're probably walking through the palace gates right now, welcomed by my father's open arms. Your love is worthless. It's your hate I need."

Rage burned the back of Niko's tongue. "Oh, you have that, *my prince*. Now leave, before I make you."

CHAPTER 27

They left Diana and Ezio's house after midnight. On their way out, Vasili tossed what remained of his courtly jewelry onto a side table as though it were worthless. Each ring would probably fetch half a year's wages for most people, and Vasili had thrown down three. He appeared eager to be free of them except for the griffin ring, which he took from his pocket and slid back onto his finger.

Shedding more layers, Niko thought.

Niko had caught glimpses of the real Vasili—when he'd told stories to the boy, chopping wood, settling Adamo with a touch and word—but that prince was so deeply buried beneath his Caville exterior he might as well not be real. Now they were heading back to the palace, and with the prince's harsh words still ringing in his ears, the more vulnerable Vasili was a distant memory.

They rode double on Adamo, Niko pressed tightly enough to Vasili's back that he felt every shift in the prince's tense muscles. The silence between them sharpened to an edge until they reached the rolling fields outside Loreen. Vasili reined Adamo back, taking a moment to survey the land and the palace beyond. The horse shifted from hoof to hoof, eager to gallop home.

The city and its granite palace shimmered like a crown of glass propped on distant hills.

"There are old service tunnels that cut through the rock. They lead into the northern face of the palace," Vasili said. "We'll use them to get inside."

Mention of the secret tunnels would have been useful when they'd fled the palace. "If you're ever under siege, that palace will be a nightmare to defend."

He caught a hint of a smile at the corner of the prince's mouth. "We have other means of deterring attackers."

"Your personality?" Niko mumbled.

Vasili huffed a short, sharp laugh. It was fleeting, but real. It almost made Niko smile, but then the sun caught the glistening palace and his mood soured.

He eased his grip on Vasili and the prince's shoulders dropped a little, tension easing. The prince hadn't mentioned his discomfort at being touched, but hadn't needed to.

"Getting inside the palace will be easier than getting close to my father."

They had to assume there were elves nearby. Talos was compromised. And Julian had the ear of the palace guards, probably the ear of the king himself. Allies within those walls would be difficult to root out, but Niko knew of one.

"Lady Maria will conceal us," Niko said, "if we can reach her rooms without being seen."

Vasili was quiet for a moment. "My aunt?"

"She's helped me in the past, in a Cavilles typically backwards way."

"I'd overlooked her," Vasili admitted, sounding as though he'd relish the opportunity to have another relative to manipulate.

"She has not overlooked you. In fact, she's been paying attention more than most. She told me of the flame, and she called you the cuckoo in the nest."

Vasili made a noise that was probably part disgust, part surprise. "Cuckoos are horrible birds."

"Then she's not wrong."

Adamo snorted. "Hush you," Vasili said, either to Adamo or Niko. The horse pulled on his reins, chewing on the bit, and pawed the soil.

Unless Niko was mistaken, Vasili was delaying. He didn't want to go back, and Niko couldn't blame him. For all its beauty, the Cavilles' home was the last place Niko wanted to be, and he'd spent eight years on the front.

"I hate you, your highness," Vasili tensed again, his back straightened, "but you have my blade," Niko said softly. He didn't mean to speak the words directly into the prince's ear, but given their proximity, it was difficult not to be intimate. He noted Vasili's short, sharp inhale, and expected a wicked retort.

"Good, because there is more at stake than a black-smith's broken heart. Now hold on." Vasili gave Adamo a sharp kick, and Niko grabbed Vasili around the waist as Adamo took off.

LADY MARIA FROZE in her chamber doorway, eyes blown wide. The glass she was holding fell from her fingers and shattered against the marble floor.

Niko quickly stepped forward, a hand out to placate her. "We're not here to hurt you. Please, don't alert the guards."

"We?" She glanced behind Niko to where Vasili still stood in shadow. Her brow pinched. Gathering her skirts to avoid the broken glass, she glided across the room to a sideboard and poured herself a fresh glass of wine. Niko didn't miss how her hand shook.

"Well, this is an unexpected surprise. Two handsome, if rugged men inside my chambers." She brought the glass to her lips and sipped, then turned to face them. "The king will kill me if he learns you are both here."

"He won't know." Niko stepped closer and glanced behind him for aid, but Vasili remained in shadow, gauging his aunt, carefully calculating the woman he'd to-date barely glanced at.

"Why are you here?" Maria asked. "Why aren't you a thousand miles away, Nikolas?"

"I've asked myself that a great deal these past few days. We—*Vasili* needs your help."

She cradled her glass to her chest and slid her gaze to Vasili. "Your Highness."

"Aunt," Vasili acknowledged, slithering from the shadows into the light. "My advisor tells me you are to be trusted. Know that if you reveal my presence here, you will not see the light of day for a very long time."

Niko closed his eyes. Did the prince not know how to be cordial at all? Threats would only push her away. But when he opened his eyes again, Maria smiled.

"Always the Caville," she said. "I came to love that wicked streak in your uncle."

"My uncle spent more time outside the palace than in it—"

"I wonder why," Niko muttered, receiving a razorlike glance from Vasili.

"It is good that you're here, Vasili." Maria bowed her head. "The king's madness has grown worse in your absence. Court is rife with rumors of elves in the city, but he ignores the reports in favor of ludicrous feasts and debauchery. Your family, your staff—forgive my bluntness, Your Highness—are terrified of him."

"We intend to rectify the situation with your help" Vasili drew up alongside Niko. "We will need proper attire, and paper. Can I trust you to hand-deliver a number of letters?"

"Of course. I've been waiting for you to spread your wings, Vasili. I'm honored and relieved you've chosen me."

He inclined his head, the gesture regal. "You have my advisor, Nikolas, to thank. He trusts you." His aunt smiled warmly in return.

Maria left some paper for them and went to find fresh clothing. Vasili was quick to take up a pen and begin writing, leaving Niko to strip off his shirt and drag a cloth down his face, arms, and chest. He found a shaving kit and smoothed his chin. With the rugged look gone, he could pretend the farmhouse and all its revelations hadn't happened. He was the same Nikolas as before, advisor to the prince, nothing more or less.

With his letters written and stacked on the side of his aunt's dresser, Vasili pulled off his shirt and washed without comment.

Niko approached the window and scanned the palace's many maze-like walkways, gardens, and courtyards stretching down the hill. Beyond the grounds, Loreen glittered in the sun, deceptively beautiful and serene, belying the tension that must by now be thick in the streets.

Vasili's reflection drew Niko's eye. Niko watched his long fingers gather up the washcloth and stroke it down corded arms.

Niko blinked and looked away, thinking instead of the elves who had infiltrated the city through Julian's treachery. They were likely waiting to strike. It was the nightmare Niko had spent eight years trying to prevent.

Niko squeezed his eyes closed, thinking of the things Julian had said. *Will you have me?* He'd spoken words of love and kindness. His touch had been so gentle. He was supposed to be good. He was supposed to be the hope in Niko's life. And to think Niko had dreamed of rebuilding the forge with him. The man had deceived him, but in many ways, he'd done worse to Vasili.

"He said he held your hand," Niko said softly.

Vasili's reflection in the window paused. He gripped the washbasin sides and bowed his head, spreading his shoulders, making the scars on his back stretch. "That is true."

Vasili's harsh words about not caring—Niko wondered now if they were true, or a barrier the prince had erected to protect himself and keep others out. Julian had lured him into a relationship at a time when Vasili was at his most vulnerable and used him to get inside the court.

"What else did he say?" Vasili asked casually, resuming his washing.

They kept you in a cage, bled you, held you down... Niko swallowed. "Nothing."

Niko still loved Julian and wanted to forgive him. To find the reason behind it all. To rescue him. They were foolish thoughts. The man might have been good, once, but whatever the elves had done to him had tainted him, turned him, made him wicked. Julian hadn't survived the elves. It was a miracle Vasili had.

Lady Maria returned with armfuls of neatly folded clothes. She and Vasili discussed the delivery of the letters, and then she was gone again. Vasili armored himself in his courtly attire, applying layer after layer of Caville poise until there was nothing left of the man who'd told stories of glass palaces. In royal blue and gold, his good eye regained its sharp, deadly spark of intelligence.

Niko donned a black and gold lord's suit, similar to the style he'd worn when he'd been promoted. He stared at his reflection, wanting to rip it all off again and burn it, along with the rest of this place.

"What was in the letters?" Niko asked, observing Vasili's reflection beside his own. Niko was dark to Vasili's light, but neither of them could be called good.

"A call to arms," Vasili drawled, like such things were routine.

There had only been eight letters. Were eight allies enough to overthrow the king? Vasili knew what he was doing. He'd been away a long time, but he'd also had fourteen years inside these walls, surviving his own family before the elves had captured him. He'd already tried to murder the king once, and he'd been manipulating the spy at his side. He was more than capable of doing what needed to be done.

Vasili twisted the griffin ring on his finger. It was a symbol of protection. Niko had followed the banner into battle, and he'd follow it again now. Not for the prince, but because it was the right thing to do. Loreen's people deserved to have someone fight for them, and Vasili shouldn't have to be alone.

"So, how do we play this?" Niko asked.

Vasili smiled his sinister Caville smile. "Carefully."

CHAPTER 28

They were to meet their co-conspirators in Vasili's little-used library. Niko's fingers twitched at his sides, eager for his sword as he walked beside the prince through shadowy back corridors, but the weapon remained in Lady Maria's care for now.

Appearing in person was dangerous, but necessary. Vasili needed to build trust. His written words were not enough to convince his allies of his good intentions, and there was no better way for a prince to rally his troops than in close quarters.

The small library smelled of dust and books, just as it had when Niko first visited, searching for information on the family and its curse. It was busier now. He recognized some of the lords and ladies of the court, and Lady Maria herself, wrapped in red and brown silks. She stood perfectly still with her hands clasped in front of her. She'd always been in motion when he'd met with her before. Instincts warned him too late.

Niko gripped Vasili's shoulder and yanked him to a stop. "This isn't—"

The door they'd just passed through slammed shut. Bolts rang home. Guards poured from behind the bookshelves, their ambush sprung.

Niko shoved Vasili aside and took a swing at a guard rushing in, knocking the man to the ground. Another lunged. A steel fist struck Niko's chin, whipping his head back. Shouts and scuffling filled the room. Someone kicked Niko's leg out, shoved him to his knees, and yanked his head back. Steel licked his throat. Niko froze.

Three guards had Vasili pinned against a bookcase. The prince hissed through his teeth, his eye wild with fury, but they held him fast.

The lords and ladies had scattered, fleeing to the far corners. Amir emerged from one of them to join Lady Maria's side. He stroked his aunt's shoulder and she smiled at him with more heat in her eyes than was right for an aunt.

"Oh, isn't this absolutely perfect?" Amir grinned. He towered over Niko. His eyes narrowed into dagger-like slits. "I finally have you on your knees."

Niko pulled on the hands clamping his arms behind him, but the blade at his throat dug in.

"The dog returns," Amir purred. "Loyal and stupid."

Niko glanced behind Amir at Lady Maria and found her expression one of mild amusement. Was nobody in this palace honorable, or was Niko the fool to look for honor in such a dark place?

He'd made a terrible mistake. Amir and Lady Maria— they were more closely aligned than he'd thought.

"Don't do this, Amir," Vasili growled. "Father is insane. He plans to hand the court to the elves. You know—"

Amir nodded, and a guard thrust a mailed fist into Vasili's gut. The prince doubled over, choking on his words.

Amir purred in delight. The tip of his tongue stroked his top lip. "Do I keep you for myself or gift you to my father?" He straightened. "Perhaps some fun first." He snapped his fingers. "Gag my brother and cover his head." Looking up, he addressed the courtly fools cowering in the corners. "If any of you speak a word of this, I'll take your tongues. Vasili did not return, and this dog"—he flung a finger at Niko—"is mine." Turning to the guards holding Vasili back, he snarled, "Put my brother in the deepest, darkest hole you can find and let him rot."

"Amir," Vasili wheezed. "You are a Caville. We are protectors. Stop father's madness. Stop the elves before it's too late."

Amir gripped his brother's chin. Vasili's eye widened, his nostrils flaring. Ragged breaths hissed through his clenched teeth. "That day the elves took you," Amir said, "I was there. I saw them come, watched them tie you up and carry you away. I could have told the guards, and they might have been able to stop them. Instead, I played in the garden until the sun set. By the time your absence was noticed, the elves were hours away and I sent the palace guards searching in the wrong direction." Amir paused, letting his words sink in. "You should have died in their cage, dear brother. Now you will die in mine."

A guard thrust a rag into Vasili's mouth. He thrashed his head and kicked out, but then Amir spread his hand on

Vasili's chest. Vasili stilled, as though Amir had snuffed out all his rage with a single touch.

"There, brother," Amir said. "You know it's easier to just lie back and give up. I hear that's what you did for years."

Vasili's head dropped, his body falling limply. The guards dragged him past Niko. He didn't look up.

Niko watched him go, fearing that without Vasili, there would be nobody left to stop the madness to come.

"You wretched son of a whore—"

A guard punched Niko in his gut, the heavy gauntlet stealing all of Niko's breath, making him choke. Hands pulled him onto his back. A kick to his wounded rib sent pain cracking through Niko like a whip. He gasped, curling around the agony. More armored blows landed to the sound of Amir's laughter.

HE CAME BACK to consciousness dangling from the beam of a four-poster bed with the screams of doomed soldiers in his ears. But those were old ghosts, and only in his head. Fire burned through his biceps and down his back. His own bodyweight tried to pop his shoulders from their sockets.

He twisted uselessly, and looked up. The thick rope tying his wrists together had been thrown over the beam and tied off. He couldn't help but think of the poor girl hung from her ceiling by a rope just like this one.

His legs were bound at the ankle, the toes of his boots barely brushing the floor.

Whoever had strung him up like a butchered pig

hadn't gagged him. Niko called for help, for anyone, until he was out of breath, his voice torn. The door opened and a brief flicker of hope quickly died at the sight of Amir. Julian following behind brought a snarl to Niko's lips.

Niko's gaze bounced between them. Amir headed for a sideboard and poured a drink from a decanter. He removed a coin pouch from the cupboard below. Blue powder puffed from the top when he set it down next to his drink.

Spice.

"The Bastard Butcher." Amir grinned, leaning against the sideboard, drink in hand. "Makes me wonder if your daddy fucked you up before you went to war, huh? Did you always like cutting bits off animals before you tried it on elves?"

"You piece of shit, Amir. Come closer and I'll fuck *you* up, you rat bastard."

He chuckled. "I do so love that mouth. You were right to leave him ungagged, Julian."

Niko turned his face away. He would not look at Julian. Couldn't. "That guard is a traitor. He works with elves."

Amir laughed again and sprinkled some spice into his drink. "This war with the elves is so unnecessary. They are simple creatures. Give them what they want and they'll go away."

"And what do you think they want?"

"You won't believe it, but they want my father. They had a taste of Vasili and found they liked Caville ass. Some ridiculous mythical nonsense about a flame. Who knows? Who cares?" He drank and appraised Niko. "Julian speaks for them and we have an understanding. When the time is right, the elves will take Talos. A terrible tragedy." He gestured, coming forward a few strides. "And with poor Vasili incapacitated by madness, Carlo tragically lost to a riding accident..." He glanced at Julian, his sly eyes making it clear Carlo's death was no accident. "That just leaves me." Sighing dramatically, he pressed a hand to his chest in mock-humbleness. "The crown is a heavy burden, but one I shall be honored to wear."

Niko barked a shallow laugh. "You're so selfish, you can't see what's really happening."

"Says the dog tied to my bed."

"Elves don't negotiate. They'll take the king, then they'll take you, this palace, and everyone in Loreen."

Amir moved closer still, his face so close Niko saw spice sparkling on his lips. "Where did you even come from? Vasili scraped you off the floor of some whorehouse, I hear." He reached up to touch Niko's face. Niko tore his head away. The prince's fingers sank behind Niko's shirt collar, and with a vicious burst of spice-induced strength, he tugged the collar apart. Buttons pinged and the fabric tore. Niko swung from his wrists, snarling.

"You going to fuck me, Amir? Finally going to use that little princely cock of yours? If you can find it."

Amir tilted his head and laughed. "Not me. Him." He jerked his thumb over his shoulder. "And you'll be so high on spice, you'll beg him for more."

The words hooked in like nothing else the prince had said. He could endure Amir's short-lived thrusting, but not Julian's. It would rip out the last pieces of Niko's heart. "Don't." The word slipped free.

"Oh, he got you good, didn't he? You love him." Amir pouted. "Poor, beaten dog." Amir grabbed Niko's hair and yanked his head back. Like before, during Amir's orgy, wine poured over his mouth and nose and ran down his neck, soaking into his clothes.

"Hold his nose!" Amir snapped.

Julian was suddenly in sight, his smile hungry and hurtful. He dutifully pinched Niko's nose and it felt like a betrayal all over again.

"Breathe, damn you," Amir cursed. "Open once for me, you little bitch."

Defiance was pointless, but he held out until his heart pounded in his ears and his vision darkened. He gasped. Bitter wine poured in, choking him. He spluttered it up, but more wine went down until Amir clamped a hand under Niko's jaw, ramming his teeth closed.

"There's a good dog." The prince grinned, his face wet and flushed with spilled wine and spice.

The second Amir's grip eased, Niko spat in his face. Amir slammed his mouth into Niko's, withdrawing just as quickly to avoid losing his tongue between Niko's teeth. "Oh, you're going to take his cock, dog, and then, when you're writhing in his seed, you're going to take mine in that troublesome mouth of yours, and you're going to *fucking beg for it!*"

Spice crackled along Niko's veins, and his nerves awoke with a tingle. Pain sparked, the rising bite of it tipping toward unwanted desire.

Julian's soft hand stroked down Niko's cheek, and Niko moaned out all the hurt. Yes, Julian's touch was everything. No, Julian wasn't Julian. He wasn't Niko's Julian.

"Hard for me already," Julian whispered over Niko's lips. His hand found Niko's straining erection. "Spice is so accommodating."

Niko opened his eyes and fell into Julian's beautiful gaze. "Bastard," he slurred. "I love you."

"I know."

"Why do this?"

"Because..." His hand molded to Niko's cock, rubbing, and Niko arched into it, seeking friction and the buzz of pleasure. "I died in that fucking war for nothing."

"You didn't die," Niko whispered. "I'd have saved you. We could have had something... a life together. You said... you wanted it."

Julian snorted. "The Julian you love died alone, crying for help. No heroes came for him, just elves. They had a prince in a cage. They licked the blood right off his skin and drank it from his veins. I drank it too, though he never knew—"

Niko thought of the brief slips in Vasili's hard mask and the vulnerable prince those glimpses revealed. "He knows."

"He tasted of strength and power. I did not have to be weak anymore. They gave me life..." Julian's tongue traced Niko's lips. "And a power unlike anything else in the world. Mostly, they gave me a chance at revenge against the royals who abandoned every single one of us at that godsforsaken killing ground."

The words were horrible and wrong but Niko couldn't unhear them, and with Julian's hand rubbing him through his clothes, he just wanted that touch, his beautifully soft mouth on Niko's skin. He knew revenge. Knew the sour taste of betrayal too. He'd been betrayed by a king, and now by a lover.

Julian eased around behind Niko's prone form, trailing breaths against his neck and shoulder. He briefly knelt and using a pocketknife taken from his pants pocket, he sliced the ties holding Niko's ankles together. As he rose, his gloved hands stroked up Niko's thighs, tucked into his trouser waist, and pulled them down. Cool air kissed Niko's back. Spice made the cold feel heavenly against his hot skin.

Julian knelt on the bed behind Niko. His fingers spread Niko's ass. Niko opened his eyes. Julian's right hand swept over his hip and pulled Niko's erection free of his clothes. Amir watched from the sideboard across the room, eyes glassy and pupils blown wide from spice, his cock an untouched rod in his trousers.

Hate scorched Niko's soul. Hate for all of them, for this prison palace, and for the Cavilles within it. But even in hate, he understood it. Niko could have been Julian. He might even have been worse. War changed people. It had changed Niko, made him dark inside. Julian was a victim too.

Julian's hard cock pushed at Niko's hole and his hand pumped Niko's erection, summoning waves of heat and disgust. The spice-induced lust overrode everything, made Niko breathless and maddened with desperation. Julian's slick shaft entered, the pressure too much—until it wasn't.

Pleasure spiked. Niko gasped. Julian bit down into his shoulder, grunting and thrusting. Niko spiraled over the edge, losing his seed in Julian's hand, and stared Amir in the eyes, issuing a challenge. *Fuck me then, prince. If you dare touch the Butcher.*

"Cut him down," Amir barked, clumsily setting his drink aside.

Julian's grunts built. His thrusts came faster, hips slapping Niko's ass, rocking Niko's body.

Niko stared into Amir's brittle blue eyes.

"Cut him down now!" Amir ordered.

"I'm not fucking... finished," Julian responded.

"You'll finish when I order it!"

Julian growled low and pulled out, reached up and used the pocketknife to slash Niko free. Niko slumped into his arms, heart and body throbbing hot.

"Lay him down."

Julian arranged Niko on the bed. A moment passed between them as their gazes locked. It was nothing intimate; more an understanding. This was the real Julian. A man tossed aside in war. A man desperate for vengeance by any means necessary. He didn't care about any of this and certainly didn't care about the Cavilles and their politics.

Amir hastily climbed onto the bed, unlaced his trousers, and clasped his swollen erection. He straddled Niko's chest, pointing his cock at Niko's chin. "Suck me off, dog."

Niko bared his teeth.

Amir gripped Niko's cheeks, dug his fingers in and pried open his mouth. "Hm... more spice, maybe? Julian—"

Julian's pocketknife suddenly came around Amir's throat from behind the prince to press against his vulnerable throat. "I said I wasn't finished." Julian sneered against Amir's cheek, his eyes flicking to Niko.

Amir froze, cock still in his hand, grip still on Niko's face. He swallowed. "Cut me and I'll have the rest of your fingers taken!"

"You princes are so fucking *pathetic*." Julian hauled Amir backward, off Niko and threw him to the floor. "I don't follow Caville orders anymore, you sniveling worm. When the elves get here, you're as dead as the rest of your people. There's no deal, no peace, no nothing... Now Talos is within reach, they'll take your daddy, bleed him and consume the flame."

"W-what? You said... Talos...you were going to take Talos away!"

"I am. *We* are. And everything else, including you, just like Niko said. If you thought more with your head and less with your dick, prince, you'd have seen all the work I've done to undermine everything you thought was yours. You even removed Vasili, the most dangerous weapon you Cavilles have."

Amir scrabbled to his feet and dashed out the door in a blur, leaving Julian cursing. "Fucking Cavilles!"

"Go after him?" Niko mumbled, his tongue heavy. "He likes to... talk."

"He's as high as a kite. Nobody will listen to his ranting." Julian leaned forward. "I'm far more interested in having you right where I want you. You never saw the lies... thought I was naïve and shy." Julian's heated attention crawled all over Niko. "I'm going to fuck you so hard, Nikolas Yazdan, you'll taste me in your dreams. It's just a shame Vasili isn't here. He's so desperate for love, even the twisted kind, he'd beg to watch. The whip that so shocked you... It was delicious, every time, and Vasili liked it. He can't get off like you and me, eight years of having your body carved up does shit to a man's head, but oh how he loves to bring that whip down and I fucking loved to take it."

The words swam in Niko's addled mind, striking his heart like their own kind of lashing.

He reached beneath Niko and sliced the ropes from his wrists. His mouth brushed Niko's, sealing against it in a slow, lavish kiss. "Poor broken prince. They're all broken. Every single one. Driven mad by their own blood. Carlo was fucking terrifying. But the runt watched me too damn closely. He had to die. It was a mercy, really. But you? You were a challenge I relished. The gentle, but deadly Nikolas Yazdan."

With his hands freed, Niko clasped Julian's face and kissed him back, their tongues and teeth clashing. He then gripped harder, hooking his legs around Julian's to hold him close. Spice tried to convince him this was right, but he hadn't consumed as much as Amir had planned. Despite the lust, he still had control. Enough to know this was wrong, and it had to end. Now.

He smashed his forehead hard against Julian's nose. Pain flashed. Julian screeched and tried to buck free, but Niko dug his thumbs into Julian's pretty blue eyes.

I won't leave Vasili. I can't. I'm asking if you'll still have me, even with the horrible parts of me I can't ignore. It's who I am.

Niko heard Julian's words again. Desperate words hidden in lies. A cry for help from a soldier lost so long ago. In the beginning—before the farmhouse—he'd released Niko from the prison cells, a moment of weakness? Or proof, perhaps, of the good man Julian must have once been. But drinking the Caville blood, the war—that good solider was too far gone. Nobody had saved Julian then, but Niko could now. In the only way left for him.

I love you.

Spice tried to wreck his mind, tearing it to shreds, bringing old horrors into the room—memories of his own hands drowned in elf blood, hearing his own laugh as he'd torn open elf chest cavities and ripped elf hearts from their chests to crush them in his fist—and Niko needed

312

those memories. He needed to be that man again, that butcher, the soldier he'd left behind at the front. He pushed his thumbs deeper into the slippery, resisting orbs. Julian howled and tried to stab wildly with the pocketknife, but Niko had clamped him too close. The short blade nicked Niko's shoulder and his neck.

Julian's eyes collapsed. He screamed—screamed like the soldiers had screamed when the elves cut them down —and dropped the knife. Niko freed him. He scrambled backward on the bed, clawing at his face, screams turning to mumbles.

Niko gulped air, mind and body adrift. He snatched the fallen pocketknife.

The mumbling ceased. Julian's lips curved into a smile and he began to whisper. The sounds were familiar, rising up like the wind through the trees.

A breeze tore through the room, slamming the open window against the wall. Julian's gloved fingers danced, his whispers growing louder, and wispy, inky smoke gathered in his palms. Dark power. Rare. Impossible. But *real* and born of Vasili's blood.

It was true, all of it. Julian had played everyone—for the elves.

Niko grabbed Julian's scalp, held him firm, and thrust the blade into Julian's throat, tearing it out, taking the sorcerer's words with it.

Blood bubbled from Julian's lips. He clutched at his blood-soaked neck, and smiled.

"I'm sorry," Niko choked out. "So sorry..." By the three gods, what had he done?

The wind tossed the open window into the wall again.

Niko crawled from Julian's twitching body and stumbled from the bed, thumping onto the floor. The chilling wind whirled inside the chamber. With bloody, trembling hands, Niko tried to climb to his feet and right his clothes, still throbbing and raw from abuse. He sobbed again, mind breaking apart, but he could do this, just hang onto the pieces of himself and keep them together, just a little while longer.

Gods, Julian's blood painted his hands. His gut heaved. He reached for the bed post.

A blur of blackness— with claws and a wide, gaping mouth—slammed into him. Niko brought his forearm up, blocking the creature from clamping onto his chest, but it dug its thin fingers in and pulled. Niko rolled, plunging the small knife into its flimsy form over and over. It wailed and skittered across the floor, then whipped its head around and hissed. Red eyes burned with animal viciousness.

Niko scrabbled to his feet and sprinted out the door. He hit the hallway wall, almost fell, and stumbled on, recognizing the awful colored walls as Amir's wing of the palace. He dragged his bruised, spice-addled body toward a set of stairs.

The fiend slammed into his back. Niko's head struck a wall, stunning him. Fingers wrapped around his throat. Niko dug under them, tried to pry them off. The floor vanished, becoming a set of stairs leading down, and he fell again, tumbling with the creature clutched close until hitting the landing. He'd lost the knife but the fiend's grip eased. Niko slammed his head back, felt something give, and the fiend's grip vanished.

He didn't look. Couldn't. He staggered on, falling into a sloppy lope, then plowed into Lady Maria's chamber door. It flew open, and he stumbled inside.

Maria let out a sharp cry.

"Sword!" he barked.

"Nikolas! What—"

The fiend crawled around the door, up the wall, and sprang. Niko tried to twist away, but the creature's fingers found his throat again, and its mouth closed over his. Ice poured down his throat and into his chest. He staggered backward, still trying to prize it off, but the spice was addling his head and his body was ruined and by the three, this was how he died, having the life sucked out of him by a summoned nightmare.

Niko's sword blade flashed and Maria roared. The fiend fell limp and slipped from Niko's body into a heap on the floor. Its shadowy form dissipated, leaving behind something twisted and warped, like an elf, but its skin hung limp off jagged bones.

Niko dragged himself to the nearby bed and propped himself against it. *Breathe in, breathe out...* but everything hurt. Maria stood trembling, the sword pointed downward, her face frozen in shock.

"Nikolas," she breathed his name in desperation, "I had to tell Amir you were back," she said, "I didn't want any of this. Please, you must believe me."

He didn't. He'd never believe a Caville again. But it hardly mattered. "Vasili," he rasped. "Take me to him."

CHAPTER 29

*M*aria clutched at the bars to the empty cell. "He was supposed to be here. Amir said he'd keep him here."

Niko leaned against the cold, damp wall outside the cell and tried to keep his trembling legs from giving out. Vasili wasn't where he was supposed to be. Laughter tried to bubble free. Of course Vasili had slithered off somewhere. He'd probably planned this all along. Had the library been a distraction? Was *Niko* the distraction?

"You're a grunt. A tool. My tool."

He'd always served the Cavilles, both willingly and not. It didn't matter. Vasili cracked the whip and Niko danced. The prince had told him the truth, but Niko kept on trying to make Vasili into something reasonable, something normal. Why? Why did Niko fall into the same trap?

He looked at the dried blood under his nails and crusted between the creases of his palms, and let the manic, spice-induced laughter go.

Lady Maria leaned a shoulder against the cell bars, her

face pensive. She lifted her sultry eyes, but instead of conveying fear or regret, she looked at him in defiance. And Niko realized she hadn't been surprised Vasili wasn't here. Her earlier words had been as flat as a poor actress playing her role. She *knew* he wouldn't be here.

"You let him go."

She stared back, the answer loud in her silence.

"He set it up... All of it. Amir brought him here and you, my lady, let him go." Yes, it was perfect. Maria *was* loyal to Vasili, but slept in Amir's bed. Oh Vasili played a dangerous game. Fuck the princes and their lies. The Cavilles, Julian, this godsforsaken palace. "I'm going to burn this whole place to the ground with all you bastards in it," he growled, shoving past Lady Maria.

He returned to Lady Maria's room, grabbed his sword in one hand and the fiend's limp carcass in the other, and dragged the creature behind him, stopping only when he caught sight of his reflection in Maria's mirror. Blood splatters had dried on his face. His lips bore a mad sneer and his eyes were wild. Those mad eyes belonged to someone who shouldn't have come back from the front line.

Amir wanted the Butcher. He'd fucking have him now.

"Nikolas, where are you going?" Maria demanded. "Wait... If you act too soon he won't be ready!"

He really didn't give a shit whether Vasili was ready or not, and left her far behind as he pulled the dead fiend through the corridors.

There were no guards outside the feasting hall, and those inside didn't see him in the crowd until he almost reached the king. Gasps accompanied his arrival. A lord swore and drew his blade. Niko bared his teeth. Maybe it was the madness in his eyes, or the carcass in his wake, but the lord quickly backed off.

Talos's laughter rang bright and striking at the end of the feasting table. It soon died as the people fell silent. He grabbed his cane and pushed to his feet. *"What is this?!"* the king bellowed.

Niko stalked forward and no guard dared move in to stop him. They hung back, waiting for instructions. They weren't fools. Some would have served the Cavilles in the war, and they might recognize the creature Niko had brought them. They'd certainly recognize the wild look on Niko's face. Maybe they'd even heard of the Butcher. A soldier so wild he'd cut up elf carcasses and left them rotting on stakes as a warning—just like the elves.

He flung the body down in front of Talos and scowled at the shocked faces in the room. "Your king is a traitor!" All of them, in their fine lace and jewelry were living a luxurious fantasy. But they couldn't pretend the fiends didn't exist when one was leaking blood on the floor. "The elves are among us. Your king and Prince Amir invited them in!"

Talos blustered, face reddening. "Guards, detain him!"

The guards hesitated. Niko searched their faces, seeing their external and internal scars. They were fellow soldiers. Men who had seen the horrors and fought in spite of them. Loyalty born in battle was stronger than that paid for by coin.

"Detain him or I'll execute all of you!"

A few hesitantly moved in. "Stop!" Niko ordered. "In the name of Prince Vasili Caville, the true protector of this city, *I command you to stop.*"

The dead fiend, the blood on Niko's face and clothes,

and the urgency in his voice commandeered the guards' attention. They were listening to him.

"How dare you come into my court"—the king stabbed his cane against the shining marble floor— "and accuse me, your king! This man is a liar, a fraud, and my son's whore. Get him out of my sight."

Niko stepped closer, fingers tightening on his sword. "Your orders saw tens of thousands of good men and women die in your name. I'll not let that stand. You are not fit to rule."

The king lifted his cane, raising it high, and then swept it down in a sudden arc. Niko parried it and pressed the tip of his sword to the king's chest amidst a chorus of shouts. The desire to kill raced through his veins, made sharper by spice. He forced the king back a step, then another. Talos's blue eyes flashed with malice.

"Who do you think you are?" the king vehemently demanded.

"Just a soldier." He jabbed him hard and the king fell back into his throne-like chair.

"Guards," a smooth, proud voice rang out behind Niko. "Detain my father!"

Niko's nerves twitched at Vasili's unannounced presence.

The guards came closer, but not for Niko.

Vasili's hand settled on Niko's shoulder and wordlessly, Niko lowered the sword. He stepped back, swallowed, and took another step. And there was Vasili, not in chains, nor hunched over in pain. He looked like he always did when on public display, the prince regent, dressed in royal clothes, the epitome of regal control.

The plan.

It had always been this.

Niko, the library, Vasili's capture—it was all a distraction. *A misdirection.*

Niko was the beaten dog they all focused on while the prince moved the pieces of his game behind the scenes. It didn't matter. The outcome was the same. Vasili would command the guards. They'd control Talos. And now Julian—Carlo's killer and the sorcerer— was dead, it was all over.

Niko brushed the prince's hand from his shoulder and moved away as the guards closed in. He could leave. It was finally done.

"My lords, my ladies, be calm now." Vasili raised his smooth voice, addressing those present. "All will be explained." He turned to the guard nearest him and issued orders to search the palace for his brother and any intruders.

Niko fell toward a chair, frightened a lord out of it, and slumped into the fine cushions with relief. Vasili would take the king away, dose him up with spice so he never woke again, and Vasili could control the flame. Vasili would fight the elves. Niko trusted him in that, if little else.

But Niko's part in it all was over. He was done. Physically, mentally and emotionally done.

The laughter, when it came, didn't sound like any laughter a man could make. The thickness of it boiled out of Talos and filled the room, its creeping sound seeking Niko's soul.

"My treacherous son!" the king boomed in a strangely echoing voice. A few of the guards stepped back.

Vasili took a few careful steps backward too, uncharacteristically retreating. "Father—"

The thing that rose out of the chair was Talos, but also wasn't. Wisps of blackness rose from his body, growing thicker with every breath he took. Niko had seen the same inky thickness in Julian's hands, the same inky thickness wrapped around the fiends. But this was heavier, as though Talos's body was the heart of something much larger.

"I should thank you, dear child." The king laughed some more. "For revealing your intentions so soon."

Vasili backed up again. "My only intention has always been to protect Loreen from you."

The king stepped forward. The smoke coiled about his boots and lashed the air as it climbed his body. Niko rose to his feet, transfixed by the sight of the raw power made visceral and real. Tendrils of the darkness slithered outward, creeping over the table, knocking over wine, sending people running and screaming.

The main door slammed shut, sealing everyone inside.

The king took another step, closing the distance to Vasili.

Vasili's fingers twitched at his sides. He stared wide-eyed at the thing his father was becoming.

Dark flame. It licked and boiled and consumed everything it touched, moving outward, climbing the walls, creeping over the floor.

"Did you think I planned to give the elves all this...?" The king opened his hand, the flame dripping from his fingers. "Darling boy, you were always too afraid to go further, cowering in the dark instead of embracing it. They were going to come to me, their stupid minds too hungry for this power to see the threat. I'll destroy them all."

"And Loreen with them!" Vasili replied.

A guard struck at the flame, and for a brief moment it seemed as though it worked. The flame recoiled, rearing up, then plunged forward in a great wave and washed over the guard, swallowing his screams inside its boiling mass.

The people didn't stand a chance.

Niko lurched for the doors. People shoved and clawed at him in their panic to get away. He wrapped his fingers around the handles and tugged, but the doors didn't give. They were trapped.

"Stay back!" He pushed back through the crowd and stood between them and the dark flame King Talos had become. A man *inside* a dark monster much bigger than him. The dark flame boiled and hissed, not with heat, but with power.

The king approached Vasili, each step forcing the prince to retreat toward Niko. Vasili had produced his favored dagger but in the face of something so vast, it wouldn't be enough.

Niko had only his sword at his side. Cold steel had worked on the fiend, which appeared to be animated by the same smoky tendrils. Would it be enough here?

"*The elves will kneel to me,*" the king announced, then drilled his glare into Vasili. "*You will kneel to me, boy. The whole world will kneel to me!*"

"Father, that is not the Caville legacy." Vasili stood firm. "We protect the flame, we do not—"

"*Legacy? I am that legacy!*" He grabbed Vasili by the throat and lifted him off his feet. "*I will rule all of the lands.*"

There were shouts behind and Niko turned to look. The door swung outward and the crowd surged, desperate to be free.

Niko could run too. Run and not look back. Julian had told him to, perhaps in a moment of weakness, but Niko had never fled in fear.

He'd followed the griffin into battle, knowing each time might be his last.

And he'd follow it again now, for the countless innocent Loreen lives.

But the living flame would not stop at Talos, or Vasili, or the palace. It was too wild a thing, too powerful. It would consume Talos and Loreen. It truly was a curse. But one Niko hoped could be stopped.

A narrow strip of floor along the wall remained uncovered by the rippling darkness. Niko ducked around the table, following the edges of the room. Dark flame sizzled and hissed, closing off any retreat. The table groaned beneath its weight. Crystal glasses shattered. It didn't matter. He raised his sword, launching into a run, and came up behind the king's rippling form.

Dark flame looped behind him and lashed down his back.

Agony blasted through him.

He heard a shout—not his own—but he was already falling. The flame swallowed his sword, coiled around his hand, looped around his waist, and constricted, squeezing ribs against ribs. Niko opened his mouth to gasp, or scream. Flame poured over his tongue, boiling its way down his throat. It choked off his air and filled him with poison a thousand times worse than any spice.

Talos twisted, still holding Vasili aloft. Nothing human radiated from the king's smile. "*The doulos who would be a lord,*" his warped voice said. "*A weak and feeble thing you are—*"

Talos's body's jerked. Words lodged in the king's throat.

His head swiveled toward his son. Vasili gripped the handle of his dagger and shoved, burying the knife deeper into his father's chest.

The king's smile twitched. "My boy?"

He dropped Vasili.

The dark flame withdrew, tearing out of Niko and recoiling from the room like waves receding from a beach, all of its terrible presence vanishing inside Talos's skin.

The king collapsed, first to his knees, then to his hands. He lifted his head and looked into his son's eye. "Vasili?" he whispered. "Finish it."

Vasili gripped his father's hair, drew the bloody dagger back. A moment passed, just a breath of time, then another, in which father and son understood what needed to be done.

"Don't let it destroy you," Talos whispered. Vasili slashed the blade across his father's throat, opening a terrible slash that instantly gushed blood.

The king slumped into Vasili's arms, and they sank together to the floor.

Niko pushed himself up. He could still taste it—the dark flame—like the touch of true darkness had burned through him, into his soul.

"Get away from him!" Amir dashed up behind Vasili. Whether to kill him or to reach their father, Niko would never know, because the dark flame exploded from Talos's body, hot and fast, and funneled into the air, where it split and plunged back down, smothering the two princes under its enormous weight.

It ended in silence, as battles inevitably did.

The Caville princes lay on the floor, unmoving, the flame having either burned itself out or buried in them both.

Maybe Niko could take up his sword and end the pair of them now, but Vasili's words regarding an untethered flame and what it might do to Loreen held him back. That, and the fact he could barely lift his sword.

Three Cavilles lay before him. The king was definitely dead. And it seemed like justice, finally, for all those who had fought and died for the ungrateful griffin.

Niko thrust the tip of his sword against the floor, levered himself to his feet, limping from the feast hall, through the palace, and past its gates. He walked, growing stronger with every step that carried him away from the cursed palace, and didn't look back.

CHAPTER 30

*N*iko beat the hammer against the glowing hot horseshoe, turning it with tongs to control the change in shape. Satisfied it would fit, he presented it to the horse's hoof to gauge the fit, and tossed it back into the forge to make a few minor adjustments. After fixing all four new shoes to the animal, he tied it to the post outside to await its owner.

Sweat poured off him. The day wasn't hot, but the forge roared. He stole a moment to catch some fresh air outside, at the front of the workshop and idly watched other workers nearby. They carried bricks to rebuild their homes and led their horses trotting by, heavily laden with goods. The scene was unhurried and curiously domestic. He should have gone inside, but small moments like this were worth lingering in.

That's when he heard the familiar clopping of heavy hooves striking the road.

His breath hitched, his body quick to remember the sound and what it meant.

Retreating inside wouldn't help. Princes didn't give up so easily.

He took up a metal bar, plunged it into the roaring forge, wiped sweat from his brow, and focused on what he could control instead of what was about to happen.

Niko ignored the new arrivals and hammered out a rough shoe as the train of guards, along with their charge, halted outside the forge. He quenched the shoe in a bucket and through the steam, saw Vasili tying Adamo to the hitching post.

"Adamo has lost a shoe," Vasili announced.

Niko threw the hammer down, making it ring, and sucked his teeth, clearing the words "fuck off," from his tongue before he could speak them. He didn't think Vasili would stoop to throwing him back inside the palace cells, but Niko had left him and his brother out cold on the palace floor.

The prince wore a grey riding cloak with fancy white ruffles that hugged his neck. His hair had grown longer, enough for him to tie some of it back, but leaving a few locks to cover the grey patch over his eye.

Would he ask for help? Niko wondered, leaning against the post and wiping metal dust, mud, and horse hair from his hands. Or would Vasili just stand there and stare until Niko gave in?

He knew how he looked next to Vasili, caked in sweat, a few days' worth of beard shadowing his jaw. He scratched his filthy fingers through it now, still waiting for the prince to ask.

There seemed to be a moment happening, some kind of push and pull. Niko raked an assessing gaze over the loitering mounted guards. They all wore the griffin on their chests. Were they truly loyal? Perhaps as loyal as anyone could be in the palace.

He'd stupidly thought the prince would move on, and as the winter had passed and Niko had rebuilt the forge and cottage, he'd convinced himself he'd never see Prince Vasili Caville again.

King Vasili Caville now, he supposed.

He should kneel and kiss that fucking ring.

"Will you help, Nikolas?"

Niko arched an eyebrow. "Do you have the shoe?"

"No."

With a huff, Niko approached Adamo and stroked a hand down the horse's nose. The horse snuffled at his palm, velvety nostrils fluttering, and Niko regretted not having any carrots at hand. He liked this horse a whole lot more than its owner.

A glance at the beast's hooves revealed four sound shoes.

Niko didn't bother hiding his wry smile.

"Invite me in," Vasili said.

He could tell him no, but saying no to Vasili was a slippery slope, eventually ending in pain.

With a jerk of his head, Niko pushed through the door into his cottage. "And do I address you as king?"

"No." Vasili's heeled boots clipped the floorboards and Niko turned to find Vasili removing his riding gloves and cloak, taking off the Caville layers. "Amir is contesting my claim to the throne, claiming I am tainted by years of imprisonment." He placed the garments on the table and coolly regarded the small room with its rustic furniture and basic amenities. His gaze finally settled on Niko. "I am still your prince."

Niko snorted and folded his arms over his chest. Vasili wasn't his anything.

Vasili drifted about the room, either fascinated by Niko's quaint little life or desperate to appear interested so he didn't have to look Niko in the eyes. "Julian's body was discovered in Amir's room."

It took a moment for Niko to level himself as the memories came swarming back. Spice had muddled the past, but it had been a nightmare, with or without spice to blur the edges. He still saw the blood on his hands sometimes.

"I assume that's where you got the fiend you dumped at my father's feet. Curiously, there have been no more sightings of fiends in the palace since Julian's death."

He wasn't going to ask if Vasili had deliberately used him as bait to occupy Julian and Amir while he rallied his forces. Lady Maria had practically confirmed it. Asking would imply he cared how Vasili used him like a tool, giving Vasili too much power.

"The elves from the farmhouse were not found," Vasili continued. "It's likely, without Julian to unlock all the palace doors for them, they reconsidered."

"I killed the man who murdered your brother, as you demanded. Our agreement—if there ever was such a thing —is over. I don't care about any of this, Vasili." A lie. He tried not to care, but alone in his bed, he'd looked for Julian beside him, dreamed of Vasili chopping wood, and watched for fiends in the shadows. At least he had new horrors to haunt him now. "Say what you came to say and leave."

"It's not over." The prince cruised around the room, halting at Niko's side.

"It never is." He knew what was coming. Vasili was kind and approachable only when he wanted something. He straightened and met the man's glare. "Don't order me to go back there."

"And if I ask you?"

"Vasili..."

Vasili's fingers brushed Niko's cheek. The gentle intimacy of it had Niko gasping. There had been... moments. Dreams. Times when he'd remembered the kiss in the field, when Vasili had shoved him away in one breath and pulled him close in the next. Thoughts of how this terrible prince set Niko's heart racing in anger and fear, and also in ways that made him hate himself more. He could never reveal such fantasies, never give them voice. Not least because he'd already fallen in love with one liar and almost died for his mistake.

"There is a madness in my head," Vasili said softly. "I don't know if it's always been there, or if it's new. Loreen is kingless. The elves are rallying, their forces bolstered. Their horrid king senses weakness. Our army is beleaguered, scattered. I fear I understand how my father succumbed to the lure of the dark flame." He pulled his fingers back. "I will not rest until every last elf is dead and Loreen safe." His fine throat undulated in a swallow. "But I cannot guard the city from the flame."

"That, Your Highness, is not my concern."

Vasili stepped back, breaking himself out of the softness, replacing it with ice. "You witnessed the same as I. The flame is real and half resides within me."

"Isn't that what you wanted?"

Vasili blinked. "You act like I had a choice." He swept

his gaze about the cottage again, perhaps seeing deeper this time. "I cannot have this," he said softly.

Niko watched the prince's brows pinch. Vasili had lived through terrible things through no fault of his own. He'd survived, and he'd vowed to keep his people safe, but it was for everyone else, not him. Amir wanted power. What did Vasili want? "*Would* you want this life?"

Vasili tensed as though caught with his thoughts open. He scooped up his cloak and gloves, suddenly eager to leave. And perhaps that was for the best, even if Niko's treacherous heart ached for company. Maybe he wanted the quiet side of Vasili to sit with him and tell him stories of glass palaces until the fire died.

Vasili paused in the doorway. "I will not ask or order you, Nikolas Yazdan, but you will return, all the same."

"I sincerely doubt that."

He left, and when Niko made it to the door, Vasili had already unhitched Adamo. He mounted in a swirl of grey cloak, and with a few tongue clicks, trotted the restless animal onto the road. The guards moved off, leaving Vasili a few strides behind them, allowing the prince a moment's breathing room.

Niko leaned against the hitching post and shielded his eyes from the sun, catching Vasili in silhouette. Adamo shifted, and the sun caught Vasili's sharp mouth, revealing a small, crooked smile. The smile he'd shown only to Niko. He gathered the horse's reins, kicked his heels into Adamo's sides, and launched Adamo down the road.

Perhaps this would be the last he ever saw of Vasili. The thought should have been comforting, but if he'd learned anything from his time with the prince, it was Vasili always got what he wanted, one way or another.

"A free lesson, from me to you. Call it a gift. I'm always one step ahead."

The memory lifted the fine hairs on the back of Niko's neck and sent a ripple of pleasurable shivers down his spine, leaving him with no doubt he'd been given a reprieve. The prince wasn't done with him, but Niko wasn't done with the prince either.

The elves weren't gone.

War would come again. And unlike his father, Vasili wouldn't surrender.

Until that day, Niko wasn't a soldier, or an assassin, or the prince's advisor. He was just a blacksmith, shaping iron and shoeing horses. It wouldn't last, but for now, it was enough.

CHAPTER 31

*M*arket day brought Loreen's crowds to Niko's village, which wouldn't have been so bad if they didn't drink too much mead and blame their horses for their poor riding. Too many thrown shoes and restless animals kept Niko's head buried in the forge.

He could have stayed that way if the rumors didn't reach him. Rumors he was sick of hearing.

He hammered a glowing shoe on the anvil, listening to the metal sing and feeling his way around the curve, but the noise and heat weren't enough to drown out the two men talking by the hitching post.

Prince Vasili was tainted, they said. Scarred and cut up like butcher's meat. But that wasn't what made Niko's skin itch.

"Half elf, they reckon," Thomas said. He was a man prone to gossip. He'd rebuilt the baker's shop six months ago and, along with many new folks moving in, he'd garnered himself quite the trade, in addition to a reputation as someone whose mouth was bigger than his brain.

"Nah, that's just talk." His companion huffed. "Vasili ain't done nothin' but good."

"Eight years, though? How did he survive that long, eh? Them elves, they don't take prisoners. So what, he just escapes and walks back to Loreen? Come on now, what's more likely? A pretty, courtly lad like him escapes elves? Or they let him go because his mother was an elf?"

Niko's hammer swing missed the shoe, struck the anvil and twanged up his arm. He swore, figured the shoe was done, and dumped it in a metal bucket of water to quench.

"What do you reckon, Niko, eh?" Thomas folded his arms and jerked his chin. "He has you shoe his horse, right?"

Adamo occasionally appeared at the hitching post for sets of shoes, but without the prince. He'd have ignored it if it didn't mean word had gotten around that he was the prince's preferred farrier and blacksmith, boosting trade.

"What the Cavilles do is no business of mine." It cost him to deny any interest, but getting into a fight with the baker on market day over Vasili wouldn't win any favors. There was also talk of his *special* relationship with Vasili, rumors he'd prefer to quash.

"Sure it is. You're a soldier. You've seen them elves up close," Thomas said. "Some toff like Vasili ain't gonna walk free, so they had to let him go, right?"

Niko plucked the cooled shoe from the bucket and headed toward the horse. Fuck if he knew why Thomas had picked the forge to spread his gossip. Maybe it had something to do with how Niko had told him to quit bulking out his bread with chalk. Hopefully he'd leave if Niko didn't rise to the bait.

"Amir has a petition to oust Vasili. Wants to exile him. Says he has evidence too. You hear about that?"

"Yeah, I heard." Niko picked up the horse's hoof and nailed the shoe home. He'd heard a lot of things in the last few months, none of them good.

"Says Vasili was behind some plot to kill the king."

"Amir is a fucking dickless prat of a man who doesn't know his ass from his elbow, and Talos was a danger to himself and his people." He straightened, hammer in hand, and squared up to Thomas. The baker wasn't a small man, shorter than Niko by a few inches, but heavier in all other ways. Small eyes gave him a rodent-like face that suited his disposition well. "Vasili is the only decent thing in that cesspit of a palace, and believe me, that's not a good thing, but it's better than the alternative. So take your bullshit rumors elsewhere. I'll not hear them here."

Thomas's friend tried to pull him away, but Thomas had rooted his boots to the ground.

"Leave it, Tom," his friend urged.

Tom wet his thick lips. "Heard some things about you too, Nikolas. Like maybe you spent some time in the palace last year. Folks can't decide if you were a slave or Vasili's personal whore. Me? I don't know what to think. You seem like a decent fella, but the way I hear it, Amir gave it to you hard." Tom's gaze dropped to the hammer in Niko's hand, daring Niko to take a swing.

Niko smiled, and turned away to set the hammer down on the anvil. "Walk away, Tom."

"You soldiers like it a bit rough, eh?"

"I won't warn you again."

The warning worked, or the friend did, because when

337

Niko turned back, Thomas was backing off, hands up, like all this was just some joke to pass the time.

"Don't matter what you think. Vasili is on his way out. Nobody wants a half-elf cocksucker on the throne."

Niko watched him go, grateful he no longer had the hammer in his hand, or he'd be tempted to throw it. Maybe Thomas the baker might meet with an unfortunate accident later.

Niko frowned at his own dark thoughts and carefully pushed the anger aside. He'd been better, of late, more able to shrug off the rage, but sometimes the dark still slipped through his armor. Besides, Vasili wasn't worth the fallout. The prince had gotten himself into this shit. It had nothing to do with Niko, nothing at all. He told himself the same that night. And the next day, when he went to market to buy coal and instead heard how Amir was calling for a public trial. Vasili had refused. Which, according to everyday Loreen folk, meant Vasili was guilty, and not that the prince didn't want to drag eight years of gruesome torture into the public sphere. Either way, in the eyes of Loreen's citizens, he was condemned.

It still had nothing to do with Niko.

He'd avoided the palace and the prince for almost a year.

He told himself the same, over and over, sitting alone in his cottage, his sword resting by the door. He'd tried storing it away once, but had taken it out the next day and returned it to its spot by the door.

He wasn't going back, ever.

That palace and that family had taken too much from him. He couldn't go through it again.

A week later, the village was abuzz with word that Vasili was sick. Niko recalled all too easily how he'd seen the dark flame split and pour into the two princes, and how that thing, whatever it was, had consumed their father. It was real and alive, and the elves would stop at nothing to get it. And Vasili was the only one who had taken it seriously.

If he died, that left Amir with the flame. For all his bluster, the elves would chew up the middle prince and spit him out, unleashing all that devastating power.

The Loreen bells rang out one evening. Their sound roused him from staring into his fireplace. The bells were only rung for a threat to the city. Had the elves returned in force?

He grabbed his sword, mounted up, and galloped toward the city, the bells growing louder with every racing beat of his heart.

Orange flames licked from the highest palace towers, making the palace throb against the night sky. The bells continued to chime more frantically as Niko rode closer. Vasili was in the palace, and whatever Niko would find, he knew it would drag him back into the horrors of the prince's world. But Vasili was right. He had to go back. For Loreen.

And perhaps for Vasili.

Niko kicked his horse into a gallop and raced toward the screaming.

NIKO AND VASILI return in Reign of Darkness, Prince's Assassin #2. Sign up to Ariana's mailing list for al the news as soon as it happens, and to be notified of the Reign of Darkness release.

NOW READ on for a snippet of the award winning Silk & Steel series.

ACKNOWLEDGMENTS

A huge thank you to all my readers in the Ariana Nash Silkies Facebook group, who keep the stories alive long after they've been released into the wild. A special mention for reader Anel Pieterse from the group, who provided the name "Adamo" for Vasili's horse, meaning: *to find pleasure in.* Vasili struggles to find pleasure in life, but while riding Adamo, he's more himself and free of the burden of his crown and his past. So the name "Adamo" was perfect.

Please join my Facebook group for more insights like this and to chat with fellow readers.

Now read on for a snippet of the award winning Silk & Steel series.

Eroan

The iron door rattled on its hinges and groaned open, spilling silvery light inside. Gloom fled to the corners, leaving behind a figure with broad shoulders. *Male*, Eroan thought. Curious scents of warm leather and citrus tickled his nose. After the wet and rotted smell of the prison, he welcomed any change in the air, even if it meant his visitor had returned.

Eroan kept his head low and his eyes down, hiding any signs of relief on his face. The shackles holding his wrists high bit deeper. He'd been so long in the dark, he'd almost forgotten he was a living thing. The constant, beating pain was a cruel reminder. This visitor was a cruel reminder too.

He knew what happened next. It had been the same for hours now. Days, even.

The male came forward, blocking more light, lessening its stab against Eroan's light-sensitive eyes. He turned his face away, but the male's proud outline still burned in his mind. Other images burned there too. The male's half-smile, the glitter of dragon-sight in his green eyes. Eroan had rarely gotten so close to their kind without killing them.

His mission would have been successful if not for this one.

"You need to eat." The male's gravelly undertone rumbled.

He needed nothing from *him*.

A tray clattered against the stone floor. The sweet smell of fruit turned Eroan's hollow stomach.

Moments passed. The male's rhythmic breathing, slow and steady, accompanied the scent of warm leather rising from his hooded cloak, and with it the lemony bite of all dragonkin. A scent most elves were taught to flee from.

"Were you alone, elf?" the dragonkin asked. The questions were the same every time. "Will there be another attempt on her life? How many of your kind are left in our lands?" More questions.

Always the same. And not once had Eroan answered.

Steely fingers suddenly dug into Eroan's chin, forcing him to look, to *see*. Up close, the dragonkin's green eyes seemed as brittle and sharp as glass, like a glance could cut. His smile was a sharp thing too.

"I could torture you." The dragonkin's smile vanished behind a sneer.

Eroan's straining arms twitched, and the chains slung above his head rattled against stone. *He has me in body, but not in spirit.* He gave him nothing, no sneer, no wince, just peered deep into the dragonkin's eyes. Eyes that had undoubtedly seen the death of a thousand elves, that had witnessed villages burn. If they had souls, this dragon's would be dark. *He could torture me. He should. Why does he wait?*

Eroan recalled that cold look when their swords had clashed. He'd cut through countless tower guards, severing them from their life-strings as easily as snipping at thread, but not this one. This one had refused to fall. This dragonkin had fought with a passion not found in the others, as though their battle were a personal one. Either he truly loved the queen he protected, or he was a creature full of fiery hate that scorched whatever he touched.

The dragonkin's fingers tightened, digging in, hurting, but just as the pain became too sharp, he tore his hand free and stepped back, grunting dismissively.

Eroan collapsed against the wall, letting the chains hold him. Cold stone burned into raw skin. His shoulder muscles strained and twitched. Pain throbbed down his neck too, but he kept his head up, kept it turned away.

"I cannot..." Whatever the dragon had been about to say, he let it trail off and reached for the ornate brooch fixing the cloak around his neck, teasing his fingers over the serpent design.

Eroan wondered idly if he could kill him with that brooch pin. Of course, to do that, he'd need to be free.

The dragon saw him watching and dropped his hand. "You do not have long, elf." His jeweled eyes glowed. Myths told of how the dragonkin were made of glass and forged inside great fire-spewing mountains in a frozen land. Not this one. This one had something else inside. Some other wildfire fueling him.

The dragon turned, sweeping his cloak around him, and headed out the door.

"What is your name?" The question growled over Eroan's tongue and scratched over cracked lips. He almost didn't recognize the rumbling voice as his own.

The dragon hesitated, then partially turned his head to peer over his shoulder. The fire was gone from his eyes, and something else lurked there now, some softer weakness that belied everything Eroan had seen. His cheek fluttered, an inner war raging.

The answer would have a cost, Eroan realized. He shouldn't have asked. He let his head drop, tired of holding it up, of holding himself up. Tiredness ate at his body and bones. The shivers started up again, rattling the chains and weakening his defiance. This dragonkin was right. He did not have long.

"My name is Lysander."

The door slammed, the lock clunked, and Eroan was plunged into darkness.

Download Silk & Steel from Amazon here. Also available in paperback and audio.

Also by Ariana Nash

Silk & Steel Series

(Complete Series)

"I would expect this series (Silk & Steel) to appeal to fans of CS Pacat's Captive Prince and Jex Lane's Beautiful Monsters." *R. A. Steffan, author of The Last Vampire.*

"A few pages in and I'm already hooked. I can't wait to see the deliciously dark world Ariana has created." *~ Jex Lane, author of Beautiful Monsters.*

"The characters yank, twist, and shatter your heartstrings." *~ Goodreads review*

Click here to start the adventure with Silk & Steel, Silk & Steel #1

⌇

Primal Sin Series

"A story of star-crossed lovers, of two men, two enemies, who should never have fallen in love."

Primal Sin, Primal Sin #1 (out now)
Eternal Sin, Primal Sin #2 (coming soon)
Infernal Sin, Primal Sin #3 (coming soon)

ABOUT THE AUTHOR

Born to wolves, Rainbow Award winner Ariana Nash only ventures from the Cornish moors when the moon is fat and the night alive with myths and legends. She captures those myths in glass jars and returning home, weaves them into stories filled with forbidden desires, fantasy realms, and wicked delights.

Sign up to her newsletter and get a free ebook here: https://www.subscribepage.com/silk-steel

Milton Keynes UK
Ingram Content Group UK Ltd.
UKHW012108240124
436635UK00001B/10

9 781916 009288